# A Love Like Wildfire

## R.J. Groves

A LOVE LIKE WILDFIRE

Copyright © 2025 R.J. Groves

Paperback Edition

ISBN: 978-0-6457792-8-8



This is a work of fiction. Names, characters, businesses, places, events and incidents are products of the author's imagination and used in a fictitious manner. Any resemblance to actual persons, living or dead, or actual events is purely coincidental.

*For Nene.*
*This one's for you, bestie!*

# Chapter 1

Hattie scrutinised the list in front of her and came to the same conclusion she'd come to many times before.

There must be something seriously wrong with her.

How else could she explain the lack of a relationship that was actually going somewhere? The lack of a *Let's do this again* and kisses at the end of the date? The lack of a spark.

Hattie pinched the bridge of her nose between her eyes, pressed her fingertips into the corners and exhaled slowly. Was there a moment in her date where things had started going south? As far as she'd known, it had been going great for a first date. On paper, they were a good fit. In person, conversation was easy enough. She wasn't uncomfortable. He was good-looking. But there was no spark. No electricity flying between them.

Not that she believed in that. She'd heard women talking about sparks flying and how their date simply smiling could make their toes tingle.

But Hattie had never experienced it herself. And she knew as well as the next hairdresser that salon talk was often exaggerated, making things sound more glamorous than they really were.

And until she felt it herself, perhaps it was better to just assume that those kinds of unexplainable reactions didn't really exist. For now, she'd keep to her lists.

She nudged her glasses up her nose and dropped her hands to her lap, fiddling with the blanket as she stared down at the list again. She bit her lip, working it between her teeth. Tonight's date wasn't the only one-and-done she'd been on lately. Now that she'd finished her hairdressing apprenticeship and found a salon she loved working at, she was increasingly aware of the loneliness she felt when she came home after work.

But it didn't make sense. She spent all day talking to people at work, and she was the kind of person who needed to recover from socialising. But while she'd sit on the couch absently staring at the television or in her bed escaping to the land of whatever book she was reading, she'd wish she wasn't doing it alone. She wanted someone to share her evenings with. Someone who recharged her social battery instead of draining it.

Someone she could be herself around.

Who didn't mind that she made lists and mapped out her day in her diary so she would actually get things done. Who didn't care that she forgot most details and names unless she wrote them down.

Of course, no one knew any of that about her unless they got to know her beyond a superficial first date. Which only reiterated the fact something else must be wrong with her for it to not make it past that. Sighing, she gathered up her papers into a neat pile and placed them in the drawer of her bedside table. She was reaching for her lamp to turn it off when something solid shattered through her window beside her.

She heard a scream and realised it must have come from her as she flew off the other side of the bed, spying the palm-sized rock that had rolled to the middle of her room.

'Oh, shit.'

Hattie lifted her head above her bed at the voice that carried through the hole in her window. A voice she knew all too well.

'Um ... Hattie?'

'Fitz?' She pulled herself to her feet, tiptoeing around the edge of her bed, careful of the broken glass. She peered out the broken window at her best friend and indicated towards the gaping hole. 'What the hell?'

Fitz ran a hand through his unruly brown hair, his lips pulled into a grimace, slightly higher on one side. In the poor light of the evening, she couldn't see the dimple that pressed into his cheek, but she knew it was there.

'Sorry about that. It worked when we were kids.'

Hattie's eyebrows flicked up and she tried to suppress the smile that was ever-present around him. 'Well, my parents' garden has little pebbles.' She placed her hands on her hips. 'Mine does too, by the way. You didn't have to choose a boulder.'

'It wasn't that big.'

The hint of teasing in his voice filled her with warmth. It's how it had always been with them. An easy friendship. One where they could tease each other without getting offended. He was the best friend she could have ever asked for.

'No?' She reached down and picked up the rock in the palm of her hand, holding it up with her fingers closed around it to emphasise her point. 'My fingers don't touch.'

'Yeah, but you've got small hands.' He indicated towards her front door. 'You gonna let me in?'

The smile tugged at her lips, but she tried her best to keep her expression serious. 'I should make you climb through the broken window.'

His mouth tugged high into a smile, his teeth glinting in the moonlight. 'Aw, don't be like that.' She heard the mumble of

voices she gathered must be her elderly next-door neigh-
bours seeing what was going on. He smiled at them. 'Hi,
folks, nothing to see here.' He brought his gaze back towards
her, his eyes widening with urgency. 'Hattie? Let me in.'

Unable to suppress the smile anymore, she let it widen her
mouth and left her room, still careful of the glass shattered
on the floor. By the time she'd swung her front door open
to reveal him standing there, one hand resting on the doorframe, her excitement had bubbled to the surface. It seemed
like forever since they'd seen each other. It had only been
months, but she'd hated not being able to see her best friend
whenever she wanted.

'Hey.'

His lips held the easy smile as his grey eyes held hers. Dark
enough to keep them a little mysterious. Her heart skipped a
beat. He'd let his stubble grow. It was the first time she'd seen
him like that. Since he'd first got the little tuft of whiskers
when he'd gone through puberty, he'd been clean-shaven,
preferring bare skin to being teased for the patchy growth.

Well.

It had filled in now.

And she knew it wasn't that he hadn't had time to
shave lately. The way he kept it—neatly trimmed and sharp
edges—he'd had it for a while.

And damn if it didn't suit him.

'Hey,' she said back, putting the breathy tone of her voice
down to her excitement at seeing him again.

He closed the distance between them, his smile wide. She
wrapped her arms around his neck as he lifted her in a hug,
spinning her around. She breathed him in, the scent of spice and
seawater and Fitz that was so uniquely him filling her nostrils.
She'd grown so used to it before he'd left for firefighter recruit-

ment training. Being apart had only made her notice the absence of it, fuelling her loneliness.

'Henrietta Wilson.' Only Fitz used her full name, and even then, it was an extremely rare occurrence. Everyone simply knew her as Hattie. He planted a kiss on her cheek like he'd always done and lowered her to her feet. 'God, I missed you.'

Her hand went to her cheek, her skin tingling where he'd kissed. The whiskers, obviously. It would take her a while to get used to them. 'I missed you too. But you're still fixing my window.'

He closed the door behind him, still grinning. 'Of course I will. Do you have a board? Cardboard?'

She followed him as he made his way towards her kitchen. 'I'd rather a window I can see through.'

He shot her a look that said he enjoyed her teasing as much as she enjoyed his and opened the packet of cookies sitting on her bench, helping himself to one before heading towards the bucket she kept her recycling in. 'I'll get someone around to fix it, but for now ...' He pulled out a packing box she'd had a delivery arrive in and assessed it, practically inhaling the cookie in two quick bites. 'This'll work. Tape?'

She dug through her junk drawer and pulled out a roll of sticky tape, handing it to him. His eyebrow lifted.

'No duct tape? Packing tape?'

'Used it all up on the last window,' she said sarcastically. He should know better than to think she'd have more than one kind of tape. As it was, she hardly used the one she had.

He rolled his eyes, taking the tape from her hand and heading to the corner where her vacuum cleaner charged, snatching another cookie as he passed the packet. She bit her lip, holding back the smirk as she followed him. Fitz and his brothers had always had a weakness for chocolate chip cookies. The store-bought packet was a poor substitute for his mother's home-made ones, but Fitz didn't seem particularly picky.

He flicked the main light on in her bedroom and looked around. Thankfully her room was relatively clean. Not that he'd ever cared about it before, and she'd never been embarrassed about mess around him. But she still found herself glad she'd tidied earlier that day.

He bent to the floor, picking up the larger shards of glass, and she brought her wastepaper bin closer, lowering herself to help.

'You know, you could have just knocked,' she said, glancing up at him, her head still lowered.

She eyed the lock of dark hair that fell over his face as he leaned forward to reach another shard. Her heart fluttered and her fingers itched to push it to the side. But that was just because she hadn't seen him for a while. And the ache in her fingers was because he needed a haircut, and she'd be the one giving it to him. They itched in anticipation. That's all.

She tucked a lock of her own hair behind her ear instead and nudged her glasses up her nose.

'I didn't want to interrupt anything.'

She worked her lower lip between her teeth. He'd known about her date tonight. And all the others over the last few weeks. While they hadn't seen each other in a while, they'd still spoken almost every day in one way or another. Sometimes just texting, but it still filled the need to talk to her best friend. He'd wished her luck on all of her dates, and commiserated with her as she'd said there wouldn't be a second.

'This wouldn't have interrupted?' She held up the rock before putting it aside to take out later.

He flashed her a grin that filled her with happiness, still not bothering to brush the hair out of his face. 'Fair point.' He dumped a handful of shards in the bin and reached for the vacuum cleaner.

Hattie sat on the edge of her bed, watching as he made quick work of vacuuming up the remainder of the broken glass. She let herself observe how different he looked now. The stubble wasn't the only thing that was new. The hint of a tattoo on his right triceps peeked out from underneath the sleeve of his shirt, what looked to be the feathery tip of wings the only part visible. His shoulders seemed broader now, stronger. He'd built a lot of muscle during his training, his shape having developed into something a lot more masculine than the slim frame she'd known her whole life. In such a short time, he'd changed so much. Before, he'd had a boyish charm. He'd been the teenage heartthrob of their school. Now he was devilishly handsome.

'What are you doing here?' she blurted, ignoring the tug in her core. It might take her a little bit to get used to his new look, but he was still her best friend. He was still Fitz.

He glanced her way before continuing with the vacuuming. 'I know your memory is shit, Hat, but in case you've forgotten, I'm fixing your window. That I broke.'

She rolled her eyes. 'Idiot.' She caught his grin, even though he tried to hide it from her. 'I mean here. In town. I thought you weren't coming back for a few more days.'

'I wanted to see you,' he said simply.

Her heart skipped a beat. She'd wanted to see him too. There was never a time where she didn't. She'd missed him terribly while he'd been away, and no words could express how happy she was that he was back in town. Fitz had been one of the few who recharged her spirits. Her sister, Charlotte, the other, along with Fitz's family. But Charlie had moved to the city to follow her big dreams, their hometown of Port Pirie not enough for her, and Hattie didn't hear from her often. And with Hattie's parents travelling more than they were home, it really narrowed down her list.

'I gather your date didn't go well,' he said, turning the vacuum cleaner off and placing it to the side.

She shook her head. 'I don't think I'll be hearing from him again.'

'Why's that?'

'Because he high-fived me at the end of it.'

Fitz's laugh rippled through her. She'd still heard it over the phone while he'd been away, but it was different when he was here. It filled the air around them, vibrated through her body.

She grabbed a pillow, hugging it to her chest. 'It's not funny.' Though she couldn't help the smile. His laughter was contagious. 'And the date before didn't bother with anything afterwards. He just walked off.'

'Well, that's just rude,' Fitz said, folding and tearing the cardboard to the right size for the window. She thought she caught a glint of amusement in his mysterious eyes before he looked away.

'I think there's something wrong with me.'

She'd thought it multiple times. She'd even come to the conclusion that there was no other explanation. But saying it out loud—saying it to Fitz—it really hit home.

'Why would you think that?' he said, his tone sobering. His hands stilled for the briefest of moments before he continued with his task.

'The string of single dates with nothing to show for it,' she said, shifting her position. There was a lump beneath her, and she reached to remove it, fisting the silk dress she'd worn for tonight's date. She dangled it between them to emphasise her point. 'I even wore the flimsiest dress I could find in case it was the way I dressed, but did it change anything? No.'

He glanced towards her, to the dress, and fumbled with the cardboard, juggling it and the tape awkwardly until they both fell. He sighed, running a hand through his hair.

'There's nothing wrong with you.' His voice rasped as he reached for the cardboard and tape again.

'How do you know?'

He swallowed, then turned to the window. 'Because they're jerks.' He pressed the cardboard to the window, paused, then glanced over his shoulder towards her, his grey eyes piercing her. 'And you're Hattie.'

She pressed her weight into her toes as she gripped the side of the bed. Was the crackling in her ears glass that had evaded the vacuum cleaner? And was the sudden warmth that filled the room because he'd covered the broken window, stopping the slight breeze from flowing in? That had to be the cause of her flushed cheeks. The prickle that crept down her spine, awakening every nerve.

There could be no other reason for it.

Because this was Fitz. Her lifelong best friend. The only person she truly couldn't live without. And she was Hattie. Just Hattie.

She cleared her throat, sure she'd imagined the tightness in his shoulders as he focused back on the task at hand. 'I'll put the kettle on.'

# Chapter 2

Fitz squeezed his eyes shut, forcing himself to take a few deep breaths as he heard Hattie fill the kettle and switch it on. The image of Hattie in that flimsy black number flickered across his vision and he swore, his eyes snapping open as he heard the cracking of the glass beneath the carboard. He hadn't even realised he'd been pressing into what was left of the window.

The room had grown hot, seemingly cooling down since she'd left it. But that could just be the knee-jerk reaction that had taken him by surprise when she'd dangled the garment between them, convinced it was her fault none of the dates had gone well. God knows it couldn't be her. If anything, the jerks she'd gone on dates with simply thought she was too good for them. He couldn't see any other reason for it. No explanation that would be good enough. It sure as hell wasn't the other way around, he knew that much.

Hattie was one of the best people he knew, if not the best. She was tender, kind-hearted, fun, compassionate. Pretty. He glanced towards the dress thrown carelessly on the bed and swallowed. More than pretty. Her heart-shaped face was framed with long golden blonde hair that fell over her shoulders in soft waves. The gentle curve of her chin was only emphasised by the stunning broad smile that brought light into any room. And those baby blues behind the soft pink frames could fill anyone with hope. Could make even the darkest person believe in a better world.

She was Hattie.

He could list off all things good and it still wouldn't come close to describing her, describing who she was to him.

They'd known each other forever, their parents already being friends before they'd been born. But they'd been best friends since primary school. Since Fitz had defended her against the other boys teasing her and pulling on her pigtails and helped her out of what he now realised was a panic attack. They'd been inseparable since. And the rest was simply history. They'd gone through everything together. The highs and lows of growing up. The rollercoaster of high school and the crushes that came with it. Life. They'd done life together. And he couldn't imagine one without her in it. Without the happiness that follows her like a bee to a flower.

She's his best friend. Closer to him than his own brothers.

Which is why the sudden wave that had surged through him when she'd dangled the dress between them had thrown him. He couldn't quite identify the wave. Jealousy? The thought that someone else had seen her in that had certainly irked him. The wanting to see her in it himself had surprised him. And the desire that coursed through his very being the second the scent of the perfume she'd worn tonight wafted towards him from the dress, from the smell of coconut he'd grown used to as hers that had surrounded him when he'd swung her around earlier

…

That just fucking scared him.

'Get a grip,' he ground out, taping the cardboard to the window as best he could. He steadied his shaking breath, his hands. More tape. 'It's Hattie.' One last strip. 'Your best friend.' He stepped back, assessing his handiwork. It would hold for a few days. Though it wouldn't protect much if it rained. He swallowed hard, glancing at the dress again. 'You'd be a fool to fuck that up.'

And he would be. No one in their right mind would mess with what he and Hattie had. That kind of friendship was irreplaceable. He cared more for her than he could put into words. She deserved more than the world had to offer. Nothing but the best. And he'd do everything he could to make sure she got it. Frankly, he was glad those jerks had never got back to her about a second date. He didn't particularly feel like chasing anyone up for treating his best friend wrong. He'd rather she found the right person straight off the bat and lived happily ever after, never knowing what heartbreak was like. Never having a reason for that flicker of light she wore like a robe to be snuffed. God help the man who ever did *that* to her.

He cleaned up the torn cardboard and the mess he'd made while fixing her window, tucked the bin with the shards of glass under one arm, and grabbed hold of the vacuum cleaner with his free hand. He glanced around him before leaving the room to make sure it was all exactly as it should be. His gaze lingered on the broken window, now covered over with cardboard and sticky tape.

He wasn't exactly sure what he'd been thinking when he'd thrown the rock through her window. He'd simply just been so excited to see his best friend that he hadn't thought twice about picking up a stone and tossing it against her window like he'd done when they were teenagers. He hadn't realised how big it was until it was already flying through the air, and by then it had been too late.

But he'd wanted to see her.

The closer he'd got to his hometown, Port Pirie, the less he could hold in his excitement to see her again, to hear her voice and see her easy smile. Feel her touch. He'd come straight here instead of going to stay the night at his parents' place. He could crash on her couch for the night like he'd done many times before. Then he'd go see his parents in the morning before he ducked over to the fire station to chase up some work. He'd also have to start looking for a place of his own. He couldn't expect to keep staying at his parents' place now that he'd finished his training. He needed something to call his own. To stand on his own two feet.

By the time he'd left Hattie's bedroom, dumped the rubbish in the bin and put the vacuum cleaner on the charger, Hattie was pouring tea out of the teapot he'd bought her for her twenty-first. He smiled at the memory of when he'd given it to her. He'd never seen her so happy with a present. She'd always been a tea drinker, preferring leaves over bags. And he'd known that teapot was made for her when he'd seen it.

'So there's that new action movie with that guy we like I've been waiting to watch. Want to put it on?'

He chuckled. He didn't need the names to know exactly which movie she meant. And frankly, he was so used to her struggling to remember names that decoding her statements had become second nature to him. He accepted the cup from her hand, their fingers brushing. It wasn't the first time they'd touched hands. Far from it. But he was more aware of the warmth that spread up his arm from the contact than he'd been before.

'You haven't seen it yet?'

She flicked him a grin, her eyes twinkling. 'I was waiting for you.' She held his gaze, squinted, then frowned. 'Have you?'

And risk seeing the disappointment on her face? Never. He leaned in close as he came level with her.

'No time for movies while training.'

He nudged his arm against hers, ignoring the warmth that filled him again, and made his way to the couch, picking up the remote and turning the television on.

Hattie settled on the couch next to him, tucking her legs beneath her. She was leaning slightly towards him, and he could feel her through the few inches she'd left between them.

'How was training? You look'—she squeezed his arm that was closest to her—'different.'

He relaxed his arm, unaware of why he'd tensed it in the first place. It was Hattie. He never needed to show off to her.

'Training was full on,' he said, watching the symbol on the television as the streaming channel loaded. 'Exhausting. But good.' He turned to face her, reaching a hand up to tuck her hair behind her ear. 'Missed this, though.' He let his arm drop to the couch, resting along the back behind her. 'I'm glad to be back.'

Her lips lifted in a smile and she leaned into him. 'Yeah. Me too.'

Something stirred inside him as the coconut scent of her shampoo filled his nostrils again. He rested his cheek against the top of her head. They'd known each other so long that being close like this was normal for them. And her shifting her position to drape her legs over his at some point through the movie, his fingers drawing lazy circles on her thigh ...

Completely normal.

It'd be odd if it didn't happen.

And yet ...

Something nudged at him.

Perhaps it was only because they'd just spent more time apart than they ever had before. That had to be why the touches and the closeness that had always been normal were now … different. It made sense, he supposed. It would only be a matter of time before everything went back to feeling how it usually did.

He ignored the throbbing in his jeans as she absentmindedly twisted a finger through his hair. Put it down to the fact the only women he'd been around during training had been completely off limits. Not that he'd had time or energy for anything sexual while he'd been away. The hyperawareness he felt now could only be from that.

Because there was no way in hell he was attracted to his best friend.

Fitz slipped through the door of his parents' house the next morning, his muscles aching from his earlier gym session. Hattie was still asleep by the time he'd left her house. And since it was late by the time she'd made her way to her bedroom and he'd settled down on her couch, he'd let her sleep. She had work today, and he had a lot to do as well.

He'd pushed himself at the gym. He'd skipped it the day before, deciding instead to get everything sorted for his trip back home. And considering the dream of his best friend in a little black dress he'd had while sleeping on Hattie's couch, he'd decided he needed to work off some extra steam.

The smell of freshly brewed coffee and sizzling bacon and eggs surrounded him as he closed the door behind him. Laughter carried from the kitchen as he made his way towards it, bringing a smile to his face. It wasn't all that long ago when laughter had disappeared from his family. Since the fire that had affected his family in more ways than one. Slowly, they were all healing and finding joy in life again.

He was slammed into by his nine-year-old nephew, Cliff, as soon as he'd come in sight of his family.

'Fitz is back!' Cliff announced, tugging him towards what looked to be a project of some kind on the counter. 'Look what I did!'

Fitz's older brother Dave's snort from the table only explained who, exactly, had been the one to do most of the work. Fitz bit back the smile. Dave's old girlfriend who he hadn't seen in years had come back into their lives before Fitz had gone to training. She'd brought a kid with her, who had turned out to be Dave's biological son. They had been on the run from a criminal gang when Dave had found them. Now the danger had been dealt with, the whole Harrow family was thrilled to have expanded to include Cliff and Ainslie, though Ma hadn't been too happy about Dave and Ainslie eloping. With a family of five boys, two were now married, both having eloped. Ma was starting to lose hope on having a wedding that she could attend from any of her boys.

But in all honesty, Fitz was happy for Dave and Ainslie. They'd both had so much to deal with over the years. Neither of them needed the stress of a wedding, but they also hadn't wanted to wait any longer to become a family in every sense of the word.

His other brother, Nick, and his wife, Liz, now had a baby on the way. It wouldn't be long before Ma would forgive them all for eloping and would be doting on another grandchild.

'Look, Fitz,' Cliff said excitedly, ignoring his father's snort. 'It's a dinosaur fossil.'

Fitz looked down at the round of plaster imprinted with what looked like a chicken bone. He ruffled Cliff's overgrown hair. 'Good job, kid.'

Ma came around the bench, handing a plate already made up with breakfast to him. He pulled her in for a hug, leaning down to plant a kiss on her cheek. 'Morning, Ma.'

'Morning, honey.' She glanced at the watch on her wrist. 'You didn't drive back this morning, did you?'

He moved to the table, set the plate down across from Dave and Ainslie and pulled a chair out. 'Got in late last night. I stayed at Hattie's.'

Ainslie made a sound as she lowered the mug from her lips. 'I've been meaning to get in touch with Hattie but I haven't seen her lately,' she said, cradling the mug between her hands.

He lifted a mouthful of eggs to his mouth, pondering the statement. Dave and Ainslie had found a place of their own, but they still spent a lot of time at his parents' place. He supposed Hattie might not have spent as much time at the house as she usually did while he'd been away.

'Cliff's hair is getting unruly. Do you think she has anything available after school today?'

Ma placed a cup of coffee in front of him and he took a swig, sending a smile and thanks her way. She patted his shoulder, her smile showing that she was glad he was home. 'I'll drop in on her after I go see McGrath and see.' Stanley McGrath was the senior station officer at the Port Pirie Fire Department.

'Thanks. I appreciate it.'

'No worries.'

He swallowed some more food, taking note of how quickly it disappeared. The Harrow boys were always fast eaters, but it seemed training had him eating even quicker. Making an effort to chew this mouthful slower, he looked at his sister-in-law.

She'd been thin and worried when she'd come back into their lives. She was at a much healthier weight now, and her worry lines had eased. She looked happy.

'How's work going?' he said to her.

She shared a look with Dave before focusing back on Fitz. 'It's good. I've finished my probation period now, and they've offered me a permanent position.' After things had settled down for them, she'd sought out a job as a bank teller.

'Glad to hear it.' He looked at his brother. The scars on the left side of his face looked silvery now instead of pink, but he looked happy too. Something Fitz had doubted he would ever be after being badly burned in the freak accident a year earlier. 'And you?'

'Work up at the cabin is progressing. All the basics are set up now for it to be manned over summer.'

Fitz rolled a mouthful of coffee around his mouth. The fire department owned a cabin up in the hills that had burned to the ground over the winter months, courtesy of the people who'd been after Ainslie. It was lucky no one had been inside when it had happened.

'And the station?'

Dave sipped his coffee, giving him a look he understood all too well. 'The weather's warming up and the heat is dry. Needless to say fire season has well and truly started. You've come back at a good time.'

Fitz finished off his breakfast, taking some time to talk with his folks even after Dave and Ainslie had gone to take Cliff to school, almost forgetting his science project.

'I wish you'd told me you were coming back so soon. I've already made plans today,' Ma said as she straightened the kitchen while he loaded the breakfast dishes into the dishwasher. Fitz's dad had already left for a day of golfing with his friends and the house seemed considerably quiet and empty with everyone gone.

He turned the dishwasher on and pressed a kiss against his mother's cheek. 'All good. I've got a lot to do today. Just wanted to see you first.'

'Look at you.' She lifted a hand and touched it to his cheek, patting it gently. Her eyes shimmered with threatening tears, though her smile was genuine. She dropped her hands to his shoulders and squeezed. 'A firefighter. All my boys are grown up.'

Fitz smiled, pulling his ma into his side. At twenty-two, he was the baby of the family. 'I've been grown up for a while now, Ma.' He pressed a kiss to the top of her head. Even at her full height, she fit snugly under his arm.

She looked up at him and shook her head. 'Not like this.'

# Chapter 3

Hattie ran her fingers through the platinum blonde hair in front of her, checking for any inconsistencies in the style. She lifted a section and trimmed the end, glancing in the mirror at the woman who must be a little older than her. She was busy studying her phone, hardly speaking to Hattie over the hours it took to dye her hair.

Which suited Hattie fine. She had enough on her mind as it was. She was grateful for the reprieve in conversation.

Despite how tired she'd been the night before, she'd struggled to fall asleep. In the stillness of the night, she'd heard Fitz's deep breathing from the lounge room, the sound travelling through the paper-thin walls and the door she'd left open. She never slept with the door closed when she was home by herself. Why would she close it when Fitz was there? It wasn't their first sleepover. And he'd seen her in less than her pyjama shorts and oversized tee.

Perhaps it was just the excitement that her best friend had surprised her by coming back to town a few days earlier than he was supposed to. Perhaps it was those little things she hadn't noticed before. The tingling that lingered wherever he touched. The warmth that filled her to her core at his closeness. The way his scent made her fuzzy on the inside. The gentle pulses that shot through her as he'd drawn patterns on her thighs with his fingertips.

Her memory must be truly terrible to not remember those little things from before he'd left for training.

But even that didn't make sense.

Fitz was the only one she'd never had trouble remembering anything about. She might be a little fuzzy on some of the minor details like dates or who else they might have been with. But with Fitz? She still clearly remembered the time he'd defended her against the boys who'd bullied her in primary school. The time she'd been so anxious from an encounter with them that she could hardly breathe. He'd plucked a dandelion from near the school playground and held it just far enough away from her mouth that she had to breathe deeper to blow the seeds away. He'd repeated the process until her breaths had steadied and she could smile again.

She could remember that. And she remembered everything they'd talked about last night. Yet she couldn't even remember the names of the guys she'd been on dates with lately, let alone most of what they'd talked about.

Fitz had been gone by the time she'd woken to get ready for work. The pillow and blanket he'd used were folded neatly at one end of the couch. She'd found herself staring at it while she'd sipped her morning coffee, wishing he'd stayed to have breakfast with her. But at the same time, she'd been glad to have more time to sort out her thoughts. Especially after all her tossing and turning through the night.

'Is it done?'

Hattie blinked at the woman with the platinum blonde hair through the mirror, her fingers still running through it. For a moment there, she'd forgotten what she was supposed to be doing. How long had she been absentmindedly running her fingers through the woman's hair? Her cheeks flushed and she gave the hair another swish. Satisfied it was all good, she removed the gown from around the woman's shoulders and gave her station a quick tidy as the woman gathered her belongings.

'Do you need another appointment?' she said as she led the way to the front desk.

The woman held out her card to pay, tapping it against the EFTPOS machine. 'I've got an event in about six weeks. I want a touch up before then. I'll call you when I know dates.' She slid the card back into her purse and snapped it closed.

'Sounds good,' Hattie muttered, scanning the appointment book as the woman left.

The salon was always busy, but they usually had last-minute appointments available. She glanced at the time and lined it up with her column in the book. She had some time before her next appointment. Marcy McGrath was coming in for a colour, followed by a couple of ladies from the nursing home. A bit of pampering for their outing. She'd have to make sure there were plenty of chocolate-coated almonds for those appointments.

She heard the ding of the bell as the door swung open. She knew who it was before she'd even looked up. She'd always been able to feel his presence like it was a sixth sense.

'Working hard?' Fitz said as he leaned over the desk, glancing at the appointment book.

'No more than usual.'

'Got time after school for Cliff?'

She examined the appointment book and nodded. 'Yeah, I'll text Ainslie the time.' She pulled out her phone and tapped out the message before she forgot. She lifted an eyebrow at her best friend, still peering at the book. He lifted his gaze to meet hers, the lock of dark hair falling over his eyes.

'And me?'

She smiled and tilted her head towards the empty salon chair she was working at for the day. The second chair in from the door. In her opinion, it had the best light and ventilation, though everyone had a favourite chair.

'I've got time now.'

He made his way to the chair and she followed him, taking a sip from her water bottle as she did. She placed it in the trolley where she kept all her tools and products and ran her fingers through his hair. Soft. Thick. She watched as the hair slid between her fingers and couldn't help but grip it gently.

'Same as usual?'

'I'm liking it a little longer,' he said, watching her through the mirror as she swung the gown around him. 'What do you think?'

She met his gaze in the mirror, those grey eyes looking bright, teasing, as they watched her. She swallowed, ignoring the fact her heart skipped a beat. It always did when he looked at her like that. Though there was something else in that look she was certain wasn't there before.

She shook her head. She was just tired. It had been a long day so far, with most of her appointments being colours. She twisted a lock around her finger and draped it over his eye where it had fallen earlier.

'Even the oldies will be swooning,' she teased, letting the back of her fingers scrape against the stubble on his cheek. How long would it take for her to get used to it? To no longer find the sensation of it brushing against her skin so enticing?

His lips curved into that smile of his, the dimple deepening on one side, and heat spread through her. 'A burden I'll just have to bear,' he muttered, holding her gaze.

She squinted at him, flicked his ear as she'd always done when he'd sat in her chair, and picked up her comb and scissors. It was only because it was getting warmer outside that made her breath shudder. She glanced up at the air conditioner. The green light said it was on, but she'd have to check what temperature it was set for. Clearly not cool enough.

Hattie ran her fingers through his hair, followed by the comb, trimming it shorter, but not as short as she usually had.

'Have you been to the station yet?' she asked, focusing on the many shades of brown in his hair rather than glancing up to meet his eyes. The stubble, she decided, with the little flecks of red through it only accentuated the grey in his eyes, making him look more mysterious than he usually did.

'Just came from there.' He pressed his hands together in front of him. 'McGrath said he'd be happy to have all the help he can get now it's fire season. He said there'd be enough work for me to do it full-time until a permanent position becomes available.'

Hattie smiled as she worked on his hair. Knowing Stanley McGrath, he'd make sure there was enough work for him to do. He'd always had a soft spot for the Harrow boys, having worked closely with their father, Jeff, before he'd retired.

'That's great,' she said, ignoring the knot that settled in her chest. The last few weeks had been hotter and drier than usual for this time of year, and the hot wind that had settled in didn't make things better. She didn't need to be a firefighter to know it was gearing up for a rough summer.

'Hear anything from your date?'

She looked at the mirror, her gaze connecting with those grey eyes. She'd imagined the slightly choked way he'd asked it. The hitch in his breath as he waited for an answer. The glint in his eyes now hidden behind clouds.

'No, believe it or not. But I did get another request on that dating app.'

His brow creased, but his expression changed so quickly it was gone with the next blink. 'Oh yeah?'

She worked her lower lip between her teeth, debating how much to tell him while she trimmed and combed his hair. Truth was, she'd been messaging the guy on and off all week, but he'd only asked to meet up that morning.

'Actually, you know him,' she said slowly. 'We went to school with him.'

His eyebrow shot up, his head jerking. She held it still, trimming carefully around his ear. 'Who is it?'

She'd thought his tone had dropped, but it could be the angle she had his neck at. She released him and picked up her phone, flicking to his profile picture. She passed it to him and went back to his hair.

Both of his eyebrows shot up and he spun in his chair to face her, not too concerned about the scissors that almost poked him in the eye.

'Jacob Terrell?'

She sighed, glancing down at the phone to make sure he was looking at the right picture. 'Yeah, that's him.'

'*Jacob Terrell*?' he repeated, annoyance in his voice.

She spread a hand out to the side as though asking what the problem was then tried to spin him to face the mirror. He didn't budge.

'What about him?'

He pinched the bridge of his nose between his thumb and forefinger, squeezing his eyes shut. 'Hattie, baby, have you forgotten the hell he put you through?' He opened his eyes and met hers, the grey stormy now.

She nudged her glasses up her nose. No. She hadn't forgotten how she'd been teased ruthlessly for the dark thick-rimmed glasses she'd worn in her early high school years. She hadn't forgotten the sneers and jibes behind her back about her roughly cut hair that time she'd thought she could cut her own hair. Or that time he'd thrown her lunch in the dirt. The fights Fitz had got in with him because of it.

'Maybe he's changed.'

'He's a bully, Hat. Bullies don't change.'

'People change. Look at Dave and Ainslie. Perfect examples.'

'That's different.'

'And you.' She waved a hand at him. 'You've changed.'

His eyes darkened further. 'No, I haven't.'

'No?' She caught him off guard, successfully spinning him to face the mirror. She ran a hand along his jaw, her fingertips scraping against the stubble. 'This is new.' She flicked the lock of hair that fell over his eye. 'And this.' She shifted the gown to the side so he could see the shirt he wore. 'Do I need to point out how your shirt hardly fits anymore?' His eyes darkened with every statement, and her heart pounded in her chest, her body heating under his gaze.

'That's different,' he repeated. 'That's physical.' Well, she wasn't about to point out how the looks he gave her were different too. She wasn't ready to admit that to him in case she'd imagined it. 'Personalities are different. The darkness in Jacob runs so deep I doubt he could ever treat someone right.'

She swallowed hard. He was probably right. But she believed in second chances. She believed people could change, that things could be better. She wasn't ready to stop believing in that. 'Well, I guess we'll find out.'

'You're serious about this?'

'I've got a date with him tomorrow.'

He studied her through the mirror while she continued snipping his hair, making quick work of the remainder of it.

'At least promise you'll text me if he's being a dick. I'll be your SOS call.' He didn't sound pleased about it, but the offer was genuine.

'I'm sure I won't need to.'

'Hattie.'

She held his gaze, those stormy grey eyes hitting her deep. She swallowed again, blinking a few times to steady her breathing. 'Okay. I promise.'

She hoped she was right about this. Jacob had seemed different in his messages. And they'd just been kids when he'd been unkind to her. Teenagers were always like that, weren't they? Didn't everyone grow up after they left school?

But a small part of her questioned it now that Fitz had mentioned it. She worked her lip, finishing Fitz's haircut just as Marcy came through the door. She swept the floor underneath the chair, tidying the space before waving Marcy over. Fitz fished his wallet out to pay, and Hattie waved a hand towards him.

'I can pay.' He ran a hand through his freshly trimmed hair.

'Why would I charge you?' she countered, angling the chair for Marcy to take her seat.

Everyone knew they were best friends, and she'd never charged him before. Besides, he hadn't even taken a full appointment slot, merely slipping in between two of her others. If she wasn't trimming his hair, she'd just be trying to look busy out the back.

'Because you did a good job.'

She grabbed a fresh gown and draped it over Marcy's shoulders. 'Go away, Fitz, before I change my mind and charge you double.'

His chuckle reverberated through her like there wasn't half a room between them. He opened the door for another customer then blew Hattie a kiss. She poked her tongue out at him, though her cheeks warmed. She watched his strong, confident stride as he made his way towards his car.

'Well,' Marcy said beside her, jerking her back to what she was supposed to be doing. 'Training did well for him.'

Yes. Yes, it did. But instead of saying that, she turned Marcy towards the mirror, giving her a shocked look. 'Marcy McGrath, what would your husband say if he heard you say that?'

Marcy giggled her Betty Rubble laugh and pressed a hand against her flushed cheek. 'I've been appreciating our firefighters for years now, dear. That's not going to change. But Stanley knows he's my favourite and I'll always be going home to him.'

Hattie smiled as she ran her hands through Marcy's fading fuchsia hair. 'Are we refreshing the colour?'

Marcy squinted at the mirror and shook her head. 'I'm thinking of changing to a rose gold. Thoughts?'

Hattie made a scene of thinking about it, though she knew in a heartbeat that rose gold would suit Marcy perfectly. 'I think that's a good idea.'

But as she worked on Marcy's hair, her thoughts drifted back to the way Fitz had blown a kiss towards her. Once again, it was completely normal behaviour for them, and everyone who knew them knew that. But she couldn't help but wonder about the happiness it filled her with, the warmth that fluttered through her every time she thought about it. The storminess in his eyes as they'd talked about her upcoming date. One she was feeling increasingly uneasy about.

# Chapter 4

Fitz sent the bowling ball down the alley one last time, turning away from it before he could see the abysmal fail it was gearing up to be. His workmates' groans indicated what he already knew.

'Gutter ball!' they chorused.

Dave slapped him on the back as Eric, the middle child of the Harrow family, brushed past him to select his ball. His oldest brother, Nick, was talking to Jeremy and Everett, two of the other permanents on their shift. Some of their other fellow fire-fighters chatted over near the pool table. They'd all just come off their shift, making a tradition of doing something together once a month now that the Harrow boys were back at the station. He supposed he was included in that now too.

He checked his phone for the thousandth time since coming out with the guys. Hattie would be on her way to the restaurant to meet her date and it rubbed him the wrong way. He was sure he wouldn't feel like this if it was with any other guy. But Jacob Terrell? The guy was as big of an asshole you could get. He'd seen him around town since they'd all graduated. Had avoided having to talk to him. But from what he'd heard, the guy hadn't changed much, if at all. Jacob had always known which buttons to press to get a rise out of Fitz. And come to think of it, most of them had been about Hattie. Because even then, he hadn't been able to stand anyone badmouthing Hattie or treating her badly.

Even then, he'd wanted to protect her from the nasty people in the world.

And here she was going on a date with the guy.

He checked his phone again, simultaneously hoping for her to send him that SOS message and dreading it. He didn't want her on the date with the guy, but he also didn't want her to be in a position on any date where she needed bailing out.

'Waiting for a call?'

He jerked as he looked up at Dave. He was still standing near him, yet Fitz had totally ignored the fact he was there. He clutched his phone in his hand, glancing down at it, then back to his brother. 'Ah. No. Not really.' He tucked his phone into his pocket, his brother not buying any of it. 'Sort of.'

'Way to be cryptic.' Dave's eyebrow lifted.

Fitz ran a hand through his hair. It was lighter, softer after Hattie had cut it. He could still feel her fingers sliding through it. Her nails scraping against his stubble. Her breasts brushing against the back of his head as she'd leaned over him to touch his cheek.

A rumble sounded at the base of his throat and he tugged his phone out again to check it. Still nothing. They'd have met up by now. Probably going through the menu to see what to order. Maybe he'd bought her a drink. Which only made Fitz more uneasy about the whole date.

Dave's second eyebrow shot up to meet the first.

'Hattie's on a date,' he ground out as though that should explain everything.

'Right,' Dave said slowly. 'And you're ... jealous?'

'What? No. I'm—' Fitz blinked. Was he? No. Surely not. He reminded himself that he wouldn't be feeling like this if she was on a date with a genuine guy. 'I'm suspicious. The guy's shady as shit.'

'Who's shady as shit?' Eric said, bouncing over to join them. It was nice to see the smile on his face again after losing his almost-fiancée in the same incident that gave Dave his scars. 'Also, I didn't win, but I crushed you two losers.' He turned to Fitz, frowning. 'What's up with you?'

'Hattie's on a date,' Dave said, his tone clearly not mimicking the way Fitz felt.

'Who's the lucky guy?'

'Fuck's sake,' Fitz muttered, rubbing his forehead as his oldest brother joined them. Thank God the last of the brothers, Sam, was firefighting in Mount Gambier. He wasn't sure he could deal with his ruthless teasing on this matter.

'Mr Shady As Shit,' Eric said, filling Nick in on the entirety of the conversation.

'Ah.'

The three of them focused on Fitz. If no one knew they were brothers, it would be easy to tell by their matching smirks.

'I'm not jealous!' he repeated, throwing his hands up, then checked his phone again. Still nothing.

'He's jealous,' Dave muttered.

'I'm concerned,' he said firmly.

'Concerned because he's shady as shit?' Nick said.

'Concerned because it's Jacob Terrell.'

The three of them stared at him in silence. Nick and Dave were too old to have gone to school with Jacob. Eric might remember him, but he was still a few years older. Sam, who was closer to Fitz's age, would be the only one of his brothers who might remember Jacob's true nature. Aside from overhearing Fitz and Hattie talking about him, Jacob was just another guy to them.

Eric rubbed a hand over his chin and swore, obviously remembering something about the guy.

'So, Jacob's bad?' Nick said, pushing further.

'Yes.'

'He's a jackass to put it nicely,' Eric muttered. He sighed, letting his hands drop to his side, and faced Fitz. 'What's the plan? Are we beating the crap out of the guy?'

'Wait, does Hattie know he's bad news?' Dave said, his expression serious. Of course they all knew Fitz would do anything to protect her. Each of them would. Hattie was practically part of the family. Always had been. She was like a little sister to his brothers.

'She knows.' He glanced at his phone once more before returning it to his pocket. 'But she wants to see if he's changed.'

'You're her SOS right?' Nick said.

'What do you know about SOSes?' Dave said to Nick, Eric laughing by his side.

Nick shrugged. 'Liz told me.'

Fitz scratched his stubble, the part where Hattie had touched earlier still feeling sensitive. 'I'm her SOS. But I don't trust the guy.'

'But you trust Hattie,' Eric pointed out.

He nodded. He didn't need to think about it. Never did. He'd always trust Hattie. Always had.

'Yeah, I trust Hattie.'

'Well, it's sorted then,' Nick said, taking charge of the situation as was his nature. It really was no surprise he'd ended up as a station officer. He slapped Fitz on the back. 'Let's get a beer to celebrate this guy finishing his training. And if Hattie sends her SOS, then Jacob has to deal with the four of us.'

They all agreed and waved goodbye to their colleagues. It had been a while since Fitz had been out with just his brothers. This was the first time since the fire. And for good reason. Out of the four of them, Fitz was the only one who hadn't been directly affected by it. He admired his brothers for their courage and strength. If he'd been through what they had, he wasn't sure he'd have been able to smile again so soon.

It didn't take long for them to head around the corner towards the pub, and before he knew it, they were lining up for a beer.

He heard a voice from the other end of the bar that set him on edge. It took him a moment to find where it came from, and he must have spotted him just as Eric had, his hand fisting by his side.

'Well, if it isn't Shady As Shit,' Eric muttered beside him. 'Fitz—'

But Fitz was already halfway to the douchebag who was half off his face by the time Eric had called after him. He heard his brothers calling him, trying to get his attention, but he only saw red.

'Hey, asshole,' he said behind Jacob, not trusting himself to touch him. Never throw the first punch. That's what their cop friend, Craig, had always told them. He silently dared Jacob to strike first, desperate to wipe that smirk off his face.

'Fitz,' he drawled, throwing his hands up in the air. 'Didn't know you were back in town.'

Fitz clenched his jaw. He'd bet he didn't know. He'd also bet the guy had targeted Hattie because he thought Fitz wasn't in town.

'Aren't you supposed to be somewhere?' he ground out.

Jacob feigned realisation, but Fitz knew he was full of it. 'Oh, right. You know about the date. Yeah, I'm not going to that.' Fitz's vision darkened, fury building inside him like a blaze about to take off. 'But don't worry,' Jacob slurred, oblivious of the danger he was in, his friends laughing behind him. 'Bitch won't remember. In fact, she probably forgot she had a date.' He pressed a hand to his chest, feigning innocence. 'She stood me up.'

Fuck waiting for the first punch.

Fitz swung his fist back, ready to plant it directly on Jacob's jaw, when it was stopped mid-air. He blinked through the haze, glancing up at the scarred hand that stopped his fist near his shoulder. Dave.

Eric came between him and Jacob, forcing Fitz to look at him. 'Go to Hattie.'

Jacob laughed over Eric's shoulder, taunting him. 'Hit a soft spot, did I? Lucky your brothers are here to keep you on a leash.'

Something flickered in Eric's eyes. Like he'd been aching for a fight for a while. The slow smile that followed was something Fitz was glad he wouldn't be on the receiving end of. Eric turned towards Jacob, Jacob's expression changing quickly.

'Remember that time,' Eric ground out. 'Where you snuck in a cheap shot while playing footy?'

Eric's fist connected with Jacob's jaw in one swift blow, the man staggering backwards into his friends. Eric shook his hand out beside him, nodding towards a dazed Jacob.

'He struck first.' He frowned at Fitz. 'What are you still doing here?'

He didn't need to be told twice.

# Chapter 5

F itz was right. Jacob Terrell hadn't changed at all.

Hattie snapped a breadstick in half, nibbling on one end of it. She hated that Fitz had been right, though by the time she'd left for the restaurant, she'd been convinced he probably would be.

But to be stood up?

The first half hour she'd waited had been for the benefit of the doubt. Perhaps he'd thought he'd said six-thirty instead of six. Or perhaps he'd been caught up with work or something had happened that had delayed him a little.

The next fifteen minutes were from seething annoyance at falling for his lies and trying to figure out how the hell she'd tell Fitz. She knew he was out with the guys tonight celebrating his first day of work at the station post-training. He'd be keeping an eye out for a message if she needed help, but he'd be enjoying his evening with his brothers. And so he should. He didn't need to be worrying about how some loser he'd warned her about had stood her up.

She'd let him enjoy his evening and tell him about the date—or lack thereof—later. No need to send out an alert when one technically wasn't needed.

She picked at the edge of the menu. She'd decided on the baked barramundi, but she wasn't sure she felt like eating alone. The glances she'd got from other patrons had been full of pity, despite her muttering that she was early. And she'd noticed the uneasiness in the way the waiter approached her every so often to see if he could get her anything. At the fifteen-minute mark, she'd been tempted to order a bourbon but asked for water instead. She didn't want to be half-drunk by the time he showed up. If he deemed to show up at all. Which he didn't.

The waiter approached carefully, and Hattie polished off the rest of her water. She knew what he was coming over for. She knew he'd taken it upon himself to tell her she'd been stood up, just in case she didn't already know. She'd seen the couples that had been turned away because there were no free tables. The table she occupied could be put to better use.

Her eyes burned. Being humiliated like this hurt. And she couldn't believe she'd let Jacob hurt her again. She should have listened to Fitz.

'I'm sorry, ma'am, but if you're not going to order ...' The young waiter trailed off cautiously.

She nodded, stood, and reached for her bag. 'Yep. Got it.'

The waiter had already picked up her glass and reached for the menus before she'd slung her bag over her shoulder.

'Wait! Hold up.' There was a thump and a clatter as Hattie glanced towards the door, recognising the voice. 'Sorry. So sorry,' he said to the waiter he'd bumped into. Then those warm grey eyes met hers as he closed the distance between them. 'Hattie, baby, sorry I'm late. There was an incident I had to deal with before I could get away.'

Hattie blinked once, twice, trying to process what was happening as Fitz brushed his lips against her cheek, his hands on her upper arms. She caught the hint of sweat and smoke and spice as he'd leaned in, and it took her a second to realise he still wore his work clothes, minus the jacket. The tee he wore was snug against him, leaving little to the imagination for what hid beneath. There was a black smear of grease or soot across his side, but he was here. Fitz was here. He'd known she'd been stood up.

Her vision blurred, her eyes stinging with unshed tears. He pulled back, holding her gaze, concern—not pity—in his eyes.

'Okay?' he said quietly, one hand dropping to link his fingers with hers and the other to cradle the small of her back.

She blinked back the tears, swallowed, and nodded.

'Sir?' the waiter said, clearly confused about what was happening.

'Leave the menus, please,' Fitz said to the waiter, not removing his hand. 'And we'll have two bourbons and a garlic bread to start.'

The waiter nodded and retreated quickly, seemingly relieved by the turn of events. In a way, so was she.

'Fitz—' she started, letting her best friend guide her back to her chair, his hand still pressing against the small of her back, though her fingers noticed the absence of his as he let go of her hand. The gentle touch sent a ripple of warmth through her and she ... liked it.

'My dear.'

He tugged her chair out, letting his hand slide across her side, her arm. Her hand. He held it as she lowered herself to the chair, very aware of the contact. The trail of flickering embers left wherever his hand had touched.

He rounded the table, taking his seat opposite her, and smiled.

Smiled.

Like this date had always been for them and not with another guy.

'Fitz, what are you doing?' she said, careful to keep her tone low so the busybodies around her couldn't hear.

His lips curved higher on one side, that dimple appearing as he did, his eyes sparkling. Her heart skipped a beat. And she could still feel his touch on her arm. Her side. Her fingers still tingled with the warmth of his. He leaned forward, that lock of hair dropping over his eye as he held her gaze.

'I'm on a date with my best friend.'

Her breath caught. When he looked at her like that ...

She must have seen every side of Fitz. God knows he'd seen every side of her. And yet.

Before she could dissect that gaze and look too far into it, the waiter came back over, placing two glasses of bourbon on the table between them and a plate of garlic bread. 'Are you ready to order?' he said, more to Fitz than her, though he did shoot a cautious look in her direction.

'Do you know what you're having?' Fitz said, not removing his eyes from hers as he flipped his menu open.

She cleared her throat and nodded, adjusting the glasses on her nose. 'Um, the barramundi, please.'

The waiter nodded, scribbling the order down on his notepad. 'And you, sir?'

Fitz quickly scanned the menu and snapped it shut. 'I'll have the porterhouse, medium. Barbecue sauce if you've got it.'

Hattie waited until the waiter had gathered the menus and left, then lifted an eyebrow.

'What?' Fitz said, his eyebrow matching hers.

'Barbecue sauce?'

He squinted. 'Yes?'

'You get steak at a restaurant, you're supposed to get gravy.'

Fitz shrugged, his lips curving. 'Gravy is for chips and roasts. I like barbecue sauce.'

She chuckled, shaking her head. 'I shouldn't be surprised.'

His eyes glinted as he reached for his bourbon. 'No, you shouldn't.' He held the glass up between them. She lifted hers. 'Good riddance to dickheads.'

She somehow managed to contain the bark of laughter, stifling it with a sip of her drink. The comforting warmth of the spirit eased down her throat, settling in her stomach.

Fitz nudged the plate of garlic bread towards her. She took a piece, watching as he helped himself after it. He'd always been a gentleman. He and his brothers had been raised right. But to fill in on a date that just wasn't going to happen ...

That was something else. Even for her best friend.

That was genuine. Compassionate. And the way he'd pretended he'd been the one she'd been waiting for all along, like that might make the whole thing less humiliating ...

Well, it did.

Even the patrons around her had seemed relieved when he'd rocked up, seemingly forgiving him as soon as they'd seen his uniform.

She swallowed, pressing the cool glass to her lips but not taking a sip. 'How did you know?'

His eyes lifted to meet hers, something flickering like smoke in the grey, like he burned from the inside, something simmering deep. He chewed the garlic bread slowly and swallowed.

'I saw him in the bar.'

It was like a bucket of ice had been dumped on her. Not only had the guy stood her up, but he'd gone out elsewhere to laugh about it. Had he had any intention of trying to be the guy he'd led her to believe he was? She sipped her drink and lowered her glass to the table. She picked at her piece of garlic bread, not particularly feeling like eating it after partaking in the bread sticks earlier.

'Is he still there?'

'If he is, he's nursing a sore jaw.'

She glanced at his knuckles. They looked fine. She looked up at him, her eyes wide. 'Did you—'

'I wanted to.'

He held her gaze, something intense in the way he looked at her. He hadn't reminded her that he'd warned her about the guy. As much as they teased each other, they were never into saying *I told you so*.

'But?'

He shrugged, lifting another piece of garlic bread. 'But Eric beat me to it. Think he had a score to settle.'

Warmth flooded her again and she took another sip of her drink. She tried not to smile at the thought that Jacob had got what was coming. Right now, she couldn't bring herself to care about him. Not after he'd humiliated her.

She sat back in her chair as the waiter brought over their meals and placed it before them. He held a large bottle of barbecue sauce towards Fitz. 'I wasn't sure how much you wanted.'

'Thank you,' Fitz said, taking the bottle. He squirted it all over his dinner. The waiter's eyes were wide as he handed the bottle back.

Hattie bit her lip, trying not to laugh. Fitz lifted an eyebrow as he glanced back at her, not holding back his smile at all.

She shook her head, picking up her knife and fork. 'You're such a child.'

'Don't act like you don't like it.'

She wouldn't. Because she did like it.

She loved Fitz's carefree attitude. The way he could make her laugh even when she was feeling miserable. How simply his presence could make everything better. He was the reason she still believed nice guys existed. That she had a chance of finding one.

After they'd eaten, he paid the bill, not giving her a chance to protest. He was only there, after all, because of her. If anything, she should have paid. And when they decided to go home together so they could watch that other movie they'd talked about, she handed him her car keys so he could drive.

He took the long way home, detouring through the main street so they could see the lights like they always did. But somehow it meant more now. And she couldn't quite place how.

She reached across the middle console and took his hand, lacing her fingers through his. She watched him as he drove, memorising the outline of his jaw, the shape of his nose. The shadow of his stubble. She could still feel the brush of that stubble against her cheek. Something flickered in her stomach at the memory.

'Thank you.' She'd said it quietly, but he'd obviously heard her.

He brought his gaze to meet hers for just a moment before focusing back on the road, his smile so genuine. He squeezed her hand once and didn't let go.

'Anytime, Hattie, baby.'

# Chapter 6

**W**hen Fitz had seen the look on Hattie's face when he'd rushed into the restaurant, fury had bubbled inside him. That resignation. The embarrassment. The disappointment. Not at Jacob, he realised, but at herself. And knowing the guy had made her feel like that only made Fitz wish he'd been the one to land the blow, not Eric.

But his brothers had been right. He could have wasted time making Jacob regret what he'd done, but Hattie needed him more.

He'd been ready to simply be her ride. To pick up some food and a bottle of bourbon on the way home. To let her vent and talk everything out while they watched a movie. To reassure her that she wasn't the problem.

Then he'd laid eyes on her across the room wearing a dark blue knee-length dress that had a slit in the side and hugged her in all the right places. Modest and simple. Yet it awakened something inside of him. Some innate desire to wipe that disappointment off her face and make her evening memorable in a good way. To make sure she smiled every time she put that dress on rather than tossing it to the back of her wardrobe because she didn't want the memory of being stood up.

To be the man who brought the smile back on her face.

It's only because he cared about her. Because she was his best friend. And he couldn't stand to see her hurt. He couldn't let himself think it was for any other reason, because the only other alternative was too dangerous. He'd have time to process it all more later. When he was alone. But for now, Hattie came first. She always would for him.

He flexed his fingers by his side as he followed her to the door, watching the sashay of her hips as she walked. She'd held his hand in the car. It wasn't a first. They'd held hands many times before. But tonight …

His hand still seared from the contact, and his fingers itched to twine their way through hers again. He pressed his nails into his palm as though that would smother the thought and glanced to the window still patched up with cardboard rather than watching her hips sway.

'Thought you were gonna fix that.'

He swallowed, glancing back towards her. She'd opened the front door, but she'd glanced back at him before going through. She must have noticed him staring at it.

He cleared his throat. 'They'll be here Monday to replace it. They couldn't get here before then.' He followed her through the door, closing it behind him.

'I have to work on Monday.' She dropped her purse and keys on the hall table near the door and rummaged around in the drawer.

He crouched down, removing his work boots before he got too far into her house. She'd never had a thing about removing shoes in her place before, and he knew she wouldn't now. But he was aware of the soot that smudged them. Not to mention he'd been aching to get out of the boots he'd been wearing all day. By the time his boots were off and he'd stood again, she was facing him with a hand outstretched. A silver key with an orange tag dangled from one finger.

'What's this?' He held a hand out and she dropped it into his palm.

'A key.' She lifted an eyebrow, her eyes shimmering with amusement as though the answer should be obvious. 'Did you have to trade some brain cells for those muscles?'

There was a challenge in the teasing way she looked at him, and damn if it didn't do things to him he just refused to think about right now. He lifted both eyebrows, his eyes widening as he tucked the key into his pocket.

'Oh, is that how you want to play it?'

Hattie took a step back, then another, a sexy sway to her hips with each step. Her grin was wide, easy, even while she fought it. 'Maybe,' she said slowly, not taking those baby blues off him. 'How many did you have to sacrifice, Caveman?'

A switch flicked inside him, igniting the childish part of him, and his grin widened. He could tell she knew the moment she'd triggered him, and he understood what she wanted without her needing to state it.

For just a moment, she wanted to forget how her evening had started.

'Let's see,' he said, closing the distance between them.

Her eyes widened, excitement threading through them, and she took another step back. Another swish of her hips. Her tongue darted out to slide along the edge of her teeth. Something rumbled deep inside him, and he caught her arm as she stumbled on her next step backwards, her heel catching on the edge of the mat.

In one swift movement, he bent forward, slinging her arm over one shoulder and hooking his elbow behind one of her knees so she draped across his shoulders. She squealed as he swooped her up and spun around in a circle for good measure.

'Fitz!' she shrieked, laughing, gripping him wherever she could so she wouldn't fall.

He'd never let her, of course. 'Me caveman,' he growled, stomping around her house to find somewhere to plonk her.

The couch had a laundry basket sitting on it, the clothes that had previously been in it spread beside it. He swore as one of her heels came dangerously close to his eye and he grabbed at her foot, slipping the shoe off, and swatted at her other foot until that heel slid off to join the other. Her laughter hit a higher note as he slid his thumbnail along the sole of her foot. She always had been ticklish.

Deciding the couch was a no-plonk zone, he turned for her bedroom instead, pushing the door open with his foot. In a couple of steps, he'd closed the distance between the door and the bed and dropped a laughing Hattie into a pile of pillows. He let out a playful growl as he flopped on the bed beside her, stealing one of the pillows she'd landed on to put behind his head.

'You're incorrigible,' she said, swatting his arm as she rolled to her stomach to face him better.

Her hair had been messed up in the tussle, the waves framing her face in a way that made his heart skip a beat. Her eyes were dancing and her smile was wide, the tension that had lingered in her shoulders no longer there. She adjusted her glasses, a lightness to her movements again.

'And you're happy,' he pointed out, flashing her a grin despite the knot that tightened in his stomach. 'You're welcome.'

He pulled the key she'd given him out of his pocket, along with his car keys, and threaded it on the same link. 'Why the key?'

'So you don't have to break my window again.'

Her eyebrow lifted, that teasing in them that he loved so much. His eyes lowered as she shifted her arms to trace the pattern on her blanket, giving him a direct view of her cleavage. The soft curves of the inside of her creamy breasts ...

He felt the nudge against his pants, the wave of yearning that surged through him, and cleared his throat, shifting his gaze back to focus on the keys. 'I'll try to remember I've got the key,' he said, bringing his gaze to meet hers. It took more effort than he cared to admit to stop his gaze from lowering again. 'But remember, I am missing some brain cells.'

She laughed again, slapping his arm, but not removing her hand. 'You had too many to start with anyway.' She focused on his arm, her fingertips sliding across his biceps, his forearm, and he couldn't help but notice the blue in her eyes dim a little. She sighed, pressing her hand flat against his arm. 'I should've listened to you. About tonight.'

He shifted his position to face her better. 'Don't, Hat. We don't do that.'

'No, but I am doing that.' Her gaze flicked up to meet his, something in there he couldn't quite discern before she lowered her gaze again. 'You were right. I was wrong. The guy's still a dick. People don't change.'

'Some people change,' he muttered, though he knew all too well he'd been on the other side of that argument only the day before.

She gave him a look that said she knew what he was thinking too. Fact of the matter was, he could see the downward spiral she was heading towards. And he needed to stop it. Stop her.

Bring her back to the present. He couldn't let her lose that light, that hope in the world.

'The thing is,' she persisted, shifting her hands to trace the pattern on her bedspread again. His arm was suddenly cool, noticing the absence of her hand and how the simple touch had felt … right. 'You knew the guy was a walking red flag and I was too naïve to believe it.'

'There's nothing wrong with hoping for the best in people.'

'Come on, Fitz, be real with me. Call me the pathetic idiot I am and tell me that I should always listen to you.'

'No.'

'Why not?'

'Because there's nothing wrong with you.' He rolled onto his side, propping himself on an elbow, urging his best friend to understand exactly what he was saying. 'You're the kindest, funniest, smartest woman I know. And you have this joy that follows you everywhere you go and gives everyone who's lucky enough to brush shoulders with you a little bit of hope and happiness in their lives.' He placed a hand on hers, stilling it, and gave it a squeeze. 'You're far from pathetic. You're the whole package. Any guy would be lucky to be with you. Trust me.'

And they would, he realised as though for the first time. She held his gaze for a heated second, her eyes glistening over. And when she looked at him like that, he could have sworn time stopped. If just for a moment.

Hattie turned her hand over, squeezing his back. Holding it like it was her lifeline. She sighed, dropping her gaze to stare at their joined hands, tracing the lines on the back of his with her free one.

'Well, I'm still shit at picking them. You can't argue with that.' He tilted his head, scrunching his nose. She was right on that one. He couldn't deny that her last picks had been bad.

'Maybe you should pick them for me.' She held her breath, casting her gaze up to meet his, that blue in her eyes rippling like looking into a blue pond.

He frowned. 'What?'

'Hear me out,' she said, releasing his hand and pulling herself up onto her knees. Reluctantly, he pulled himself upright too. 'You're a guy, so you can read them, right?' He blinked at her, uncertain how to answer. 'You'd be able to pick who's genuine or not. Who would be good for me. So will you?'

He opened his mouth to answer, then closed it. Exhaled. Tried again to no avail. He pressed his lips together, trying desperately to analyse everything that was running through his head.

Her theory made sense. As a guy, he should know who was serious about her or not. He should be able to see the signs. Whether they were looking to just get their rocks off or for someone to spend the rest of forever with. And don't get him started on why he hated the sound of either of those.

'Fitz?' she said, still waiting for an answer.

His mouth worked, but no words formed. Just a tightening in his chest that he couldn't explain. He wanted the absolute best for Hattie, and if he could help her find that, he would. But the thought of choosing someone for her had his heart squeezing.

'I can't.' He'd said the words before he could stop himself.

She jerked back, her brow furrowing, and blinked a few times before answering. 'Why not?'

Why not, indeed. He should help her. He should want to help her. But his mouth clearly had a mind of its own. 'It would be weird.'

'How?'

'Me telling you who to love? How is it not weird?'

She almost laughed, the hint of it disappearing before it could settle in. 'I mean, you wouldn't be doing *that*,' she said slowly. 'You could just tell me who would be worth my time getting to know.'

He swallowed hard, a lump stuck in his throat. Even if he did help her choose someone to get to know—which any good friend might do—he would be the one living with the guilt if that guy ended up hurting her. But how could he tell her his concerns when he was trying to help her believe there was nothing wrong with her?

He ran a hand through his hair, feeling the grit of dirt and smoke as he did, then rubbed his stubble. 'I don't know, Hat. I don't think I'd be the best judge of that.'

Her lips tweaked, uncertainty written all over her face. She shook her head. 'You know me better than anyone. How does that not make you the best judge?'

'Because there is no one who deserves you.'

She frowned. Swallowed. And he rubbed his hand over his chin, knowing it came out completely wrong.

'Gee, thanks for the vote of confidence.'

She made to move off the bed and he reached for her arm, pulling her back to look at him. 'That's not what I meant.'

She brought those eyes up to meet his, that blue swimming with unshed tears. He swallowed hard, the lump growing in his throat. The last thing he wanted was to hurt Hattie. But going off the sadness that now sat in place of the light that usually shimmered in her eyes, he had.

'Hattie, baby, there's no one alive who I'm going to think is good enough for you.'

He lifted a hand to swipe an errant tear from her cheek. Her skin was smooth against the callused pad of his thumb. He swallowed again, that lump in his throat stubborn as hell.

'Only those who'll be willing to do anything to try to deserve you.'

He pushed aside the dread that filled him at the thought of someone else treating her the way she should be treated. That wasn't something he could let himself think about. Not here. Not now. Not ever.

Her lips parted, and his mouth dried. He brushed his knuckle underneath her chin and gave her a weak smile.

'And that's okay. That's how it should be. You should be treated like a fucking queen. And even then, they still wouldn't deserve you.'

'You know that's bullshit.' She'd whispered it, her voice shaking, but he knew she understood what he was saying.

'No, it's not.'

She sighed, gripping his hand in hers, and swiped her hair away from her face. Her lips quirked up in a faint smile. 'Well, what if you come on my dates with me?' She put a hand up between them before he could tell her how ridiculous that idea would be. Clearly his expression had already given it away. 'Not *with* me, but there. At the same place. Where you can see us. He won't even know that we know each other. And maybe—' She took another shaky breath, her shoulders lifting as she did. 'Maybe you can see what's going wrong with the date.'

'Hat—'

'Humour me.'

He pressed his lips together, knowing he would hate seeing her with someone else more than he'd hate picking them out for her. But if it's what she wanted ...

She squeezed his hand harder, not letting him go. 'Please?'

He looked into those pleading eyes, the warmth returning to them. That glimmer of hope. And he knew that when she looked at him like that, he could never say no.

# Chapter 7

Hattie pulled the curler through the woman's hair, letting the lock of hair fall in a soft curl, guiding it into place to frame the bride-to-be's face. Her makeup and nail artist colleague, Beatrice, had already finished the bride's makeup and was now working on the bridesmaids. Hattie had already twirled the bridesmaids' hair into simple updos before her and Bea had swapped places.

They'd been asked by one of Hattie's regulars if they could do a home visit for the big day. So here she was now, turning Imogen's dead-straight hair into gorgeous wavy curls that looked natural so she could walk down the aisle to her new husband in the backyard of her family's huge home.

Bea was chatting easily with the bridesmaids as she applied the makeup, yet Hattie didn't feel particularly chatty. Even if she did love doing bridal jobs—especially if they were home visits instead of at the salon. It was the kind of jobs she'd dreamed about when she'd first wanted to be a hairdresser. The icing on the cake, so to speak.

But somehow, today just didn't quite have the same ring to it as it usually did.

Fitz hadn't stayed the night before. He'd left shortly after she'd talked him into going on her dates with her. A turn of events, considering they'd planned to watch a movie and he was going to crash on her couch like he usually did. Not to mention that he'd left his car in town and had simply started walking in that direction rather than accepting a lift from her or calling a taxi. She couldn't help but shake the feeling that something was off with him. That he just couldn't have waited any longer to get out of her place. Away from her.

What he'd said still rung in her ears.

He didn't think anyone deserved her.

And while he'd explained it in a way that didn't hurt—not like her initial response had been—she knew it was all bull.

There was a lot wrong with her, and he knew that. How could he not? She was far from perfect. Felt like she stumbled her way through most of her days. But he'd seemed so convinced.

It was a normal reaction for a best friend, right? If Fitz had been a woman instead, the response would have been the same, surely.

But he wasn't a woman.

He was very much a man.

And she still felt the brush of his thumb against her cheek. His knuckle nudging her chin. The way holding his hand had made her feel safe, brought her clarity. Like she could think straight.

And the way her breath had caught when she'd noticed the grey in his eyes darken ever so slightly.

She let another curl frame Imogen's face, looking at it through the mirror of the duchess to make sure it was perfectly placed. Imogen was watching her, and for the first time that morning, Hattie realised the one thing that was completely missing from this bridal party.

'Are you nervous?' she said, quietly enough that only Imogen could hear. The bridesmaids and Bea were all engrossed in their own conversation anyway.

Imogen smiled easily, the picture of grace. 'About today?' Hattie nodded, gathering up another cluster of straight hair to curl it against its will. Imogen shook her head carefully, her smile widening. 'Not at all. I guess you could say it was a long time coming.'

'How so?'

The little Hattie knew about their relationship was enough to garner that they hadn't had a long engagement.

Imogen shrugged, her silk robe draping off one shoulder. 'We've known each other a long time. I guess we were in denial for a lot of our friendship.' Imogen laughed, no hesitation in her expression. She truly wasn't nervous about her wedding day. 'Everyone knew we were meant for each other but us. He's been my best friend for a long time. You know how it is.'

Hattie's hand slipped, her fingertip brushing against the hot curling iron. She shook her hand in an attempt to ease the burning in her fingertip and tried her best to mask the pain. She forced a smile, focusing back on Imogen's hair, her words ringing through her head.

This woman was marrying her best friend. And she had no qualms at all. No wedding day jitters. Just an eagerness to start the rest of her life with the person who knew her best.

'How did you know?'

'One day it just clicked.' Imogen studied her carefully through the mirror, not getting distracted by the laughter that filled the room between them. 'Is your best friend a guy?'

Hattie's cheeks warmed, but she took a deep breath, hoping the colour wasn't obvious, and nodded. 'We've known each other forever. But it's not like that,' she added quickly.

'Hmm.' Imogen studied her a moment longer, then smiled. 'Well, I'm not saying it's for everyone. But having a strong friendship is the best kind of foundation for a good relationship. Paul had already seen me at my worst, and he'd stuck by me even then. There really is nothing else to scare him away.'

'I'm glad it's worked out for you.' Hattie let the final curl fall and positioned it carefully, putting the curling iron down.

'How's it going in here, Gin? Ladies.'

Hattie startled at the masculine voice. It had just been the girls this side of the house all morning. The groom and his men were getting ready on the other side. The man with thick ash-blond hair a little on the long side and a sharp jawline let out a low whistle as he surveyed the room.

'You all look beautiful.'

His gaze lingered a moment on Hattie, and her cheeks heated.

'Just doing the finishing touches,' Bea answered, leaning back to assess the last of the bridesmaids. 'Hattie?'

His eyes didn't sway, his lips curving into a hint of a grin. She cleared her throat, lifting up the bottle of hairspray. 'Same here.'

'Good,' he said. 'It's getting harder to keep Paul from crossing the midline of the house.'

Imogen laughed, rising to her feet once Hattie gave her a tap on her shoulder. 'My brother is dramatic as always,' she laughed, saying it more to Hattie than anyone else. 'It won't take long to slip into my dress, and after a few photos ...' She made a point of checking the clock on the wall. 'Oh, look. We'll be precisely on time.'

'Yeah, but you know how he is with standing in front of crowds.'

'He only has to look at me,' Imogen countered, picking up the earrings she'd chosen and slipping them on.

Imogen's brother laughed, tapping on the doorframe. 'You're absolutely right. I'll tell him that.'

'Oh, and Noah?' Imogen called after him before he left. He turned to face her again. Imogen nudged her thumb towards Hattie. 'This is the hairdresser I told you to go to.'

He held Hattie's gaze again, and she shifted her weight to one side. 'Good to know,' he said. 'I'll call to book in, shall I?'

'We accept walk-ins,' Bea chimed in, oblivious of the suggestive look on his face. 'If you don't mind waiting.'

'I'll keep that in mind.'

And then he was gone. And Hattie could breathe a little easier. She avoided looking directly at Imogen afterwards, and soon enough, they were all too busy bustling around in their dresses and having photos taken to worry about her anyway.

She'd intended to stay and watch the ceremony. But she slipped out unnoticed instead, claiming to Bea that she had a headache coming on.

Imogen's brother—Noah—was good-looking. And if she read the look he'd given her correctly, perhaps he thought the same of her. But she had other things to worry about right now. Like why her best friend still hadn't answered her text from early that morning. The one she'd tapped out in the wee hours before dawn when she'd been unable to sleep all night. The one where she'd told him how grateful she was that he was her best friend. How much she appreciated that he'd shown up at the restaurant.

Strictly speaking, she didn't need a response from him. She'd asked no questions in her message. And if he'd seen it when she'd sent the message, he'd probably been half asleep. He might have even forgotten to message back by the morning.

But he'd never once not responded, and he'd usually sent a message of his own by lunchtime. Not today. So she'd busied herself with doing her laundry and giving her house a deep clean, scrubbing until there was no dirty surface left to scrub.

And by the time she'd tucked herself into bed later that night with every item on her to-do list ticked off, there'd still been no contact from him. Her eyes drifted to the cardboard taped over the broken window and she couldn't help but think that perhaps she'd said something to piss him off.

Fitz rolled his phone over in his hand, facing the screen away from him. He'd read and reread Hattie's message too many times to count and he still didn't have a response. He'd tapped out multiple replies, deleting them before he could hit the send button. And each time he read it, the knot in his stomach tightened. A knot that surely wouldn't have been there before he'd left for training. Before she'd asked him to screen her dates.

Hell, before yesterday.

He couldn't quite place it. Couldn't explain what it meant. And wasn't sure he had the energy to try to understand it either.

He'd been walking back into town after leaving her place when Dave had picked him up on his way home, giving him a lift back to his car. Apparently things had died down after Eric had punched Jacob, the latter and his crew leaving shortly after, and the rest of their evening had been relatively normal.

Fitz couldn't remember the last time he'd needed to put some distance between he and Hattie. If ever. They'd always been able to work things out. But in this case, there really wasn't anything to work out. She'd asked him to do something for her, and he'd agreed. Even if he regretted it now, there was no argument about it. But the thought of sitting through a movie with her like they'd originally planned, knowing she'd sit as close as she usually did ...

He had never wanted the space between them as much as he had in that moment. And that thought confused him more than anything.

Hattie is his best friend. The one person in his life he'd never wanted or needed space from. Who he'd never been at a loss of words for.

Yet here he was.

Rereading the text once again. The stark reminder of what he'd agreed to as her friend.

'Friend-zoned. Yikes.'

Fitz jerked, turning the screen of his phone off as he looked up at Justin, one of the two firefighters who'd been brought in to replace those they'd lost in the accident a year before. The other, Justin's dark-haired counterpart, Gene, was right beside him. No surprise there. The two had initially only been subs but had cemented their place in the Port Pirie station, despite their inexperience and being the youngest in the station. Fitz supposed he filled that spot now.

He'd clearly been so lost in his thoughts that he hadn't heard them creep up behind him.

'We are friends,' he muttered, tucking his phone into his pocket. He made a mental note not to look at his phone too long at work. There was no rule against using their phones at the station as long as it wasn't a waste of time, though Fitz was more concerned about the stickybeaks peering over his shoulder.

'Not with that expression,' Gene pointed out, nodding towards Fitz.

Fitz frowned. 'What expression?'

'The look of denial.'

'You want more, and she friend-zoned you,' Justin explained.

'I don't—' Fitz pinched the bridge of his nose, a headache forming. 'Anyone ever mention how annoying you two are?'

'Many times,' Justin said, indicating towards the phone in his pocket. 'Why has she friend-zoned you?'

Fitz dropped his hand, glaring at his colleagues. 'She's my best friend. We've always been friend-zoned.'

'Because of your date last night?' Gene said, ignoring him.

His frown deepened. 'How much did you manage to read?'

'We saw you when we walked past the restaurant. I'm assuming that date was with her,' Justin said with a frown of his own. 'We're not snoops, you know.'

'It wasn't a date.'

'It looked like a date.'

Fitz sighed. 'She was supposed to be on one. He didn't show.'

'And the hero you are swooped right in to save the day.'

Fitz eyed his colleagues, not missing the deliberate pause as they waited for his response. Like they were waiting for something to click.

Which sure as hell wasn't going to happen. Because it wasn't a date. Yes, he'd filled in for her no-show. Yes, she looked absolutely beautiful dressed up for her date. Sure, he'd pretended for appearances' sake that he was the one she'd been waiting for. And yes, he'd enjoyed it more than he should have.

But it wasn't the first time they'd eaten at a restaurant together. Even if it had been more intimate than it usual. Even if he hadn't been able to tear his gaze away from her. Or how the feel of her hand in his had stirred him in ways he hadn't felt before. Even if—

He blinked slowly, his eyes widening. Were these two assholes right? Had he been properly friend-zoned? And why did that bother him?

The white of Gene's teeth as he grinned was a stark contrast to his tanned skin.

'There it is,' he said slowly, nudging Justin.

Fitz quickly recovered, frowning again as he rose to his feet. He couldn't stand to be around his colleagues right now. 'It wasn't a date.'

Because if it was, then damn it, they were right. And he wasn't sure why that irked him as much as it did. Hattie is his best friend. That's how it's supposed to be. Anything else just doesn't make sense. He'd do well to remember that.

# Chapter 8

The tinkle of the bell rang out as Fitz shoved through the door of the salon, still agitated from what Justin and Gene had said to him on the weekend. He'd been grateful work had given him enough to distract his mind during his shift. But at home, sleep evaded him. And he realised how much he needed to find a place of his own. He loved his parents and the home he'd grown up in. But there were, quite frankly, too many people frequenting the house for the mood he'd been in.

If he eventually did fall asleep after convincing himself that his colleagues were completely and utterly wrong, his dreams only threw him out again.

Dreams of her silky golden hair sliding through his fingers. The coconut scent of her shampoo dancing around them while they explored each other. Her dress sliding higher up her tanned thighs. Tantalising. Tempting. The suppleness of her lips pressing against his.

Then he'd wake up sweating, his heart racing and breaths quick, an ache and tightness in his groin that wouldn't let up until he'd dealt with it.

And hell if it didn't make him feel worse. Not to mention how her bedroom had affected him while he'd shown the window replacement guys to the broken window. Her bed was neatly made, save for the dimple in the blanket where she'd probably sat to put her shoes on, and the scent of her perfume still lingered. Her whole house smelled of her, and it only brought up the memory of his dreams again, fuelling the ache he hadn't been able to shake.

Hattie's eyes lit up as she glanced at him, and her smile sent his heart skipping a beat.

Damn Justin and Gene for getting in his head. Damn them both.

Hattie was with a client—an elderly regular who was deaf as a post and refused to wear hearing aids—but he didn't bother waiting for her to be free. He never had before, so why start now? Acting out of the ordinary would only prove his colleagues were right. And he sure as hell—could not possibly—have feelings for his best friend. There must be some other explanation. Had to be. And he was determined to prove that, if only to himself.

Swallowing the lump that had formed in his throat and ignoring the beads of sweat gathering at the back of his neck, he made his way over to where she worked. He couldn't help but notice the weary look in her eyes as he approached. The tightness in the corners of her smile. Her eyes drifted to the two takeaway coffee cups he held.

'One of those for me?' she said hopefully, her eyes flicking back to meet his.

'Would I dare come otherwise?'

He'd had his own coffee stolen enough to know better. He held one out to her as he sat in the empty salon chair next to them. Her eyes drifted closed as she took a sip, and he swallowed hard at the moan she let out.

'Mmm, I could kiss you for this.'

He ignored the lurch in his stomach, the prickle that ran down his spine. The wish that she would. Or the flush that darkened her cheeks. He cleared his throat instead.

'You'll be pleased to know you now have a fully functional window.'

Her eyes widened as she placed the coffee on her trolley. 'They fixed it?'

He nodded, staring at the lid of his takeaway coffee. 'They just finished up. Figured I had enough time to grab coffee and let you know before I head off to work.'

He felt her gaze on him for a second, but didn't dare meet it. She picked up her scissors and got back to work on the woman in front of her, snipping with an ease and expertise that still amazed him.

'How does it feel?'

She was focused on her job, but he could tell she was talking to him. 'The window? Hard, I guess. Like glass.'

She flicked him an exasperated look and he made the mistake of looking up at her that time. The familiar way she rolled her eyes at him, the warmth in her smile ...

His heart skipped a beat, his stomach tightening as he lost his appetite for the coffee he held and grew hungry for something else. Something very much off-limits.

'The job, idiot.'

She looked back down at her hands working, breaking the spell that had come over him. He swallowed hard. He really needed to find something to get his mind out of the gutter.

'You're officially employed now instead of volunteering, and you worked so hard to get there. Does it feel any different?'

'In a way, yes, but also no.' He took a sip of his coffee and rolled it around in his mouth before swallowing, considering his answer. 'I mean, I already know everyone I work with from before training, but I see them more now. I see the action and the lulls as well rather than only being called up when they need extra hands. The job is the same, but different.'

'Way to make sense,' she teased, a smile playing at her lips.

'I don't know how else to explain it,' he said, realising the truth in that statement.

How could he explain it? He saw a lot more now than he had as a volunteer. He also had the joy of doing all the jobs at the station he'd managed to mostly avoid as a volunteer. He had more responsibility now, even if he was the newest worker in the station. The most inexperienced. Training alone had shown him how much he hadn't known about firefighting, despite hearing the stories from his brothers and dad. Yet he'd revelled in the challenge. He'd worked through the harder things in training until it became instinct. He'd thrown himself into everything, and now he was back in his hometown working at the station his family had worked in for generations. And had almost been shocked when he'd returned.

His life had been so full-on during training. If he wasn't doing the training exercises, he'd been studying and working out. He'd thrown everything he had into the intensity of the exercises, and when he'd left and come back to the small-town station, it was like a shock to the system. He had free time again, lulls in the workload. And a hell of a lot more time to think.

He lifted his gaze to study the woman before him. The woman he'd been close to for most of his life. Did that explain how he'd been feeling for her? The unexplainable attraction? He swallowed, the lump in his throat still stubborn. Perhaps. And maybe if he could dissociate the two, then perhaps he could move past it and things could go back to how they'd always been.

'Well, lucky I know you,' Hattie said, running her fingers through the woman's hair in front of her before making another snip. 'Otherwise that would make no sense at all.'

He hid a grin, lifting the cup to take another sip. 'Yeah. Lucky.' He sighed, pushing himself to his feet. 'I better get to work.'

'Oh, I've been meaning to ask you something,' she said, putting the scissors on the trolley and looking up at him for a moment, her head tilting back to catch his eye. Did she realise she touched his arm now? What it did to him? He fisted his hand beside him, fighting the sudden urge to cradle the back of her neck and pull her close.

Fuck, he needed a hobby.

'Mmm?'

She swallowed, her lips parting on a sigh before she dropped her gaze. 'I met another guy on that app. He wants to meet up at the pub on Saturday. Are you free?'

His heart dropped at the reminder of what he'd agreed to do. He unclenched his fingers, running them through his hair instead. 'What time?'

'Seven.'

He nodded slowly, mentally building the wall higher around his heart. Compartmentalise. That's what he needed to do. 'I'll be there.'

'Thank you.'

He nodded again, forcing a smile, but unable to form any words. Instead, he pressed a quick kiss to the top of her head, the tropical scent of her shampoo filling his nostrils. He closed his eyes against the hunger filling him from the simple action, then made to leave.

'Will you be coming over later?' she said, turning to watch him go.

He paused, wanting more than anything to spend all his free time with his best friend. But until he got a hold on, well, everything, he had to distance himself. He glanced back over his shoulder, not turning to face her completely. If he did, distancing might be the last thing on his mind.

'I'm swamped with work this week. I'll see you Saturday.'

He thought he caught a hint of disappointment flash over her face, but he turned and left before he could tell for sure.

Hattie's heart dropped to her stomach as she watched Fitz leave the salon, disappearing out of sight as he headed for his car. She still couldn't shake the feeling that he'd been avoiding her all weekend. And while it made sense that he'd be swamped with work this week ... perhaps he was only using it as an excuse. She took in a shaky breath, the scent of his cologne lingering in the space he'd just vacated. Her skin still prickled from the warmth of how close he'd been earlier.

When he'd stood, she'd thought he might pull her close. Had felt the tension swimming in the space between them. A tension she'd been sure hadn't existed before he'd left for training. Or ever, for that matter. Had it? The fact she hadn't had even the slightest bit of resistance in her at the thought he might bring his lips to hers—pull her body flush against his—unsettled her now.

She wouldn't have pushed him away.

And part of her ... she wanted him to kiss her.

She shook her head, bringing her gaze back to the elderly woman in front of her. There had to be some explanation. And the best she could come up with was the weirdness between them lately. She couldn't trust what she was feeling because it was so obviously wrong. She hadn't been this confused about a guy for a very long time, but it was all silly anyway. He'd left for training months earlier. For the first time ever, they'd had that distance between them. And he'd come back different. Physically. And perhaps even mentally. He was still her best friend, but different. Which is probably the only reason why she'd understood what he'd meant about how work felt. Because she felt the same way about him.

She just needed to get used to the new Fitz. The Fitz who worked full-time in a very meaningful job. A dangerous one, sure. But so very important. She'd grow accustomed to seeing the muscles stretch his shirt. The hint of a tattoo peeking out from underneath the sleeve. The stubble along his jaw and the passion in his eyes.

She would get used to it.

And then she'd get used to seeing him with other women.

She fluffed her fingers through the woman's hair to style it, drawing the woman's attention to the mirror.

'What do you think?' she said, talking a little louder so the woman might hear her.

'Mmm?' The woman frowned into the mirror, then her eyes brightened. 'Oh, yes. He's a keeper all right.'

Hattie rolled her eyes, swishing the gown off the woman's shoulders. 'I meant the hair.'

# Chapter 9

T he man sitting before her looked decent, she'd give him that. Tall, dark and handsome. Tanned skin and a slightly Spanish accent. He'd been born in Australia, though his parents had come from some small town in Spain that she quite simply could not pronounce properly.

Nor could she remember his name. He'd used a username for his dating profile as a lot of people did on the app she used. With Hattie's track record of dates she'd managed to get from it, she was starting to wonder whether or not that was a good thing. He'd mentioned his name on the phone when he'd rung to organise the date. She wished he'd messaged it instead so she had a chance of remembering it. It started with an E. She knew that much. And that it wasn't a very popular name around here, though it certainly wasn't one she'd never heard of before.

Elijah?

No.

He didn't look like an Elijah. And if his parents were Spanish, he probably had a Spanish name.

Eduardo. Yes, that rang a bell. Ed for short.

She blinked as he said something to her that she realised she'd missed completely while she'd racked her brain for his name. The look in his eyes said he waited for her answer, but she hadn't heard the question. In fact, she was surprised there was a question. He'd done nothing but talk about himself since they'd met up.

Her skin prickled at the back of her neck and she opened her mouth to say something—anything—just as one of the waiters came over with their drinks. She took a shaky breath to compose herself as she eyed the cold glass of white wine placed in front of her. Her stomach twisted. She hadn't ordered a drink yet. She sure as hell wouldn't order something that was going to make her feel miserable later on.

'I didn't order this,' she said to the waiter, trying her best to sound polite rather than coming across as a grouchy customer.

The waiter looked confused for a moment, but then a warm hand was resting on her arm. She glanced across at the dark brown eyes across the table.

'I took the liberty while I was waiting for you. Hope you don't mind.' Ed flashed her a grin, his teeth whiter than she'd ever seen.

She swallowed, the prickle on her neck intensifying, and forced a smile. He had good intentions. He'd already ordered before she'd even arrived, probably to save time so they didn't waste precious time debating drinks instead of getting to know each other. He couldn't have known white wine didn't agree with her. That half a glass would have her feeling queasy for the rest of the evening and bring on a migraine by morning. Most women preferred white wine over other drinks because most people handled it better than other drinks, but Hattie could handle any drink except for white wine. But he didn't know. Statistics fuelled his decision. She couldn't fault him for that.

But she also wasn't feeling up to being knocked for six for the next couple of days. Perhaps she could manage only a few sips, or pretend to drink it at least. Maybe he wouldn't even be able to tell.

'Are you ready to order?' the waiter said.

Hattie flipped open the menu and scanned it quickly as Ed rattled off his order and handed over his debit card for payment. Deciding on the mushroom risotto, she lifted her gaze to the waiter—

Except he wasn't there.

And Ed was lifting his glass towards her. 'To an enjoyable evening with a beautiful lady,' he said, a twinkle in his eye.

She lowered the menu, realising he'd obviously taken the liberty to order her meal as well. She swallowed, lifting her wineglass to touch his. She brought it to her mouth, his eyes not leaving hers. The cool of the wine touched against her lip, though she didn't let any pass into her mouth.

Her phone vibrated in her purse beside her and she reached for it. 'Sorry, I have to check this. Could be clients.'

A flicker of annoyance shot through his eyes, but he indicated towards her phone. His smile seemed forced. 'Oh, of course. I know how it is with running your own business. Some things just can't wait.'

She lifted her lips in a smile, though she knew it was only half-hearted. Truth was, even if her clients messaged her after hours, they rarely needed an immediate response. With the appointment book being at the salon, most requests would have to wait until she was next at work for a response. She glanced down at the message.

*White wine?*

Her next inhale was one of pure relief. She hadn't seen Fitz in the pub when she'd first come in, but he must be here to see what drink she had in front of her. Another message came through and she bit her lip so her expression wouldn't give her away.

*He ordered, right? Want me to spill it on him?*

If anyone could subtly spill another person's drink on someone else entirely, it would probably be Fitz. At least he would never order a white wine for her. In fact, he knew bourbon was her drink of choice. She tapped out a quick reply and hit send.

*Not yet.*

Hattie lowered her phone to her lap and nudged her glasses to hide her glance around the room. She bit back the smile as she laid eyes on her best friend. Fitz had claimed a seat in the corner booth at a perfect angle to see everything that was happening at her table without Ed seeing him.

'You own your own business?' she said, trying to get the conversation moving. Ed's eyes lit up at the question.

'I've built some up from the ground and sold them as very profitable businesses. I'm partnered with an accounting firm right now.'

'You're an accountant?' She didn't know what to expect of him, but for some reason he'd never come across as an accountant. His smile seemed stuck as he pondered her question for the briefest of moments.

'No. I'm partnered in their firm. I work the business side of things.'

'Like what?'

'Like anything to do with business.'

Hattie's eyebrow shot up before she could control it. Could he have been more vague in his answer? 'We don't have to talk about work.'

'It's not that,' he said, sipping his drink. 'It's just difficult to explain. Most people have no idea what I'm talking about when I try to.'

'Well, I'm not most people.' She brought her glass to her mouth, pretending to take another sip. God, she could do with a real drink.

His smile was more sincere this time. 'No, you are not.'

Hattie swallowed as she lowered the glass to the table, her fingers lingering a moment before letting it go. Despite the fact he'd ordered her drink—and food—without first checking what she wanted, he seemed a nice enough guy. A little evasive of some questions, but nothing particularly coming across to her as glaring red flags.

Except for the uneasiness she felt around him.

But again, it was nothing prominent, and she could probably put it down to that she didn't know the guy. An awkwardness. Though it wasn't exactly what she would normally consider awkward.

She leaned back as the waiter placed an Asian salad in front of her and some kind of wrapped chicken dish in front of Ed. Her phone buzzed on her lap and she glanced down.

*He order that for you too?*

She replied with a quick thumbs up emoji and focused on the man in front of her. The Asian salad did look nice. He could have chosen worse. But it should have been her choice, not his. And that still didn't sit right with her. She lifted her fork as another message popped up on her screen.

*He seems like a dick. Just say the word, Hat.*

She didn't reply. Did Fitz only come up with that conclusion because Ed had ordered for her? But as she swallowed the first bite of her food, she knew Fitz was probably right. He had a sixth sense for things like that. Which is exactly why she'd asked him to tag along in the first place.

But she wouldn't end the date just yet. Perhaps things had just got off to a rough start.

She cleared her throat. 'Tell me about yourself. Do you have any hobbies?' Like he'd done anything other than talk about himself.

He took a bite of his food before replying, not even bothering to finish his mouthful before responding. 'No time for hobbies. Always on the run. Travelling for work and the like.'

'You don't get any free time while travelling?'

'I guess I do. I just ... fill it.'

'What do you fill it with?'

She took another mouthful, seriously considering risking a migraine from the wine just to get through the dinner. Getting an answer out of him was like squeezing blood from a stone. She certainly wouldn't be able to keep that up in a relationship.

'Well, I—' He paused, waving his hand as though indicating their arrangement, his smile sheepish.

Realisation dawned on her at what he meant, and her mouthful suddenly became hard to swallow. She forced it down, lowering her fork. 'You date.'

Was this just another pit stop on his travels? An attempt to find someone easy to whisk into bed with him before he shot through to the next town, the next person?

She wasn't naïve enough to think that whoever she dated would have been celibate before her, but she also wasn't into players. Which Ed was looking like more and more each time he opened his mouth.

The mischievous glint in his eyes proved it further. 'No one's tied me down yet.'

The lingering taste of the salad was suddenly bitter, her appetite deserting her. She reached for the glass of white wine and took a deep gulp.

Fitz had been watching the date from the corner booth for longer than he was comfortable with. It was clear Hattie's date had no trouble talking. But gauging from the few times Hattie had spoken, he doubted the guy had asked much—if anything—about her.

He clearly didn't give Hattie much chance to talk. He ordered for her without asking what she wanted. And quite frankly, he had an air about him—in the way he held himself—that could only be warning bells.

And that was just from what he'd observed. It had nothing to do with the strange twang that ate at him with seeing her sitting across from another man. Wasting that gorgeous smile on someone who was probably only banking on trying to get her drunk and in his bed. Or the possessive feeling that bubbled under his skin at seeing some other guy touch her.

Fitz eyed his phone again, polishing off the glass of bourbon he'd been sitting on. She still hadn't sent him a message asking for help, but the second he saw her lift the wineglass to her lips and actually drink from it, he realised she didn't need to message. That was as good as an SOS.

He rose to his feet, moving towards the jukebox along the wall. He slipped a coin into the slot and flicked through the pages until he found the song he was looking for. Then he moved towards the bar as though lining up to order another drink. And waited.

He was within earshot of her table here, and he heard her gasp as the song started playing, cutting her date off from whatever he was talking about.

'I love this song! Dance with me.'

Her date chuckled awkwardly. 'No one else is dancing.'

'So?'

'So ... I don't dance. I'm not into making a fool of myself.'

There was a beat of silence, and Fitz turned slightly so he could see Hattie's reaction. Hattie, the woman who would dance in the middle of a grocery store if a song she liked came on. Who grasped every little hint of joy and held on with both hands, letting it consume her until she was happiness personified.

'Come on, Hattie,' he murmured, watching as her face dropped at her date's proclamation. 'Spill your shitty drink on him.'

But she didn't. Instead, she lifted it to her mouth and took another drink. Fitz cringed. She was going to regret drinking that wine later. But he'd be there for her when she needed it. She glanced over towards where he'd been sitting, and a flash of confusion crossed her face as she let her gaze roam the tables surrounding where he'd been. He didn't even have time to think before he'd arrived at their table, looking only at his best friend as though it was the first time he'd seen her.

'Sorry to interrupt.' He wasn't. And he wasn't going to look any further into Hattie's expression except for it being one of relief. 'I heard you say you love this song.' He reached a hand towards her. 'Care to dance?'

She'd been about to reach for his hand when her date grabbed Fitz's arm, trying to turn him to face him.

'No, she doesn't,' the date said firmly.

Fitz didn't remove his gaze from Hattie's. And there was no way in hell he could read that look wrong. Of course she wanted to dance. And yes, she wanted out of the date. The slightest nod of her head only confirmed his thoughts. He finally turned his gaze from hers, levelling her date with a look.

'Wasn't talking to you, buddy.'

Her date's face reddened, and Fitz could have sworn he saw steam coming from his ears. He held back a smirk. The guy had the potential to be unhinged. Fitz had never seen him around town before, but his whole persona screamed out-of-towner. And his eyes bore nothing but hatred for Fitz. He clearly did not like someone stepping on what he thought was his turf, and he certainly wasn't used to not getting what he wanted.

Fitz had come across his sort before.

In fact, most of his fistfights had been with guys just like the one fuming before him.

'Now, listen here, *buddy*—'

'If you're trying to offend me, come up with something new. Reusing insults is purely unoriginal.'

More steam escaped, the guy's ears reddening. Hattie's date pushed up off his seat, standing straight like the tough guy he thought he was, and moved into Fitz's space. Fitz lifted an eyebrow, not breaking eye contact. He had a good four or five inches on Hattie's date, and Fitz wasn't sure the guy had ever been in a fight by himself before. He gave off more of a leader-of-the-pack, smack-talker vibe. The kind who instigates the fights but lets their cronies do the fighting for them.

But he sure looked like he wanted to throw a punch now.

'If you don't mind fucking off, we're in the middle of a date that's going quite well.'

The man spoke through gritted teeth, but Fitz didn't budge. He crinkled his nose, squinting at the man. 'How about we let the lovely lady decide that.'

He heard Hattie mutter a curse beside him, but he didn't dare take his eyes off her date. His jaw clenched, and in a rage of fury, the guy swung his fist back. Seeing the move coming, Fitz stepped in, their noses almost meeting.

'I'd also think really hard about throwing that punch,' he growled.

The man staggered backwards, clearly freaked by the closeness, but before anyone could do anything more, Hattie had stepped between them, her palm resting on Fitz's chest. He felt the burn of her touch like his shirt was non-existent. Surprised by the feeling, he glanced down at her manicured fingers pressing into his chest. It looked ...

Right.

Like those fingers belonged there. Always.

His breath hitched, and he shook his head, focusing on what was being said. The guy was obviously annoyed with the whole thing, talking over whatever Hattie was saying. Fitz blinked, shaking away thoughts of Hattie's hands on his body.

'Okay, you know what?' Hattie said more firmly, taking a step closer to her date, her hand falling from Fitz's chest. He refused to acknowledge the disappointment at the loss of contact. Her date snapped his mouth shut at her sudden change of tone. 'Thanks for the dinner, Eduardo, but this date is over.'

The guy blinked a few times, a deep crease forming on his brow. 'It's Mateo.'

Hattie's eyebrows shot up, her head tipping forward in disbelief. 'Really?' Mateo nodded. 'Wow. Okay. It's still over. And, by the way'—she turned to the table, picking up what was left of her drink—'I don't drink white wine.'

She shoved the glass against Mateo's chest, his hands grappling to grasp the glass before he wore it all. He somehow managed to not spill anything, though the feat caught him off guard. But Fitz's gaze was still on the woman sashaying away from both of them, his grin getting harder to hide with each of her steps. When she disappeared into the ladies' room, he cleared his throat, suddenly aware of Mateo's mumblings beside him as he gathered his things.

'Better luck next time, mate. No hard feelings.'

Mateo glared at him, his movements jerky. 'Fuck you.'

Fitz chuckled as Mateo stormed out of the pub, shaking his head. His gut feeling was spot-on with that guy. Hattie was much better to be rid of him. 'You too, buddy,' he muttered, though Mateo was long gone. 'You too.'

Fitz shot a text to Hattie to tell her it was all clear and made his way back to the booth in the corner via the bar and the jukebox.

# Chapter 10

Hattie poked her head around the door, scanning the room quickly before landing on Fitz sitting back in the corner booth, two glasses of bourbon in front of him. Relief washed over her as his gaze connected with hers and he gave a reassuring smile. He'd already sent her a text message saying Ed—*Mateo*—had left, but that smile released the remaining tension in a way only Fitz could. She'd been so convinced she'd remembered Mateo's name, but she couldn't have been further from it.

And she couldn't have been happier that Fitz was there to bail her out.

She slid into the booth across from Fitz, her leg coming to rest against his outstretched one. The tables were small and the booths cozy. It was near on impossible to fill the table without a tangle of limbs beneath it. But he didn't shift his legs.

Neither did she.

He slid the second bourbon across the table towards her, and she sipped it gratefully. There was no annoyance with Fitz ordering for her. He already knew what she liked. And because of that, she could never get frustrated with him for it.

Was it that he knew what she liked?

Or that she'd love anything coming from Fitz?

Hattie rolled the sip of bourbon around in her mouth before swallowing, mulling on that realisation. Sure, he could annoy the hell out of her when he wanted to. But it was never a serious annoyance. She'd never been so frustrated at him that she'd needed space from her best friend. Instead, whenever he was in the mood to annoy her, she'd found herself enjoying the moment, teasing him back and revelling in the fact they could stir each other up without anyone getting offended.

It had always been that way with Fitz. And she kind of hoped it always would be.

But would Fitz still be in her life like this if she formed a relationship with someone else?

The next swallow burned her throat, the rounded warmth of the drink suddenly bitter.

She had always been one to hope for the best possible outcome, but she was also realistic. And while she'd hope her and Fitz could be best friends forever, she knew how these things tend to work when one or both parties start dating. Growing apart would be inevitable. And the thought of growing apart from Fitz hurt.

'Penny for your thoughts?'

Hattie blinked through the blurriness, lifting her gaze from the amber liquid in the glass she held tightly to connect with those grey eyes she'd grown to love seeing on the regular. The ones that never failed to lighten her mood, to make her feel safe.

Home.

Those eyes were home.

And her breath caught in her throat as that thought hit her.

He'd asked her what was on her mind. He was still waiting for her answer. And yet ... she couldn't tell him what was really troubling her thoughts.

Because that just might push him away.

She cleared her throat, lifting her glass and forcing a smile. 'This is so much better than white wine.'

There was a slight hesitation before his smile, like he saw through her diversion, but he let it slide. 'I'm surprised you actually drunk it. Are you going to be okay?'

Hattie tilted her head to one side, scratching her fingernail along the edge of a cardboard coaster. She'd had about a third of the glass of wine. At that amount it could go either way. Sometimes even a sip of white wine was enough to bring on a full-blown migraine. Which, of course, Fitz knew. All she could do now was hydrate and hope for the best.

'I'll hopefully be able to avoid feeling sick later, but there's no telling with the migraine side of it.'

'Why'd you risk it?'

She glanced up at him briefly, her finger pressing the coaster onto the table now instead of picking at it. His tone was not admonishing. Never was. Only curious. And this was no exception. In a way, it should be the former. She'd known all she had to do was give Fitz the right look and he would have come straight over and saved her from the date. He'd been right there, waiting for any such signal.

Instead she'd risked the repercussions of a drink that doesn't agree with her.

'I mean, if you could hear the conversation, you would have done the same.'

His brow furrowed, his lips pressed into a thin line. 'That good, huh?'

'He basically admitted to being a player. He was only looking for a good time, nothing more. Someone he could conveniently call up anytime he was passing through. Probably has a woman in every town.'

She took another drink of the bourbon, a thousand times better than the drink Mateo had ordered her. She still couldn't believe she'd almost fallen for it. Had the signs been there before the date? She'd flicked through the messages they'd sent while she'd been in the bathroom, right before she'd blocked him. Nothing had pointed to him being a player in the messages, though he had made a lot of suggestions she must have missed the first time she'd read them. And there was a significant lack of questions coming from him. In fact, he knew hardly anything about her.

'He also talked about himself. A lot,' she added, placing the glass on the table between them.

Fitz's lips curved in one corner, a dimple forming in his cheek as he did. God, she'd witnessed many girls swooning over that dimple in their school days. He'd basically been a teenage heart-throb. And even though she'd never been the popular girl, she'd always secretly loved the fact that the guy all the girls wanted was hers. Sure, only as a best friend. But still. She was the one he spent his time with, refusing to give that up even with the few girls he'd dated pushing him to. He'd always chosen her over them, and that had always meant something to her. He'd given her the comfort she'd craved.

It wasn't as though she'd had a difficult life. She'd never really gone without anything material. Her parents had both been well off, which inevitably funded their passion for travel. But they had both worked full-time for the life they currently had. Which meant that, more often than not, Hattie's older sister, Charlotte, had been the one looking after her as soon as she'd reached an age to do so. She'd been more present than either of their parents. Until she wasn't. Until she'd got too cool to be looking after her little sister, the task more of a hindrance for her and her popular friends. And Hattie hated being around Charlie's friends.

It was then when Hattie had started spending more time at Fitz's place. Where his family had made her feel more welcome than her own family had. Where she'd spent more awake hours than she had at her own home. She'd wished she'd been born into the Harrow family, where she could experience that love and compassion and warmth that had filled their home like it was ingrained in the walls that surrounded them.

'Well, I gathered that much,' Fitz said, breaking her out of her thoughts once more. His leg nudged against hers, and she couldn't ignore the way it sent a warmth to her core. Made her feel ... full. Like it was the most natural thing. 'The guy clearly didn't like me cutting his grass.'

Hattie's eyes widened. 'You are such a shit-stirrer. I thought he was going to punch you.'

Fitz's grin widened, his teeth showing. 'He didn't stand a chance and he knew it.'

Hattie snorted, rolling her eyes. Fitz was absolutely right. He'd grown up with four older brothers who certainly acted like boys. Rough play was an everyday occurrence in their household growing up. Their mother, Rosie, had given up on telling them to cut it out and switched to merely telling them to take it outside. But Hattie couldn't resist stirring him up.

'You're so full of it.'

His eyes glistened with amusement. 'Yeah, but you love it.'

Yes, she did. She bit into her lower lip, unable to suppress her smile. She wouldn't have him any other way. Another song started on the jukebox, and she realised it was the same one as before. Her favourite. And the way Fitz's lips curved higher told her he had something to do with that.

'Did you—' She left the question hanging, knowing there was no point in finishing it. She already knew the answer. Fitz rose to his feet and stretched a hand towards her, nodding slightly.

'We didn't get to dance before.'

He said it like there was nothing else for it. So simple. So … thoughtful. And meaningful. Her heart skipped a beat. The gesture was so easy for him, so innate. And yet, she couldn't quite form the right words for what it meant for her. When he'd played it before, she'd thought he'd just been helping her out of her date. She should have known he'd been serious about dancing.

He didn't need to play it again to get the dance they'd missed before, nor did he have to buy her a drink. There was nothing saying he even had to hang around once her date had left.

But that's who Fitz is.

And she loved him for it.

She placed her hand in his, blinking back tears as he led her to the closest thing to a dance floor this pub had, her favourite song streaming through the speakers. She'd managed to pull herself together by the time they'd got there, but when he spun her into his arms and swayed them a few beats slower than the music, it almost undid her.

This is what she wanted in a relationship.

An easiness. Someone who made life better. Who lived in the moment with her and made her feel like she could take on anything the world threw at her with him by her side. Someone who loved her for all her flaws and quirks and never stepped on eggshells around her.

'You really forgot his name?' Fitz muttered, lifting an eyebrow.

She chuckled, rolling her eyes, grateful for the distraction. Her mind was not where she wanted to be right now. There was too much to process. 'I could have sworn I had it right.'

His eyebrow shot higher, the look in his eyes turning mischievous. 'You're not gonna forget who I am, are you?'

'I never forget anything to do with you, Fitz.' She held his gaze, her mood growing serious. For all their teasing, for some reason she really needed him to know this.

His expression softened, his smile gentle as he tucked a lock of hair behind her ear, his thumb brushing against her cheek. 'Same for me, Hat.'

His smile deepened, and she knew in her heart that he meant it.

'Thank you for your help tonight. I appreciate it.' He really had no idea how much.

He held her gaze, lifting his shoulder in a shrug, her hand rising with the movement too. 'That's what friends are for.'

Right. Of course. So why did that statement leave an ache in her chest, her heart dropping a little?

The song changed to a slower one, yet neither of them broke apart, both enjoying being the only ones dancing despite the pub growing busier. She wasn't sure who stepped in first or if they both did, but her hands slid from Fitz's shoulders, linking behind his neck just as his hands lowered to her waist, the rest of their bodies only a breath apart. Even now, she wasn't sure they swayed in time with the music. But quite frankly, she didn't care. Dancing with Fitz ...

It was nice.

It grounded her.

Everything made sense, even if just for a moment.

And it felt natural. Everything to do with Fitz was natural. She'd always thought that was normal. He was her best friend, after all. Natural and comfortable came hand in hand with that, didn't it?

She let her head fall slightly to the left, his cheek meeting her there, and they continued swaying. The whole world could be falling apart around them right now and she wouldn't know. And she wasn't sure what to make of that. Everything she wanted in a man, she realised, was Fitz. Yet he was the one person she could never truly have. Not like that. Because losing him—losing their friendship—would ruin her. She closed her eyes and took a shaky breath, breathing in that seawater and woodsy spice of his cologne, and it filled her with that familiar warmth.

'What's on your mind?'

His voice rumbled against her, his breath whispering against her ear. An odd pulse of desire swept through her, and she quickly shut it down. That white wine must be affecting her more than she realised, because there was no other excuse for it.

'I need to find someone just like you,' she admitted, surprising herself at her brazenness. But it was the truth, wasn't it? If she couldn't have Fitz, then she needed someone just like him. Who treated her the way he treated her.

He inhaled deeply, his cheek still pressed against the side of her head, and she felt the slightest turn of his head towards her, the hint of his lips brushing against her head. The slight tensing in his body. But his steps didn't falter, and neither did hers, both still swaying at the same pace despite a faster song playing now.

She should clarify what she meant. She should say something—anything—to make sure he didn't take what she'd said the wrong way. But she couldn't. Whether it was the wine and the bourbon or just simply the moment they shared, no words were willing to form. But in the end, she didn't need to because Fitz voiced her exact thoughts.

'There's no one else like me, Hattie, baby.'

*I know.*

But instead of saying that, she tried to swallow the lump forming in her throat.

# Chapter 11

Fitz woke with a crick in his neck and a woman in his arms. A woman who smelled of coconut and flowers and vanilla soap. He rubbed his eyes, taking in his surroundings. The early morning sunlight drifted through the space between the blinds and window frame, the birds announcing that dawn was breaking. The streaming channel's logo fluttered silently across the television. The movie they'd watched had ended hours ago. Clearly neither of them had bothered to turn the television off.

He dropped his hand from his face, landing on a smooth, feminine one splayed out across his stomach. The slender fingers tangled absently with his, though the relaxed exhale told him she was still deep in sleep. But that hold ... those fingers entwined with his ...

He'd never held a hand that felt as right as this one. Had never wanted to close his eyes and continue sleeping with a woman in his arms like this. Her body running along the length of his as he balanced on the edge of the couch, keeping her safe between him and the couch cushions. He tested his other hand, the warmth of bare skin against his fingertips as they skimmed across the small of her back, just above the line of her pyjama shorts. She let out a sleepy moan that triggered something in him as his fingertips moved, and he stilled, holding his breath until he was sure she was still deep in sleep.

A touch of sunlight caught on her golden hair as he realised exactly the position he was in. One of her legs rested between his, her head resting in the crook of his shoulder, her knee dangerously close to his hard-on. She let out another sleepy moan, his erection only growing harder. He had to fight himself to not roll her over and make love to the woman.

The woman.

Hattie.

*Fuck.*

They'd fallen asleep on the couch together before, but they'd never woken up snuggling as intimately as this. And he certainly hadn't woken right next to her with a raging hard-on wanting to do things with her a man shouldn't want to do with his best friend.

*Fuckity fuck.*

He wouldn't even be able to hide it if he tried. All she'd have to do is move her leg slightly up or her hand slightly down or even open her eyes and she'd know. They could try laughing it off, sure. But after last night ...

She'd said she wanted to be with someone just like him.

Not him.

Someone like him.

Theirs was a line neither of them were willing to cross.

And here he was, waking up with her in his arms and horny as hell.

He mouthed a curse, knowing he had to somehow untangle himself from her hold without waking her. He needed a cold shower. At the very least he needed to let off steam. Obviously his body couldn't be trusted around her, so he had to keep that in mind too.

Fitz carefully released her fingers and lifted her knee with his fingertips. He let his legs drop off the couch, careful not to shift his upper body. So far so good. But he hadn't started the hardest part yet. He took a shallow breath, wary that breathing too hard might wake her, and carefully slid his free hand beneath her head, lifting her just enough to ease his arm out. A tingle started in his arm as pins and needles filled it, making his movements a little jerky, but he managed to free his arm just in time for her to roll towards him, her head rolling off his hand and onto the pillow he'd been resting on. Her hair draped over her face as she stopped.

He didn't move, his hand still hovering near the back of her head, his chest still against the edge of the couch. His breath held.

She let out a little snore, and a smile tugged at his lips. God, she was damn cute when she slept, though she would give him shit if he ever brought it up. So for now, he would keep it to himself.

Content that she was still asleep and he could make his escape, he carefully rose to his feet, reaching for the blanket that had become tangled down where their legs had been. He draped it over her, tucking it in around her shoulders to keep her warm. While it had been quite warm when they'd watched the movie, the morning had grown cool. He paused, still bent over her as she let out a little puff of air that shifted the lock of hair that had fallen across her face.

It wasn't even a conscious action. He hadn't realised he'd reached for her until his hand had gathered up the errant silky strands and brushed them back from her face, his knuckles grazing her cheek with the lightest of touches. With his change of position, the sunlight shimmered across her face, catching on the long, thick eyelashes that fanned against her cheeks, her elegant lips in a sexy pout.

His breath caught.

She wasn't just cute when she slept.

She was fucking beautiful.

Time stopped as he taught himself to breathe again, unable to tear his eyes from the woman before him.

His best friend.

Hattie.

His pants seemed tighter, and his heart fuller, and he just did not have the capacity to unpack what all that meant right now.

So he leaned forward, brushed his lips softly against her forehead, and left.

Hattie's head was throbbing when she'd finally willed herself to try opening her eyes. That damn white wine. She let out a groan, rolling over with an arm across her eyes to block out the light glaring through the window. The fact her couch was positioned in the exact spot for sunlight to shine directly in her eyes if she happened to fall asleep on it was clearly an oversight. Hell, she'd only have to move it a few inches to avoid it happening again.

Couch.

*Fitz.*

She forced her eyes open, squinting through the pain, and scanned the room around her. The television was still on but with nothing but the streaming channel logo floating across the screen. She'd fallen asleep watching a movie, though she could have sworn Fitz had been here too.

Yet he was nowhere to be seen now.

Had he left once he'd realised she'd fallen asleep? He usually didn't. In fact, she wasn't sure if he ever had. They'd both woken up sprawled out in the lounge room more times than she could count, and he'd never disappeared without waking her first.

Hattie pulled herself up onto her elbows and glanced towards the kitchen, listening for any signs of movement. There were none. Her place was eerily quiet. A good indication she was alone.

The change of position had her head throbbing more, so she dropped it back on the cushion she'd used as a pillow and rubbed her hands over her face, willing the pain to go away.

She'd had the strangest dream last night. Strange, yet wonderful. She'd been lying against a strong, muscular body, her hand pressed against the abs hidden beneath his shirt. His leg had been resting between hers in just the right position to make her body yearn for more. The woodsy crisp scent of him had surrounded her. And the steady rise and fall of his chest beneath her head, the regular, soothing thumps of his heartbeat, had only swallowed her in a feeling of warmth. Of home. And it was that familiar feeling that told her who the mystery man in her dream was.

Fitz.

Her best friend.

Then the scene had changed. More of a feeling than a visual. The warmth of his knuckles barely touching her cheek, his fingers in her hair. The subtle press of his lips against her forehead that had fuelled her belly with desire. But when she'd opened her eyes, no one was there. Yet she could still feel the touch, the kiss, like it had been real and not a dream. Her body still remembered the feel of his fingertips sliding along her bare skin.

It was like nothing she'd ever felt before, and yet it was everything she'd always wanted. And the fact it was with Fitz—even if it was just a dream—worried her pulsing brain.

The dream could have been worse, she supposed.

They could have been having sex. Delicious, erotic sex.

But somehow, the dream she'd had seemed more intimate. More ... special. Meaningful.

Her cheeks heated with the blush she knew had overcome her. Thank God Fitz had already left. She wasn't sure she could quite look him in the eyes after that.

She could never tell him about her dream.

There had never been anything she'd been unable to tell him. He knew her deepest darkest secrets, and she knew his. But this?

This was a secret he could never know about. It could just be the one thing capable of driving a wedge between them.

But why had he left?

That question still ate at her. She was sure he didn't have to work today. Unless, of course, he'd been called in. But surely he would've let her know before leaving if that were the case. Forcing herself to a seated position, she dug around in the couch cushions until she found her phone. The brightness of the screen hurt her eyes almost as much as the sun shining through the window, but she was able to make out that there were no new messages and it was almost nine in the morning.

She needed to get up and moving. Have an electrolyte drink, a coffee, and a cool shower. That usually helped shake the worst of a white-wine migraine. God, she was glad she hadn't had more than she did. She would truly be regretting it if she had. She should have known better.

She did, she reminded herself. She'd thought long and hard about whether drinking any amount of it would be worth it. And she'd decided it was worth the risk. A stupid decision, looking back on it now. With Fitz there, she hadn't needed to have even the slightest sip. Hindsight was a funny thing.

*Fitz.*

Hattie groaned, pushing herself to her feet and making her way slowly to the kitchen to get started on the drinks. She slipped her phone on the charger as she passed it and fumbled her way through the cupboards until she found the tube with the dissolvable electrolyte tablets and dropped a couple in a glass of water. She really needed to get her head on straight, shake the memories of her dream as quickly as she could so that Fitz wouldn't think anything was off. And if she saw him before then, she'd just have to fake it.

Fake that she hadn't felt the warmth and hardness of his abs. How she'd loved the feel of his fingertips skimming across her bare skin. Or his lips pressing against her forehead. Cheeks. Neck. Lower.

She flushed again, rubbing her hands over her face once more.

'Oh, God,' she moaned, picking up her glass and heading towards the shower. Her thoughts had gone from what had happened in her dream to what more could have happened. And hell, if it didn't all seem appealing.

Except it's Fitz!

And now she couldn't shake the vision of the mischievous look he'd have in his eyes if he trailed kissed down her stomach, the way his grey eyes would darken with desire. The tilt of his lips as he gave her that signature smile of his. Her whole body suddenly burned, the very thought of him lavishing her with attention sending her into a full-body blush.

With another groan, she reached for the handle of the shower and turned it all the way cold.

# Chapter 12

Fitz's muscles ached as he strode up to Hattie's door. He'd pushed it harder than ever at the gym that morning, desperately needing the release that only came with physical exertion. He'd been only mildly successful in forgetting how perfectly Hattie's body had slotted against his as they'd slept, how his lips still tingled from the kiss he'd pressed to her forehead. But mildly successful was the best he could hope for.

He had the day off work, and he'd already agreed with Hattie the night before that they would spend the day together. And he wasn't the kind of man to break his word, let alone going back on plans he'd made with his best friend. Now that he was working at the station, he wouldn't be getting every weekend off. With a rotating roster, he would only land on a free weekend every so often, and this would be his last full weekend for a while. And considering Hattie's working hours, Sundays were just about the only days she regularly got off. Saturdays only if she didn't have a wedding or other event to work.

So he had no choice but to suck it up, bury these confusing feelings deep down, and pretend like he hadn't wanted to fuck his best friend earlier that morning.

He checked his watch as he neared her door. It was almost half past nine. He'd been gone for hours after he'd put in an extra-long workout and had dropped past the bakery to pick up breakfast. There was a good chance she might still be asleep, especially if she was trying to shake a migraine from drinking wine the night before. She'd spent the night before assuring him she was fine, but he'd still been able to tell from the tension in the corner of her lips that she'd been queasy.

Deciding he wouldn't knock in case it woke her, he slipped the key she'd given him into the lock and turned it, swinging the door open just enough to slip into her house while balancing the bag of bakery goods and takeaway coffees. He'd intended on glancing towards the couch on the right first to see if she was still asleep, but her shriek from his left meant he didn't have to.

'Oh my God. Fitz!'

His eyes widened, and he fumbled with the precariously balancing goodies as he closed the door behind him, his eyes locked on her.

Or rather, the navy blue lace panties covering her ass as she leaned forward to quickly pull on a pair of shorts.

Holy. Shit.

There goes his resolve to suppress everything deep down, straight to his tightening crotch. He barely caught the paper bag of bakery goods as it slipped from his grasp and managed to somehow catch it by slapping an arm across it, sandwiching it against his stomach. The scrolls would likely be squished, but he was lucky they hadn't scattered all over the floor.

He was unable to tear his gaze away from her. From the bronze tan of her skin. The perfect curves she kept hidden under clothes he now despised. She tugged her shorts up, turning towards him as she buttoned them, breaking his gaze from her lower half.

To her breasts.

Tucked comfortably in a matching blue bra with a lace trim.

His mouth dried, once again unable to lift his gaze, despite the only logical voice in his head screaming at him to do so. God he hoped she didn't notice his blatant staring, but he could tell from her peripherals that her head was bent forward as she fumbled with the button.

Then she reached forward to the clean laundry basket to pluck a tee out of it, her breasts threatening to spill from the bra.

*Thank you, gravity.*

Still not meeting his eyes, she pulled the shirt over her head and pushed her arms through, the shirt snagging on her glasses as she did. Her stomach and sides stretched tight as she reached high to fix it. He heard a groan, and it took him a moment to realise it had come from him.

God, he hoped she hadn't heard it.

He quickly cleared his throat, hoping to have masked the groan with a cough, and forced himself to lift his gaze now she'd covered up. 'Morning,' he managed, not missing the roughness in his voice.

'Morning.' Her voice sounded high-strung, and a blush darkened her cheeks. Whether that was because she'd noticed him staring or because he'd walked in on her getting changed, he wasn't sure. Perhaps both.

He lifted the tray holding two takeaway coffees, and her gaze fell to it, looking as though she'd only just noticed he came bearing gifts. 'I have coffee.'

'God, you're a lifesaver.' Her expression softened, her shoulders visibly relaxing as she reached for the tray and led the way towards the kitchen.

He scooped up the bag of bakery goods in his now free hand, cringing as he peeked inside to see that some of the scrolls were indeed squished.

He cleared his throat again, the vision of her in her near nothings burned in his mind even though the clothes she wore now gave no hint of her sexy underwear underneath. 'How are you feeling?'

'Better now.'

She sipped one of the coffees as she dragged a stool around to the kitchen side of the bench. He took the stool opposite her, trying not to look relieved that she'd put the bench between them, and took his own cup from the tray. He slung the bag of food on the bench between them, tearing it open to reveal the assortment of scrolls. Some were still in a semi-not-squished state, though one almost looked mangled enough to not be able to tell what it originally was.

He reached for that one just as she did, their fingers touching for the briefest of moments. Fire singed through his veins at the contact, and she inhaled sharply, snapping her hand back as though she'd been electrocuted. His hand, however, still hovered over the squished scroll.

'Sorry, I—'

'Mangled one's my fault,' he said at the same time. He picked it up, then slid one just like its original form towards her. He couldn't help but notice she didn't reach towards it until he'd pulled his hand back. 'Good thing I got a second one.'

She chuckled, though it wasn't with the usual easiness. He frowned, picking at a bit of the mangled scroll before popping it in his mouth. She was acting ... odd. Avoiding eye contact. Jumpy. Putting that space between them.

To be fair, he had walked in on her half naked.

But something told him it was more than that.

Had she noticed more from that morning than he'd thought? The next bite almost got stuck in his throat. Her eyes drifted towards him as he coughed, her eyebrow lifting as he sipped his coffee to wash it down.

'No migraine?' he said, taking another bite.

She chewed her mouthful slowly, then swallowed, the subtle movement of her slender neck drawing his attention. God, he needed to get a grip. 'A bit of a headache,' she said. 'But a shower and electrolytes helped a lot.' She lifted her cup considering it. 'Coffee, too. Should be able to shake it this time.'

'That's good.'

She nodded slowly, her eyes distant, and lowered her hands to the bench, bringing her gaze to meet his again. There was something he couldn't quite read there. Something indiscernible. His throat dried again.

'What time did you leave?'

'Hmm?' he managed over another mouthful of coffee.

'This morning. Or last night. I didn't see you leave.'

'Oh.' He picked at another bit of mangled scroll. It still tasted good, so it had that going for it. But it just didn't quite hit right. He lifted it to his lips, pulled his hand back before taking the bite. 'I'm not sure, exactly. Sun was rising, so whenever that was.'

She swallowed, worrying her lower lip with her teeth. 'You didn't wake me.'

He caught a hint of disappointment in that statement, but she looked more hesitant. 'You were out like a light, Hat. I'm not sure anything would have woken you.'

A white lie wouldn't hurt, right? She didn't need to know that he'd crept out as quietly and as quickly as he could so she wouldn't be met with a sight she couldn't unsee.

He shrugged nonchalantly, bringing the scroll to his mouth again. 'I figured you might've still been asleep by the time I got back.'

A smile, though slight, tugged at her lips. 'Sun was shining in my eyes.'

'Ah. Sorry. Forgot to move it before I left. Next time.'

Her brow pulled in confusion, then she laughed, her body seemingly growing more relaxed throughout their conversation.

God, he loved hearing her laugh. Being the one behind that glorious lilt that made his heart skip a beat and his spirits lighten.

'But you were almost right. I hadn't long woken up before you came back. I had a shower as soon as I was up.'

'Sounds like I had perfect timing then.'

She nodded, and the image of her in her knickers floated back into his vision, her body flushed pink with the blush she'd had

...

Perfect timing indeed.

'Where'd you go?'

Her tone had turned more conversational now, her eyes brightening as she took a larger bite of her scroll and nudged her glasses up her nose. He bit back the smile. Perhaps she hadn't noticed his dilemma earlier that morning after all. Perhaps nothing had to change between them. As long as he kept his feelings—whatever they were—to himself.

'The gym,' he said matter-of-factly, glad to have his best friend back. 'Kinda got in the zone. Didn't realise I'd spent so long there.'

'Ah, the cause of the muscles, obviously.' She circled the scroll towards him as though using it to take him all in. She took another bite, resting her elbows on the kitchen bench as she did, and moaned with the next mouthful. 'Mmm. I'm not sure when the last time I went to the gym was. Probably before you left.'

'Still got your membership?'

She tilted her head from side to side, her nose scrunching as though she didn't particularly like her answer. 'Well, yeah. Seemed too much effort to cancel. And every time I thought about cancelling, I figured I should probably just go. Then I was either too busy or too tired or just couldn't be bothered.'

'You could come with me.'

She scoffed, reaching for her coffee. 'I'm not that much of a morning person, Fitz. Come to think of it, neither were you before you left.'

He shrugged, finishing off his scroll and reaching for another. 'Wasn't much else to do while training. Their schedule was ... intense. Guess I just got in the habit.' He lifted an eyebrow, leaning forward. 'You could get in the habit too.'

She scrunched her nose again, looking damn cute when she did, and shook her head. 'Never said I'd like to see the sunrise.' Her eyes shimmered with amusement, and something tugged at his chest.

'It's the most glorious sight you could see,' he said, meaning every word of it. He'd never been a morning person before training. But waking up early and seeing the sunrise each morning had grounded him. He'd come to love seeing the wondrous painting spread in the sky.

He had a feeling seeing it with Hattie would make it that much more wonderful.

She ran her tongue along her teeth in thought, then pulled her lower lip between them once more, her eyebrow twitching upwards.

'Well, maybe I could be convinced.'

He'd take that as a win, his mind already plotting how he could get her out of the house to see the sunrise. She wouldn't like being dragged outside in the early hours, but he could already imagine the awe on her face as she saw what he'd come to love seeing.

'So what's the plan today, Hat?' he said, still working on getting control over his errant thoughts.

'Rosie still do Sunday roasts?'

He nodded. Fitz's mother had done Sunday roasts as long as he could remember. Being a family with five sons, she'd always loved putting on a spread to feed the bottomless pits that surrounded her. Sunday roasts were his favourite. Especially the roasted potatoes that no one else had even come close to in flavour. The late lunch tradition hadn't stopped with the boys growing up and moving out. Whoever wanted a decent feed would be there. In fact, the lunch had only gotten bigger with Nick and Dave both starting families of their own.

Hattie shrugged, finishing off her scroll and wiping her hands against each other. 'Been a while since I've had a roast. It's also been a while since I've been able to pop over for a cuppa with your mum. I've missed her.'

Fitz eyed his best friend. The one who had slotted into his family years ago like it was her own, who had developed a relationship with his ma like she was her own. Ma had told him whenever Hattie had dropped past while he'd been away. He'd been grateful that she'd still kept visiting. He'd been worried for Ma that Hattie might've pulled back on the visits completely while he'd been away.

Clearly not.

She was obviously comfortable enough around his family to keep visiting even without him. And he loved that for her.

Loved it for his ma. She'd taken Hattie under her wings like she was the daughter she'd never had. Now she had Liz and Ainslie to mother as well.

'Sunday roast it is, then.'

# Chapter 13

Hattie had always loved spending time in the Harrow household more than she had her own, and Sunday roasts was everything she loved about it. She remembered being included in the family affair like she was Rosie's own daughter, and in a way, she'd always felt like it. The whole family had welcomed her into their home with open arms, Fitz's brothers teasing her like they were her own.

This was the family she'd chosen. Sure, she still got along well enough with her own parents and sister, but they'd always been hard pressed having a simple meal together. The Harrow household had always filled the cravings she'd had to be part of something special. To be part of a big family. And this family was only getting bigger.

She scanned the room around her, the large dining table already filled to capacity. It was loud and noisy and busy and she loved every bit of it.

Fitz's eldest brother, Nick, sat with his pregnant wife, Liz, keeping her glass full of sparkling water. He'd always been protective of her, treating her like she was the most precious thing in the world. Since she'd fallen pregnant, he'd become even more so. But the smile on Liz's face as she looked at him showed that she loved it.

Dave was sitting beside his wife, Ainslie, with their son, Cliff, on Ainslie's other side. Dave held her hand under the table, and the look they shared was a look Hattie had only ever dreamed of feeling herself. The two couples made her hopeful she could still experience that herself someday.

The middle Harrow brother, Eric, had also joined them, his mood considerably improved over recent months since he'd lost his very serious girlfriend in a fire a year ago. For a while there, he'd been in a dark place—completely understandable, of course—but it was good to see him smile again.

Fitz's dad, Jeff, was at one end of the table, deep in discussion with Nick and Dave over the happenings at the station. He'd been retired for years now, but no one would guess it. Now that Fitz had completed training, all the men in the Harrow family were officially firefighters. The only brother not present was Sam, and that was only because he worked at the Mount Gambier station.

Hattie glanced to Rosie next, who was busy piling extra food on everyone's plates, making sure each person got more than their share. She smiled. Rosie looked so bright and happy being surrounded by family. It truly was a household full of love and happiness and it filled Hattie's heart just being around them.

She let her gaze drift to Fitz. Her best friend. And the man she'd dreamed about the night before. Who had also walked in on her half naked that morning. Talk about an eventful start to the day.

He was discussing Cliff's history project with him, giving the kid the kind of attention he might give another adult. From Cliff's expression, he'd grown to like being treated like an adult.

But that's how Fitz had always been.

She'd never seen him treating a kid like they might normally be treated. Rather he would talk to them in the way he would talk to anyone, giving them the same respect an adult would get. And it was just another thing she loved about him.

As a friend, of course. She loved his whole family like they were her own. Fitz was no exception. At least that's what she told herself.

But after her dream last night ...

After the flush that had covered her from head to toe when he'd seen her in her underwear ...

The pulse of electricity that had seared through her whole body after their hands had touched when they'd both reached for the scroll ...

Well, something told her that perhaps she did love him differently.

But then she told herself that going down that line of thinking was ridiculous. And perhaps that pulse that zapped through her was merely just static electricity like one would experience after going down a slide.

And yet.

Her gaze drifted to her lap, his thigh resting against hers. An unavoidable position considering how crammed everyone was around the table. But even so, the touch of his leg against hers filled her with a warmth she couldn't explain. A fullness in her core she'd never had with someone who was just a friend. Something she realised now that she'd never felt with him before he'd left for training. Had she?

She'd always been comfortable with Fitz. Like he was her home.

That hadn't changed now. It was just ... extra.

Rosie took her seat at the end of the table near Hattie and placed a hand over hers, offering her a warm smile. 'How are you going, honey? I've missed you lately.'

She squeezed the older woman's hand, her own smile genuine. 'I know. I'm sorry. I've been busy with work.'

She didn't know why she felt like she needed to apologise. But the fact was, she loved spending time with Rosie. And she'd missed it too. It wasn't until Fitz had left for training that she'd realised she'd mostly come over with Fitz here. While she'd still made an effort to visit Rosie whenever she could, her schedule had filled in Fitz's absence. She should make more of an effort to visit her now, she decided. The woman had done more for her than her own mother had at times.

'I've seen you at the salon a lot,' Rosie said, releasing her hand to pick up her knife and fork. 'I was starting to think I'd have to book an appointment to see you.'

'Sorry,' she said again. What else could she say? Since finishing her apprenticeship, she'd basically been living at the salon. 'I'll have a look at my appointments and carve some time out for a catch up. Maybe we could get a mani-pedi, pamper ourselves a little?'

Rosie gave her a soft smile, then nodded. 'I'd like that, love.'

'Sign me up,' Liz said from Fitz's other side. 'Pregnancy has sucked the life out of my nails. I could kill to have pretty nails again.'

'You're perfect just the way you are,' Nick said without missing a beat, quickly returning back to his conversation with Dave and Jeff.

Liz peered around Fitz at Hattie. 'I'm still coming.'

'Room for one more?' Ainslie piped in, curling her fingertips into her palm. 'I can't even remember the last time I got my nails done.'

Hattie felt for the woman. Before reuniting with Dave, she'd come from an abusive relationship. She smiled at the woman who certainly looked a lot healthier and happier now than when she'd first come back into Dave's life.

'Of course. Let's make a day of it, then. Just us girls.' Hattie mentally checked when she had free. 'Does Saturday work for everyone? I don't have a wedding to work next weekend.'

Liz groaned. 'No, but I do. Weekends are gonna be out for me until baby comes.'

Hattie chewed her lower lip at the reminder she wasn't the only one with a busy schedule. Liz worked as an events planner with Marcy. Usually Marcy took the weddings and Liz took parties, but in the busier wedding season, they both had to work weddings.

The four women agreed to create a group text message and post availability as soon as they were able to look at their schedules. Hattie glanced back at Rosie, her cheeks reddening from the smile she wore. Hattie smiled for her too. The woman had spent most of her life in a family of men. She'd always called Hattie the daughter she'd never had. Now she had two more. Hattie reached for Rosie's hand and gave it a squeeze, a silent acknowledgement of the changes in the family dynamic.

Instead of one-on-one time with Fitz's mother, it appeared Hattie would now be sharing her with Liz and Ainslie. Not that she minded. She loved spending time with them just as much as she had with the rest of Fitz's family.

Conversation continued around the table long after everyone had stopped eating, and Hattie could only revel in the way being included in the big family affair made her feel. She'd overheard Jeff saying Sam would be coming back for Christmas this year. It would be the first family Christmas that included wives and grandchildren, and Hattie didn't miss the excited look in Rosie's eyes.

She drifted in and out of conversations, revelling in the laughter and jesting that surrounded her, and wished she could truly call this family her own rather than being a guest.

'How's house hunting, Fitz?'

She shot her gaze towards her best friend as the keywords caught her attention. He hadn't said anything about looking for a house. She just assumed he was still happy living at home.

Dave had been the one to ask the question, and that's where Fitz's attention was focused. 'Slowly. Rentals are in short supply at the moment and there seems to be a lot of people who need it more than me. I saw a young family who were on the verge of living out of their car at one place, and the real estate agent looked more interested in me. I told her to prioritize any families over my application. Can't have kids being without homes, you know?'

'It's a tough time for housing,' Dave agreed. 'Something will come up eventually, but keep in mind there will always be families looking for homes.'

Fitz shrugged, toying with the edge of the placemat. 'I can sleep anywhere. It's not me I worry about.'

'You'll never be living out of your car, Fitz,' Rosie said chidingly. 'You've always got your room here.'

He gave his mother a smile, but Hattie could tell there was more to it. His eyes met with hers briefly, his smile not quite reaching his eyes. A promise in them to talk about this later. It obviously wasn't the time to discuss details now, yet she couldn't shake the heaviness that settled in her chest. The topic changed again, and Hattie noticed Rosie had started piling up the dirty plates. She quickly shoved to her feet and gathered up plates herself.

'Let me do the dishes, Rosie.'

The older woman smiled at her and offered her thanks. She'd clearly grown used to the idea of accepting help when it was offered. Hattie was sure any of boys would have offered if she hadn't, but if she was being honest, she needed a moment to herself. And doing the dishes would offer such a reprieve.

She watched the sink fill with hot soapy water that she could rinse the stubborn bits with before loading the dishes in the dishwasher.

She didn't know why it hurt that Fitz hadn't told her he was looking for a house. She'd thought they told each other everything, especially big decisions like moving house. So why hadn't he told her about this?

Each of the Harrow boys filed into the kitchen with their arms loaded with plates and dishes of leftover food. She smiled at each of them as they offloaded the dirty dishes near the sink, and she busied herself with sorting them into piles. She'd let the cutlery soak and rinse the cups first, then the plates, loading the dishwasher as she went. Some of the dishes would have to be handwashed, which she would do last. The kitchen was busy behind her as the men covered over leftover food and put it in the fridge. It had all happened quickly, and soon the flurry of voices trailed outside as everyone shifted out the back and she was left in the kitchen with her thoughts.

It took her a moment to realise she wasn't alone, jumping as a hand reached out beside her and took the damp cloth from the side of the sink. She was met with shining grey eyes, one of which was veiled by a lock of dark hair. Her heart skipped a beat, her mind drifting back to the dream she'd had the night before. Would she ever be able to forget that?

'Everything okay?' Fitz said as he moved to wipe down the bench. 'You jumped to doing the dishes pretty quickly.'

'Just helping out where I can,' she said as though that were the only reason. 'I don't want to be freeloading off your parents. Doing the dishes is the least I could do.'

A warm hand rested on her shoulder, gently turning her to face him. His expression had grown concerned, his brow furrowed. 'That's not what I meant. You seemed off when you left the table. Did someone say something?'

She shook her head, staring down at her hands between them. It was more of what someone—Fitz—hadn't said. But she was still trying to figure out why that should bother her in the first place.

'You never said you were looking for a house.'

She hated that she sounded like a whiny girlfriend when she'd said it, and she regretted bringing it up almost immediately. He jerked back ever so slightly, but she'd seen it. Had he noticed the tone too?

She groaned, turning back towards the sink. 'Forget it. You're entitled to your secrets.'

She cringed again. Another poor choice of words. What the hell was wrong with her?

'It's not a secret, Hat.'

He had every right to sound annoyed at her, but he didn't. He'd said it softly, and that apparently was enough to surprise her. God knows why. She shouldn't be surprised at all. Not really. Fitz had never sounded particularly annoyed at her before. She glanced at him from her peripherals, barely moving her head. But it was enough to see him run a hand through that unruly hair as he sighed.

'I guess we've both just been really busy and talking about other things. But yeah. I'm looking for a place of my own. I'm not a kid anymore, and this place doesn't offer much chance to be alone.'

'Is that what you want? To be alone?'

He tilted his head, lifting his eyebrow as he did, and didn't meet her gaze. 'You know what I mean, Hat. You moved out of your parents' place as soon as you could. I'm twenty-two and still sleeping in the same bed I did when I was eight.'

She stared at the remaining bubbles in the sink and let her vision blur. He had a point. She'd left home as soon as she could, somehow scraping enough money together to pay the rent. Now that she was fully qualified, she had no trouble making ends meet.

'You were waiting for your training,' she said as though he needed an explanation.

'Yeah, and now I've finished that.' He bumped against her shoulder, and she found herself leaning against him in the way they'd always done. Except now the scent of him stirred her insides until she craved more contact. 'I wasn't keeping it from you,' he continued, his voice rumbling through her. Engulfing her. 'It just didn't come up. Not that it matters much, since I'll never find a place at the rate I'm going.'

She closed her eyes, lapping up the warmth of his arm as he put it around her and pulled her into his side. She rested her head against his chest as she pressed into him. God, her dream had been spot-on with how it felt.

'I have a room.'

Her eyes shot open as she realised she'd been the one to say that, and for a brief moment, Fitz didn't move. Was she insane? That dream had messed with her mind. She couldn't be having feelings like that for her best friend and expect to get over them with him living in her place. But she did have a room he could use. And even though she didn't need help paying the rent, it wouldn't hurt to be able to save some of that money to one day buy a place of her own. And it would get him out of his parents' place. Not to mention she lived closer to the fire station than his parents did.

He would also be the perfect housemate. They got along well, and he was a generally clean guy who also smelled amazing. He was already over at her place a fair bit and often fell asleep on her couch. Hell, he even had a key. The more she thought about it, the more it made sense.

'What?'

He pulled back to look at her, though his hand still remained on her shoulder. She stepped out of his hold, certain she couldn't think straight if she stayed there. Though something told her that her brain—and her heart—had already made up its mind. Perhaps living with him would help her shake those odd thoughts and feelings that had pestered her all day.

'I live in a three-bedroom house and I'm really only using the spare rooms to store random crap. It wouldn't take much to shift it. We could use one room for storage and you could have the other.'

His head tilted to the side as though he was actually considering the idea. And while part of her was telling her to shut her mouth and that living with him would be a terrible idea, the other part was saying to throw all caution to the wind and go for it.

'You practically live there anyway,' she continued, busying herself with the dishes again. 'Why not make it official?'

'Well, I wouldn't exactly be *alone*.'

'What, are you planning on bringing women home?'

There was a beat of silence, and for some reason she couldn't explain, her heart plummeted to her stomach. He didn't deny it. Did that mean he did? Had she just hit the nail on the head of why he wanted his own place? It made sense, she supposed. It would be awkward bringing someone home to spend the night if he lived with his parents.

He cleared his throat, his voice sounding gruff as he spoke. 'I mean, if I did, would you be okay with that?'

*No.*

She squeezed her eyes closed, telling that little inner voice to shut up. The thought had taken her by surprise, but she realised there was an element of truth to it. The thought of seeing him bring women home to spend a night making love and having fun and seeing him treating someone else the way she wanted to be treated ... she hated it. And she shut down the brief thought that she wanted to be the one he treated right.

But considering he was her best friend, it would only be a matter of time before she had to share him—no, not share. Because when he found someone who he decided he wanted to spend his life with, she would not be sharing him. That other woman would have all of him, and Hattie would be left watching it all unfurl from the side.

And that's how it should be, she told herself.

As much as it would break her heart.

She swallowed the lump that had formed in her throat, but refused to look at him. 'I guess just give me a heads-up so I don't walk in on you. And I'll do the same for you.'

She risked a brief glance in his direction, long enough to see a darkness sweep through his eyes before it disappeared. Something she couldn't quite place in the fleeting moment it had been there.

'You already have a key,' she pointed out. 'It'd just be a matter of adding you to the lease, which I'm sure would be fine.'

'Yeah,' he said slowly, thoughtfully. He touched her arm, urging her to look at him, the warmth spreading straight to her core and nestling into place, ready to grow into something more. 'Are you sure?'

No. She absolutely was not sure. But looking up into those gorgeous grey eyes, how could she say no? She'd never been able to deny him anything when he looked at her like that, and she had a feeling that wasn't about to change. She swallowed hard, silencing all the thoughts that protested at her.

'Living with my best friend?' She forced a smile, though she didn't fully feel it. 'How could I not be sure about that?'

His Adam's apple bobbed as he swallowed. 'Okay, then yeah. Yes. I'd love to move in with you, Hattie, baby. Thank you.'

He pulled her in for a hug, her face pressing into his chest. She breathed him in, wondering how many hugs they could have like this while he lived with her. Would they still hug?

'You'll have to get a bed though,' she teased as they broke apart. 'Can't sleep on my couch forever.'

He laughed, nodding. 'I'll get one tomorrow.' His eyes gleamed, and she realised she could get used to seeing that. She could get used to a lot with Fitz. Especially if he kept calling her baby.

# Chapter 14

Fitz flicked the light switch, eliciting a groan from a sleepy Hattie. He walked over to her bed, reaching for her blanket to tug it back like he would with his brothers, then decided against it as the vision of her in her underwear filled his mind again. Instead, he reached for her shoulder and nudged her.

'Time to wake up.' He held back a smile as she swatted a hand at him, groaning again as she glanced at the time on her phone.

'Go away, Fitz,' she grumbled. 'It's not even morning.'

He smirked. Morning for Hattie was well after the sun had risen. Granted it was still dark outside, but if the sunrise was anything like it was the day before, it was gearing up to be quite spectacular.

He waved the coffee he'd brought with him near her nose, and her head lifted towards it like she was drawn to the scent.

He pulled it back just out of reach as she grabbed for it. 'Up you get.'

She groaned again, pulling herself to an almost sitting position. Her blanket fell to her waist, and she was—thankfully—wearing pyjamas. Though the singlet top sat slightly askew as she rubbed her eyes, hinting at her cleavage.

He looked away, refusing to go there this morning. Or ever. Especially if he was moving in with her. Everything between them had to be purely platonic, otherwise the living together thing wasn't going to work.

'Sunrise won't wait for you, Hattie. And we're gonna see it this morning.' He moved towards her bedroom door to give her space to get ready, stopping as she called out after him.

'Sunrise? Are you kidding me?'

He looked back at her, holding her grumpy gaze. 'You said you wanted to see it.'

'I didn't mean *now*. I have to work today.'

He dished out a smile he knew always softened her moods. 'You won't regret it.'

'You could've knocked.'

'Oh, baby, I did. You were out like a light.' He turned to leave again, then paused, tapping his fingers against the doorframe. 'Wear your workout clothes. We'll go to the gym after it.'

She blinked at him slowly, her frown deepening as she assessed whether or not he was serious. Clearly deciding he was, she groaned again, tossing back the blankets. 'I hate you.'

He flashed her another grin. 'No, you don't.'

He closed the door behind him, giving her time to get ready. After a few moments of silence, followed by some staggered thumping, he heard the running of the tap in her ensuite. Happy that she was getting ready, he made his way towards the spare bedrooms, one of which would be his. He stood in the doorway of the empty room. Hattie must have cleared out the room the day before after he'd dropped her home from his parents' place.

It was a standard room with a built-in wardrobe. Nothing flash, nothing extra. But he didn't need anything more than a room. He hadn't accumulated much while living with his parents, not wanting to fill their house with random stuff. Not that he'd ever needed to accumulate things anyway. He'd hunt down a bed and the required linens today. Aside from that, he only had a few bags of belongings and his work uniform to move, and they were already packed in his car.

Part of him said this was a bad idea. And perhaps it was. But it was somewhere to stay that wasn't his childhood home until he found something else. Hattie had made a point in saying he practically lived there anyway. More often than not, he'd slept on her couch whenever they'd hung out. Had done just that since she'd moved in to begin with.

Though the idea of him moving in had never come up before. But then, he hadn't actively been looking for a place of his own until now, not wanting to settle into a place only to have to leave for training.

Perhaps his uneasiness was just because of the odd feelings and thoughts he'd been having lately. He would get over it, surely. Because the logical part of him also told him that he could have no better housemate than Hattie. He already got along well with her, for starters. They could discuss things and approach each other with topics most housemates might not feel comfortable with, especially if they didn't know each other well.

But Hattie was his best friend.

And it was completely normal for good friends of the same sex to move in together, so why couldn't it be the same for them?

This was a normal progression.

His thoughts flickered back to the day before, when she'd asked if he planned on bringing women home. Admittedly, the thought might have crossed his mind as a point for moving out of his parents' place. But he'd found himself realising it wasn't his intention now. Especially if he was living with Hattie. On the off chance he was planning on spending the night with a woman, he'd probably favour her place over Hattie's. But the more he thought about it, the more he realised that even that thought didn't particularly appeal to him.

But he'd been curious what Hattie's reaction would be if he said he did. And for a brief moment, he'd seen a guardedness about her. Something flicker in her eyes that he hadn't quite been able to determine before she'd placed her walls up. And then she'd said she would give him a heads-up if she had anyone over.

And for some reason, that grated him.

Perhaps that's why this was a bad idea. Because although he might not bring anyone home, she very well could. And the fact she was seeking his help with her dates only showed that it could be a very real possibility. She was actively seeking a long-term relationship. He was not.

He brushed his thumb against his lower lip, considering the predicament. First sign of her in a lasting relationship, he'd probably have to move out.

Not probably.

Would.

Because while he wanted the best for Hattie—wanted her to be happy—the idea of regularly seeing her with someone else, knowing that the guy she chose would be the one touching her, kissing her, bringing her to absolute bliss every damn night ...

Well, he couldn't decide if it was anger that churned his guts or if he genuinely wouldn't be able to stomach it.

And something told him it wasn't in the way a sibling might be grossed out.

No.

The idea irked him because he—

'It's nothing extravagant, but it's clean.'

He spun to face his best friend, the incomplete thought lodging fear in his throat. She wore brown tights and a dusky pink sports bra. Her tanned stomach was bare, and the whole ensemble left nothing really to the imagination. Her smooth arms stretched up as she brought her golden locks into a high ponytail, the shorter strands that generally framed her face refusing to be tied back. God, she was beautiful.

He swallowed hard, the incomplete thought from earlier finally trickling through.

He wanted her.

He didn't want to see her with anyone else because he—

He wanted her for himself.

Holy fuck.

He suddenly couldn't breathe.

Hattie's brow creased, her lips turning into a worried frown, and even with her early morning weariness, she was still the most gorgeous woman he'd ever seen. Like another blow to his stomach, that thought forced a breath into him, his inhale shaky.

'You okay, Fitz?' Hattie said, letting her arms fall to her side. 'You look like you've seen a ghost.' Her frown deepened. 'Is it the room? I know it's not much, but—'

'It's fine,' he snapped out, her head jerking back in surprise.

He tore his gaze away, glancing back at the room. Terrible idea moving in with her. Probably the stupidest thing he'd ever planned to do. Then again, if he had his own bed in her place, there'd be no more waking up on the couch with her in his arms. And staying in another room would be preferable to that. Preferable to have her figuring out he was having feelings he absolutely should not be fucking having.

'Sorry, the room's fine. Great.' He risked looking at her, her expression confused at the sudden change in his tone. He swallowed once more. He should not be having feelings for her. He placed a hand on her shoulder, determined to keep her quite literally at arm's length. 'Thanks, Hat. You're a good friend.'

Friend being the keyword he desperately needed to remember.

Whatever it was he was supposedly feeling, it wasn't worth losing her. Which he would. If she ever found out, he would lose her. Because if she had even an inkling of feelings towards him, she would not be actively dating other people.

She blinked, her mouth working as the crease between her brow deepened. 'Right. Yeah. Sure.' She gave a hesitant smile as she seemed to purposefully step out from under his hand and head towards the hall table she kept her keys on. 'I'll drop past the real estate today and add your name to the lease. When do you think you can move in?'

He forced another breath, glancing back at the empty room pointedly, reminding himself that living with her was better than sleeping on the couch. They'd have their respective rooms for starters. And considering both of their rosters, they'd spend a lot of time not actually seeing each other.

'I'll hunt down a bed today, so depending on when I can get that delivered. But I can move the rest of my stuff today if that's okay.'

She picked up a gym bag and stuffed some clothes in it from the damned laundry basket that still sat in the corner. 'Sounds good to me. Should we celebrate tonight?'

The unwanted image of her in her lacy underwear as she straddled him on his new bed in celebration popped into his head, and he almost choked on his next breath. God, he needed to snap out of it. He couldn't let his mind go there. He forced a hand through his hair and nodded.

'I can pick up pizza for dinner,' he said instead. 'And we can figure out all the housemate stuff then.'

She glanced up at him. 'Housemate stuff?'

He shrugged. He hadn't thought about it overly much, but he'd heard of the necessities when you lived with other people. 'Cleaning rosters. Meals. That kind of thing.'

'Oh.' She cringed, looking as though she'd just been caught out. 'I sort of thought we'd wing it.'

He scrunched his nose. 'Won't be saying that when we've spent weeks fumbling around with everything.' He made his way towards her door. His door too now, he supposed. 'Coming? We're about to miss the sunrise.'

'Where are we going to see it?' She slung her bag over her shoulder and grabbed her purse and the travel mug of coffee Fitz had brought for her as she followed him.

'Just step outside the front door, Hattie, baby.' He held the door open for her and took in the look of awe on her face as she stepped out and looked up.

There was a lookout nearby that provided a stellar view of the sunrise, but they'd run out of time for that today. The sun had just peeked into view, sending bright golden rays out above them, filling the sky with orange and gold and it was—

'Breathtaking.' Hattie had whispered the word as though speaking might chase away the sun. Like she was witnessing something private and wonderful.

And breathtaking.

The sun glowed on her face, exacerbating her own glow as she lifted her face to revel in it like a sunflower might. Her eyes were wide, her smile genuine. And she looked so at peace. Like nothing could ruin that moment.

And yet, he couldn't tear his gaze away from her to look at the beauty she was witnessing. She'd hit the nail on the head when she'd whispered that one word.

She was breathtaking.

And he was totally and utterly fucked.

# Chapter 15

Hattie yawned into her shoulder as she pushed the broom over the floor, gathering up stray clusters of hair that had blown away from the neat pile when a customer had opened the salon door and let in a gush of hot wind.

She was exhausted and her whole body ached. She'd been sceptical earlier that morning when Fitz had shown up wanting to see the sunrise with her. She wasn't sure when the last time she'd been awake in time for the sunrise was. Probably in her teenage years. Probably with Fitz after they'd spent the night watching movies during the school holidays. If they'd ventured outside to see the sunrise then, she clearly hadn't taken it all in.

What she'd seen that morning was the most spectacular sight she'd ever seen. Something as simple as nature. Something that happens every single morning. And yet, she'd been breathless as she stood in awe at the painting in the sky like it was a performance put on just for her and Fitz. It grounded her.

It had washed away any remnants of a bad mood and had even put her in good spirits for a gym session straight after it. Her and Fitz had taken separate cars to the gym so she could go straight to work after utilizing the gym's showers and he could go bed hunting. Though they'd hardly spoken while they were there, both listening to music as they'd worked out and did their own routines, it had still been nice. She realised she'd missed going to the gym. She'd always known that trying to work up the energy to go there in the first place was the hardest part, but it was incredible how quickly the time went when she'd done nothing but made excuses not to go.

She wasn't much of a morning person, but perhaps she'd be able to work herself into a routine like Fitz had. Perhaps she could even hop into Fitz's routine. Being motivated was always easier with other people there to motivate you.

She swept around Bea's workstation where she'd been working on a last-minute nail appointment. Apparently the client had broken a nail at work and needed a full set replacement *since she was here*. She could see the twitch in Bea's jaw as she worked as quickly and efficiently as she could. Hattie had finished with her last client five minutes earlier, but Bea should have left almost an hour ago. She noticed Bea's gaze flicker up to the clock, worry creasing her brow. As if on cue, her phone dinged next to her. There was a slight tremor in Bea's hand as she reached to tap out a quick message.

Bea's client didn't seem particularly happy with the distraction, but then she wasn't one to talk. She'd been glued to her phone the whole time.

'Okay, Bea?'

Bea's gaze met Hattie's, and though there was the slightest shake of her head, Hattie didn't need that indication to see it wasn't okay.

Bea quickly dusted off the woman's hands, clearly having finished the job, and came straight over to Hattie while the woman gathered up her things and headed slowly towards the register.

'What's wrong? Are you late for something?'

Bea swallowed, twisting her hands together. 'Just my boyfriend. He doesn't believe that I had to work late and thinks I'm cheating on him.'

Something stuck in Hattie's throat. It sure felt like a big fat red flag.

She grasped Bea's arm so she wouldn't move away from her, and didn't fail to notice her startle. 'Is he always like that, Bea?'

She spoke only loud enough for her friend to hear. She'd seen Bea's boyfriend a few times and hadn't been impressed with him, but nothing had stood out as controlling or abusive at the time. But abuse generally happened behind closed doors, right?

Bea's mouth worked a few times, her eyes glistening with threatening tears. 'I mean, not always. It's worse now I'm picking up more hours. But we've got bills to pay and he's currently out of work. I need the money.'

Bea's voice wavered as she spoke, and Hattie held her shoulders a moment before pulling her into a hug. Her friend jumped away from her as the bell above the door dinged and they both glanced towards it as a striking man with ash-blond hair walked in. He looked strangely familiar, but Hattie couldn't quite place it.

Content that it wasn't Bea's boyfriend, she focused back on her friend. 'Why don't you go home? I'll bill your client and finish cleaning up here.'

Bea sniffed, focusing on the ceiling as though trying to blink back tears. 'You sure?'

'Yeah, absolutely.' She gave Bea a warm smile and patted her arm again. 'Just—' She paused, not sure how to broach the topic. She'd never had to point out to someone that their partner might be more than just an asshole.

'Yeah?'

Hattie swallowed, giving another reassuring smile. 'If you need to, you're welcome at my place anytime.'

Bea gave her a confused look, then nodded. 'Okay. Thanks. I owe you one. I'll see you tomorrow.'

Hattie chewed on her lower lip as she watched her friend head out the back to gather her things in record time and leave. She really hoped it was nothing. She really hoped the bright young woman she worked with wasn't having her soul destroyed at home. But all the hope in the world didn't take away the warning signs.

She made her way towards the register and billed Bea's client who didn't seem happy with having to wait. As far as Hattie was concerned, she deserved a little inconvenience. The woman huffed, not wanting to make another appointment in advance—probably so she could do a last-minute appointment when it suited her again—and swung the door to leave dramatically.

Hattie shook her head, reaching for the patience that was wearing thin, and smiled at the man. 'Can I help you?'

The man smiled pleasantly, though seemingly a little awkward. 'Ah, yeah,' he said slowly, stepping closer to the register. 'I'd like a haircut, please, if you know of anyone who might be available.'

She studied the man. His tone was ... teasing? Flirty? She glanced down at the appointment book to gather her thoughts. He looked familiar for a reason. He obviously thought she remembered who he was, but hell. She wouldn't be able to remember his name on a good day, let alone while she worried about Bea.

She checked the time and exhaled. Hopefully he wouldn't turn out like Bea's client. 'If you're after a quick trim, I can fit you in now. But if you're after a style cut, you'll have to book an appointment.'

'A quick trim would be great. Thanks.' He gave her another smile, and he genuinely seemed like a nice guy.

She cleared her throat, picking up a pen. 'Name?'

A beat of silence followed, her pen hovering above the appointment book. 'Oh. Um. Noah.'

She scribbled his name down for her records and met his gaze again. 'Great. Follow me, please.'

She walked to her station quickly, determined to finish up and head home for the day. Fitz had been moving in, and according to his earlier message, he'd been able to get his bed delivered this afternoon. Which meant she officially lived with her best friend. Her stomach twisted oddly at the thought. A weird combination of excitement and ... longing? She couldn't quite place it.

Hattie pulled the chair out and waited for Noah to sit. He lowered himself with an ease that made him look almost businesslike. Going from his suit pants and business shirt, he probably was a businessman of some kind.

His posture was straight as she wrapped the gown around him. She could feel his gaze on her, but she was focused on getting the job done. She held the hair clippers in one hand and scissors in the other where he could see them.

'What are we going for?'

'Whatever's easier for you. I need it short, I guess. I trust you. Ginny says I go too long between cuts.'

She placed the scissors down and picked up the comb, running it through his hair. It was deceptively thick, yet soft, not gritty. Like he actually washed it properly. A lot of people would be surprised if Hattie were to say how many men she'd come across who thought merely running water over their hair was washing it. It was just something that came with the job, she supposed.

'Ginny your partner?' She couldn't help her gaze drifting to his left hand. No ring.

He let out an awkward laugh. 'No, she's my sister.' There was another beat of silence, then he spoke again. 'Actually, you did her hair for her wedding recently.' She glanced up at the mirror, meeting his striking blue eyes. The sharp jawline. The easy smile. 'Imogen,' he added, as though that might prompt her memory.

*Imogen.*

Married-her-best-friend Imogen. Had a home wedding at her parents' huge place.

She lowered her hand, the clippers heavy in her hand.

Imogen's brother who'd given her a look in the bridal room that she hadn't thought much of. She'd been so distracted with her thoughts that day. Seemed today was no different.

She dished out a smile, putting on her best impression that she remembered him. 'Right. I did. Sorry, I should've recognised you. It's just been a big day.'

He visibly relaxed, and she took that as her cue to start cutting his hair. She ran the clippers up the sides, fully aware of his eyes still on her in the mirror.

'Nothing too crazy, I hope.'

She shook her head as she worked on his haircut, the ash-blond locks falling into little piles on the ground. 'Just long. How was Imogen's wedding?'

'It was good. They're still on their honeymoon.' He hesitated another second. 'I looked for you at the reception, but didn't see you.'

'I couldn't stay. Something came up.' The excuses rolled off her tongue like it was natural. She had meant to stay for the wedding, but she couldn't exactly say that she just hadn't felt like it. But then his words caught up to her. She pulled the clippers away from his head and met his gaze again. 'You looked for me?'

His cheeks darkened, and he lowered his gaze. 'Yeah. I was gonna see if you wanted to dance.'

So simple. Yet, he'd have no idea how much that meant to her. She lifted an eyebrow. 'You like dancing?'

'Well, yeah. It's what you do at weddings, isn't it?'

She chewed the inside of her cheek, focusing back on his hair. 'I guess so.'

'I'm not very good at this.'

He'd said it so quietly she'd almost missed it, and glancing at him briefly in the mirror only indicated that perhaps he hadn't realised he'd said it aloud at all. She finished up with the back and sides and worked on blending in the top of his hair.

'Sorry?'

'Just that I—I've been thinking about you since the wedding.'

Hattie jerked in surprise, a little chunk of hair falling to the ground as collateral. She grimaced, touching the patch of hair significantly shorter than the rest as though it would make it reappear.

'That bad, huh?'

She shook her head, her cheeks flushing. 'No, it's fine. Can't even tell.' She'd have to do some serious blending to make that patch not obvious, but she didn't make a habit of telling her clients to wear a hat for a while.

She worked in silence for a good while, the conversation seeming to have died down, but eventually she'd blended the patch as well as it could be and finished up the cut. It took twice as long as she'd expected, but the gouge was her own fault. Or was it? After all, he was the one who'd said he'd been thinking about her.

He followed her to the register and cleared his throat as she punched the amount into the EFTPOS machine.

'Are you free?'

She frowned, the machine literally held out between them showing exactly how much her time was worth and that she most definitely was not free. 'What?'

His eyes widened. 'To date, I mean. Not ... this.' He tapped his card against the machine and tucked it back into his wallet in one quick movement.

'I—'

Her mouth worked. Was he asking her out? She'd been on so many dates lately, yet she only realised now that she hadn't been asked out in person for a very long time. So many people opted for messages now rather than face-to-face, and she didn't realise she'd missed it.

'You've got a partner,' he said, disappointment clear in his expression.

'No, I—I'm free.'

'Really?'

Her cheeks heated as she nodded, and his whole demeanour seemed to swamp with relief. The guy was completely readable. His every expression gave away what he was thinking and feeling. An open book if ever she'd seen one.

'Well, would you like to go out with me? Coffee, dinner. Whatever you're comfortable with.'

'Sure.'

'Really? Wow. Saturday?'

She made a point of checking through the appointment book but already knew she would be free. Her, Liz, Ainslie and Rosie had agreed to a spa afternoon on Friday when they were all able to shuffle things around to make it work.

'Saturday works for me.'

Noah still looked in disbelief, but his smile widened. 'Great. Saturday, then.' He'd made it to the door before turning back towards her. 'Can I get your number?'

She bit her lip, suppressing the smile, and handed him one of her business cards from the stand at the counter.

He looked down at the card, then smiled up at her again. 'Thanks, Hattie. I'll be in touch.'

Then he was gone. She continued working her lip between her teeth for a good long while, uncertain of how she felt. He seemed a nice guy, which was always a positive. He seemed genuinely happy about her agreeing to go out with him, which indicated more towards that he wanted to get to know her rather than just have fun. Another positive. He was good-looking. Check. And he'd made her smile.

Which is more than she could say about the last string of dates she'd been on. But there was something missing. And maybe it's just because she'd been cutting his hair rather than being on a date, but she didn't feel that zing she'd been so convinced she didn't believe in. And yet, she'd felt it when her hand had brushed against Fitz's the morning before.

'Static electricity,' she voiced aloud, reminding herself that it wasn't a zing, just a scientific phenomenon.

And if it wasn't a zing, then there was no reason why she couldn't get to know the nice guy who'd just asked her out.

# Chapter 16

Fitz yanked on the final corner of the fitted sheet, but no matter how much he pulled and tugged, the blasted thing just didn't fit. He gave it another tug to no avail, then shook it in hopes it might loosen the threads or something—*something*—that would make it an easier fit. The first three corners popped free, the sheet forming a puddle in the middle of the mattress.

'Are you kidding me?'

He heard the chuckle behind him and realised he'd practically yelled at the sheet. An inanimate object. He wiped the sweat off his brow and turned to his best friend leaning against his doorframe.

'Need a hand?'

Her eyes sparkled with amusement, her grin wide, and it did nothing towards helping him suppress the thought of bending her over the edge of the damned mattress and—

'I think it's more likely a lost cause.' He waved a hand towards the fitted sheet and let out a huff. 'Never had this much trouble with the bed back home.'

'That's because it was a single.'

'King single,' he corrected. There's no way he or his brothers would have ever been able to fit in a normal single with their heights.

'You have a few things going on here.' Hattie pushed off the doorframe and made her way around to the other side of the bed. 'First, it's a new mattress, which certainly adds to the difficulty in getting the fitted sheet to slide on just right.' She indicated towards the empty packaging the sheets came in that he'd dumped on the floor. 'You also have new sheets. They haven't had time to stretch and loosen yet.'

'So it does loosen,' he said, realising only after he'd said it that she hadn't been privy to his earlier thoughts.

She lifted the scrunched edge of the fitted sheet and lifted an eyebrow as she gave it a tug. 'It's got elastic in it, Fitz. Elastic loses its spring over time, effectively loosening.'

He sucked his lips in, pressing down so he wouldn't be inclined to say something stupid and make a fool of himself. He stared at the sheet a moment, nodded, then glanced up towards her.

Hattie shook her head in amusement and they both burst out laughing at the same time. 'I sometimes forget you had to give up some brain cells for those muscles,' she teased.

His heart filled. Despite all the shit going on inside his head lately, his best friend was back. And they still had that effortlessness between them. He just had to make sure he did nothing to mess with that.

'Yeah, well, they've met their match with this sheet. Care to impart your wisdom, Hattie, baby?'

She smiled as she shook the sheet out over the bed, turning it so the corners lined up differently to how he'd had it. He could have sworn her cheeks had darkened, but he dropped his gaze so he wouldn't brew on it.

'Get that corner.'

She indicated towards the corner he stood closest too and tugged the opposite one on at the same time as he did. They did the same with the other end of the bed and the sheet miraculously went on. He narrowed his eyes at the sheet as though it mocked him.

'Hmm.'

'It's not rocket science, Fitz. But that's what you get for getting an extra deep mattress.'

He shrugged. The thought of making it hadn't crossed his mind when he'd tested it out in the store. 'It's comfy.'

She chuckled, shaking her head. 'I bet it is. Need help with the rest?'

'I think I've got it now. Thanks.'

He glanced at his watch, surprised to see what time it was. He'd meant to go pick up pizza for dinner so that it would be here by the time she got home from work, but he'd lost track of time while struggling with the sheet. As it was, he still hadn't finished making his bed or unpacking his belongings. Not that he had much to unpack, but he wanted it all squared away before he went back to work.

'Are you home later than usual?'

She sighed, staring at the corner behind him. There was nothing there, but he supposed she just needed to focus on something. Anything. He understood the feeling. After a long day, he'd often found himself staring blankly at nothing in particular.

'Yeah. I had a late walk-in that took a little longer than I thought.' She lifted a hand to her neck, rubbing the back of it. 'Actually, he asked me out. Turns out I've met him before.'

'Oh.'

Fitz swallowed, trying not to focus on the way his heart dropped to his stomach. He chewed on his lip, finding himself wishing he could be anywhere but here. But there was something in her tone that halted him.

'And?' he prompted.

'Hmm?' She blinked up at him, her gaze still distant. 'What did you say?'

'Oh. Yes. We're going out on Saturday. I don't suppose you're free then?'

Right. The vetting process she'd roped him into. Probably the worst thing he'd agreed to. Though moving in with her was starting to be up there if he might be seeing her with other people sooner than he'd been prepared for. Not that he'd be prepared for it at all, he realised.

He shook his head, hoping he looked apologetic, but was secretly glad he'd be able to get out of this one. 'I'll be working the night shift. Sorry.'

She chewed on her lower lip. 'Yeah. That's what I thought.'

She sighed again, making her way towards his door. 'I'm gonna have a shower.'

'Yeah. Sure. I'll order the pizza.'

If he ordered it for delivery, he'd be able to keep working on his room. Hattie nodded and headed out of his room. He found himself moving to his doorway, his eyes on the tension in her shoulders. The way she'd seemed a bit off.

'Hat?'

She turned towards him as she reached her bedroom, both of them now standing in their respective doorways. It felt like they were a world apart, not simply the length of the open-plan living room.

'Are you not feeling good about the date?'

She shook her head, her shoulders dropping. 'It's not that. He seems a nice guy. I just—I'm worried about Bea.'

He frowned. He didn't need her to explain who she was. He'd spent a fair bit of time in the salon himself, so he knew her colleagues by name and all the latest gossip. 'What's wrong with Bea?'

'She had to work late today too, and her boyfriend was hounding her phone. She said he thinks she's cheating on him and didn't believe that she just had to work late. She seemed really wound up about it.' She rubbed her hand over the back of her neck again, then lifted her hand to release her hair from her updo, the golden waves falling over her shoulders. 'I mean, it could be nothing, but that's a red flag, right?'

He nodded, folding his arms over his chest. 'A big one if he's micromanaging her every move.'

'That's what I thought.' She worried her lip between her teeth, and he fought the urge to cross the room and ease it with his thumb.

'Do you need my help?'

She exhaled again, puffing her cheeks as she fiddled with the hair tie in front of her. 'I'm not sure she even realises she might need it.'

'Well, tell me if she does. Don't go trying to help her by yourself.'

Her eyebrow flicked up in a challenge, amusement creeping back into her eyes. 'Don't think I can take him?'

Oh, he had no doubt his best friend could rip the guy a new one if she wanted to, but that's not what he was worried about. 'It's not that, Hat. Guys like him can be unpredictable. Unhinged. I want you safe. If she needs help, you call me.'

She considered him a moment, then nodded. 'Okay.' She turned to go into her room then paused again, glancing back at him with a mischievous smile on her face. 'Don't forget that pizza, tough guy. I'm starving.'

He chuckled as she swayed through her door, closing it behind her. A moment later, he heard her shower start. God, that woman. He shook his head as he tugged out his phone and dialled the pizza place, trying his best to not think about Hattie's date and the ache it formed in his belly.

# Chapter 17

By the time Hattie came home a couple of days later, her concerns for Bea had only increased. She'd missed work the day before and still seemed high-strung today, though she hadn't wanted to talk about it. So Hattie had given her space. Her own day was busy enough since she'd had to shuffle a few clients around to take the afternoon off on Friday.

She dragged her feet up towards her door as she carried the groceries from her car, her eyes drifting to the uniform draped over the outdoor chair beside the door. The jacket had black smudges on it, and she caught the whiff of smoke as she neared it. Fitz's boots sat neatly beneath the chair, also smudged with an assortment of colours.

Her shoulders relaxed. She hadn't realised until now that she'd been concerned about Fitz too. He'd left for work before she'd woken up, the house already seeming empty without him in it. Odd, since he'd only officially been living there for a couple of nights.

She'd found herself glancing out the window as she'd heard the sirens before the truck tore past the salon. A lump had lodged in her throat as she'd wondered if that was Fitz in the truck. As she'd worried about what the emergency was. And she'd found herself checking her phone more frequently for any word of anything serious. But if his uniform was airing outside, that meant he was home. That meant he was safe. And she hadn't realised until now that she hadn't been able to breathe easily since she'd heard the sirens.

She also hadn't realised how much she would like seeing that uniform draped across her outdoor setting.

She squeezed her eyes shut, pausing at the front door. Living with Fitz had been harder than she'd first thought, yet for reasons she could never have imagined.

Like coming out of her bedroom to find him plodding around the kitchen making two cups of coffee—one for him, one for her—breakfast sizzling on the stove.

And coming home from work to find the house had already been aired out and tidied up, the basket of clean laundry no longer sitting in the corner of the living room, but her clothes had been folded and the basket shifted to just inside her room. Not on her bed like her mother had done. But just inside her door, like he hadn't wanted to invade her privacy by stepping into her room without her there.

Like the glass acting as a vase in the middle of the table with a handful of yellow flowers in it. Yellow for friendship.

Or the house filling with the smell of dinner cooking when she'd come home from work the day before.

He'd settled into her place like he'd never not been living in her spare room, and she'd realised she liked him being there. They'd worked out the specifics of their living arrangement the night he'd moved in after she'd showered. They'd keep their respective bathrooms clean. He'd make dinner on his days off, and she'd make it on the days he worked. They'd agreed on that so they wouldn't both be cooking each night. Besides, it was easier to cook for two than it was to cook just for one. Though something told her she'd got the better end of that deal, considering he wasn't home for dinner when he worked nights. They'd split the remaining chores between them, and bills would be split fifty-fifty.

He was the perfect housemate.

Yet she couldn't help but notice the way his pyjama pants hung low on his hips, his shirt fitting snugly. The way his hair was mussed as he'd left his bedroom with sleepy eyes. How he'd dish out that signature grin of his, dimple and all, no matter what time of day it was. Like he was happy to see her. The roughness in his voice as he'd say good morning to her as he sought out coffee.

She reached for the door handle and met nothing but air as the door swung open, Fitz on the other side of it. She swallowed as she took in the water droplets still lingering on his hair like he'd just got out of the shower, his shirt sticking to him in a way that said he'd dressed quickly. The smell of soap and aftershave and Fitz met her, and her breath caught as she took in the smooth skin across his jawline. The glint in his eyes. And that smile. She wouldn't be a woman if that didn't affect her in any way. At least, that's what she told herself.

'Thought I heard your car,' he said, seemingly oblivious of the fact she struggled to remember how to breathe.

He reached for the grocery bags, and she let him take them all in one hand. He stepped aside to let her through, his free hand still on the door. She paused as she came level with him, still unable to tear her gaze away from his face, surprising herself when her hand pressed flat against his cheek, her thumb rubbing against his chin. Warmth travelled up her arm and to her core. The simple gesture seemed so natural. Normal. And she found herself aching to feel that whenever she came this close to him.

No. Not him, she told herself.

It was what she wanted to feel with her partner.

And Fitz was her best friend.

And housemate.

His lips parted, the grey in his eyes darkening. She swallowed, then smiled, forcing herself to move forward, her hand accidentally brushing down his chest as she lowered it. God, she needed to put distance between them.

'I like the stubble better,' she threw over her shoulder as she deposited her handbag in its usual spot and kicked off her shoes. Her eyes lingered on the way the shoes were neatly lined up against the wall, and she adjusted the ones she'd just taken off to match them.

His laugh rippled through her, deep and wholesome. And she refused to look back at him, even as she heard the click of the door closing. God, the last thing she needed was for him to see the flush that warmed her cheeks as her fingers ached to touch him more. Especially if she got to feel the rumble of his laughter beneath her fingertips.

'Could be a fire hazard.'

Her gaze shot towards him, assessing his cheeks as he passed. She couldn't see any visible burns, so that was a good sign. 'Just don't stick your face near any fires.'

He laughed again as he deposited the groceries on the kitchen bench and began putting them away. 'Noted.'

Hattie chewed on her lower lip as she slid onto a stool and rested her forearms on the bench. 'I saw a truck go past the salon today.'

She let the question linger unasked. She'd started speaking before she'd had a chance to think better of it, but now that she'd started, she wondered if she could really ask him those questions. If she had the right to worry about him the way she had all day.

Part of her said she absolutely did. He's her best friend. She cared about him. Therefore she could worry about him. Especially since she'd seen how his whole family had been affected by the fire incident almost a year earlier that had left Dave with burn scars on his face, neck and hands, and Eric with a broken heart. If she was being honest, she wasn't sure she could think about another fire without worrying whether someone would be hurt, particularly with the knowledge that someone she knew and cared about was probably fighting it.

But the other part of her ...

She'd almost panicked when she'd heard the sirens. The way she'd imagined someone might feel for someone they were in a relationship with. And that part ... it scared her.

'Small fire on the wharf. A lot of smoke, not a lot of fire. Didn't take us long to get it under control,' he said, clearly not noticing the way her thoughts bothered her.

So he had been there. He'd been one of the few firefighters in the truck that had practically flown past the salon. She'd been within her rights to worry about him. Hadn't she? He finished putting the groceries away and pulled out a container of leftover pasta from the night before.

'Eat or shower first?'

She worked her lip between her teeth again, hiding the blush that threatened to form. She shouldn't be surprised he already knew her routine. It hadn't really changed since she'd started hairdressing. Nothing felt better than peeling off the clothes she wore for work and eating her food in her pyjamas.

But tonight would be different.

She'd already worked later than usual and had gone to the supermarket on the way home. Honestly, she was spent. She worried that if she were to shower now, she'd simply lie down on her bed afterwards and sleep till the morning. And she was hungry. And certainly not in the mood to wake up in the middle of the night with her stomach rumbling.

'Food first,' she said, folding one leg over the other, relieved to be off her feet. Fitz pulled two plates out of the cupboard and started dishing up. 'I think I'll have an early night tonight though. I am looking forward to that spa afternoon with the girls.'

'I bet.'

He put one plate in the microwave to heat up the food and turned back towards her. A droplet of water fell from his wet hair onto his shoulder, and she forced herself to look away. Being swept up in Fitz's charm and good looks would not work well for her. It wouldn't have before, and it certainly wouldn't now they were living together.

'Any news on Bea?'

He gave her his undivided attention. Hattie had always loved that about him. But the fact he also asked about her friends like he cared about the same people she did, it just made it all that much better.

She released her hair from the ponytail she wore and ran her fingers through it, the release on her scalp already rejuvenating. 'She missed work yesterday, and still seemed out of sorts today, but she didn't want to talk about it.'

'What are your instincts telling you?'

'That her boyfriend is a big jerk.'

The microwave dinged as though it agreed with her too, and Fitz swapped out the plates, putting the heated one in front of her. He handed her a fork, and she accepted it, careful not to let their fingers touch. She was not in the mood to assess whether or not the tingle whenever they touched was static electricity or not.

He leaned on the bench, resting his weight on his forearms, and focused on her. The grey of his irises darkened, his expression serious. 'Remember what I said, Hat. Don't go putting yourself in danger with him.'

She stabbed the fork into some pasta and lifted it to her lips, blowing the steam off it. 'Do you think he's dangerous?'

'I don't want to take that risk.'

He'd held her gaze as he'd said it, and he'd spoken quietly. Yet it ... it did things to her she couldn't quite discern. Her main concern was for Bea. And while she could tell that he was worried about Bea too, he stretched that concern to encompass her. And well, it made her want to launch herself over the bench into his arms and have him show her why he didn't want to risk her being in danger.

She shoved the steaming pasta in her mouth, forcing herself to break eye contact with him. He was concerned about her. She was concerned about him. They could both be concerned about each other.

That's what friends do.

Doesn't mean she should throw herself at him and kiss his face off. She lifted her plate as the microwave finished heating his food and shifted to the table, her eyes on the flowers displayed in the middle.

Yellow for friendship.

As if he couldn't be more obvious than that.

Her phone dinged just as she placed it on the table next to her as she sat. She opened the message with a frown, the number not in her phone. It only took her a moment to realise it was from Noah.

'Something wrong?'

She glanced up at her best friend while he took a seat opposite her, already scooping pasta into his mouth despite the fact it was piping hot. She glanced back down at the message, not sure she believed what she was seeing. She'd almost given up hope that Noah would end up messaging her to confirm their date on Saturday and decide where and when. But she hadn't expected this.

'My date just cancelled on me.'

'How very mean of him.'

She lowered her phone, sending him a glare. 'Fitz.'

He held his hands out in surrender, his eyes shimmering with amusement, and a lightness to his manner she'd missed the last few days. 'What? Were you actually looking forward to it?'

'Well, yeah, I was.' She stared down at her pasta, her appetite subsiding as her inner voice reminded her of all her failed dates lately. 'He was already looking better than the dates from the app. I kinda thought this one might not be a dud.'

There was a beat of silence, the pasta her sole focus. Then Fitz's hand was on hers, squeezing it briefly before letting go. 'Sorry, Hattie.'

Her hand burned from his touch. And she told herself it was because he'd just been holding his piping hot plate with it. But she was finding the excuses harder to believe.

'Did he say why?'

She checked the message again and shook her head. 'He just said that something came up and he'd have to cancel.'

'Well, that's his loss.'

She wanted to believe Fitz. But was it really Noah's loss? Or was there something wrong with her? Her phone dinged again, and she glanced down at the message that popped up.

*Cancel might have been the wrong word. I meant reschedule. Are you free next Saturday?*

Her heart skipped a beat as she mentally stamped down the intrusive thoughts. She really did need to stop thinking there was something wrong with her. The previous dates didn't work because it wasn't with the right person. She just needed to remember that.

'Him again?'

She glanced up at Fitz and nodded, noting the flicker of disappointment in his eyes before he looked down at his food. 'He says he meant to reschedule. Wants to know if I'm free next Saturday.' She didn't bother asking if Fitz would be free to tag along this time. She got the vibe he didn't want to be there.

'Will you go?'

'Yeah, I think so.'

She chewed her bottom lip, watching as Fitz shovelled in another mouthful of pasta. She wanted to give Noah the benefit of the doubt. It was in her nature to do that. But she couldn't shake the shift in her when he'd cancelled. Maybe it was Fitz's reaction that influenced her. Or perhaps she just genuinely didn't feel as keen to go now.

'He might have a legitimate excuse for rescheduling.' It felt as though she was saying it more for herself than Fitz, the emphasis on *rescheduling* instead of *cancelling*.

'Mmm. Maybe.'

# Chapter 18

'How are you going with the heat, Liz?'

Hattie glanced towards the end of the row at the pregnant woman leaning her head closer to the fan the nail artist had placed there for her. It was a particularly hot day, and even though Liz still had a few months to go with her pregnancy, she looked like she was feeling it. Even the spa's air conditioning couldn't quite beat the heat.

Thankfully, this particular spa had the availability for the four women—Hattie, Liz, Ainslie and Rosie—to have their nails done all at the same time, straight after having had facials done together. Hattie's face felt amazing and rejuvenated. The best it's been in a very long time, if she was being honest with herself. She probably should carve out more time for self-care. But that's what the four of them were doing now, wasn't it? Perhaps they should make it a regular thing. She'd bet the ladies would all be up for it.

'I am dying,' Liz said dramatically. 'Clearly we had terrible timing. I'll be spending the tail end of this pregnancy in the hottest part of the summer.'

Hattie cringed, making a mental note for any pregnancies she might have in the future. Either aim to avoid the summer months or invest in a really good air conditioner.

'I had the early months over the summer with Cliff. Morning sickness and heat? I would strongly recommend against that,' Ainslie said from beside her, her eyes bright as she watched her nail artist work.

Hattie changed her mental note to just invest in the air conditioning. Then reminded herself she'd need to have a partner to have children with in the first place. Her thoughts drifted to the man who now lived in her spare bedroom. Fitz would make a great dad. She'd seen how he was with Ainslie and Dave's son, Cliff. She could imagine him play wrestling with his children, giving piggyback rides to a little blonde-haired girl with her hair in pigtails.

She shook her head as though the movement could send those thoughts flying. While she truly did hope that her and Fitz would be in each other's lives when they were married with children—and she knew he would treat her children as his own—she just could not let herself imagine that those children would be theirs together. Because that ...

That scenario was too picture perfect. It would only consume her if she dwelled on it.

So, no. She would not let herself dream about a life with her best friend. If she did, she would be ruined for anyone else.

Liz groaned, breaking Hattie out of the downward spiral she was headed towards. 'I am so glad I'm over the morning sickness. I could not have dealt with being sick in this heat.'

Rosie scoffed from Hattie's other side. 'You want to talk about morning sickness? I was sick for nine months with Nick, and Dave wasn't much better. And I'm telling you, that sickness wasn't just in the morning either. God knows where they got that name from.'

'I bet we're turning you off having babies,' Ainslie said, grimacing as she glanced at Hattie. 'Trust me, it's worth it.'

Hattie laughed. 'I'm sure it is. I'll need to check a few more boxes between now and then though. Like a man, for starters.'

Ainslie's eyes went wide. 'Oh, you're not—' Ainslie's gaze drifted towards Rosie, she frowned, and then looked back at her. 'I mean, I thought—'

Liz cleared her throat, trying to get Ainslie's attention, and shook her head. Ainslie's cheeks flushed red, realisation dawning on her, and she focused her gaze back on her nails.

'Oh. Sorry. Never mind.'

Irritation irked her. The last thing Hattie wanted was for the women in this family to start tiptoeing around her. Sure, she wasn't technically part of the family like they were, but she'd always felt like she was. They were the people she'd thought she could come to about anything, particularly relationship advice. Had they heard about her terrible luck with dates?

'You may as well say it,' she said flatly, Ainslie still not meeting her gaze. 'Otherwise I'll spend all day freaking out about it.'

Ainslie's eyes widened as she jerked her head up, finally looking at her. 'I didn't mean to freak you out. It's just, well, you and Fitz are always together. I guess I assumed you two were, you know, a thing.'

Hattie's breath caught in her throat. She would find it amusing if Ainslie was the first one to assume that. But she wasn't. It had made sense for people to assume when they were still in school. But now that they lived their own lives and there was no way they would have been seen together as often as when they were kids? Couldn't two people of the opposite sex be friends without people assuming otherwise?

Her thoughts drifted to the smile that had sent her heart aflutter, the way his hair dropped over his eye, tempting her to brush it out of his face.

The dreams she hadn't been able to shake.

They'd hardly seen each other over the past few days, their schedules not quite lining up to allow spending quality time together. Sure, they'd both been home for the evenings, but he'd had an earlier start in the mornings than she did, so an earlier bedtime was a priority. She understood it. She knew he worked long hours. Had even considered that they might not see each other much except for on his days off. But she'd found herself missing him. Had been bored plodding around the house knowing he was just behind his closed door.

She lived with her best friend, and she still found herself missing him.

'I mean, he just moved in, didn't he?' Ainslie continued, her tone hesitant, wary.

Hattie blinked back the thoughts that had dampened her mood. 'We're just friends.'

Ainslie's expression turned puzzled. 'You've never thought about being more?'

A lump wedged in her throat. Yes. She had. She hadn't truly realised it until now, but since he'd come back from training, she'd thought about it a hell of a lot. And it terrified her. Everyone knew you couldn't cross that line with your best friend. If you valued the friendship, you would not cross that line. Though Imogen had with her best friend, and now they were married.

'No,' she lied, shaking the thought. 'Actually, I have a date next Saturday with a client's brother. So there's that.' Yet saying it aloud left a bitter taste in her mouth.

'Oh.' Ainslie didn't look totally convinced, but she would have to deal with it.

Hattie and Fitz were just friends. And she would not risk that.

'Have you all heard about the Flinders' fire?' Liz said, changing the topic completely.

'Dave told me about it,' Ainslie said, accepting the change wholeheartedly. 'He said it could get really bad.'

'With the weather we're having over the next few days, it very well could,' Rosie said. Hattie only just realised how quiet Rosie had been through the last part of the conversation.

Hattie's brow furrowed as she processed what Liz had said. The Flinders Ranges spanned a good portion of South Australia, starting not far from Port Pirie. Depending on the location of the fire would depend on which stations would be called to it. But if it got particularly bad …

'I didn't hear about it,' Hattie said, wondering if Fitz knew. Odds were he did. He probably hadn't told her about it because they simply hadn't had much time together. But if it had been bothering him, that could explain the tension she'd noticed in his shoulders when she had seen him.

'The fire is a couple of hours away from us,' Liz said, leaning around Ainslie to see her better. 'But if it gets bad, our boys could be headed up there.'

*Our boys.*

Because she did consider Fitz and all of the Harrow men in that category. Worry settled in her stomach. Fitz could be among those going up to the fire, and he wouldn't think twice about going. It's what he was born to do. Yet she'd been almost going out of her mind with worry when she'd simply seen a truck pass the salon with lights and sirens blaring.

She knew they were friends. She knew that was likely all they would ever be.

But the depths of the feelings that plagued her now …

That was something else.

'When could they leave?' Like anyone would know the answer.

'They're pretty much on call now.'

She wasn't sure which one of the women said it. She was too gobsmacked at the way her stomach twisted with the thought he could leave at any moment. How her insides wanted to scream at the thought of him in danger.

'It's all part of the life, dears,' Rosie said, though her voice sounded distant behind the thudding in Hattie's ears.

The life.

What it was like being with a firefighter.

Could Hattie handle that?

Hattie was late coming home. She'd texted Fitz to let him know her and the girls were going out for dinner. He hoped they'd had a nice time together. He knew they would have. She fit into his family like she'd always meant to be part of it. And that was only part of what scared him about her.

Fitz heard the front door open and close, the click of the lock shortly after, and the gentle padding of her feet across the floor growing louder until they stopped just outside his closed door. There was a pause. A hesitation. Going from the shift of the shadow he could see in the gap under his door, she may have even retreated before coming back. She tapped lightly on the door.

'Fitz?'

It was barely over a whisper, the considerate way she spoke when she wasn't sure if he was asleep or not. When she didn't want to wake him if he was. He swallowed the lump forming in his throat, his jaw tense, and forced himself to stare at the ceiling. Particularly unappealing, especially with only the moonlight shining on it.

But he ... couldn't.

He'd never deliberately ignored his best friend. And he'd never intended to. But he just couldn't bring himself to respond. To show that he was still lying in bed awake, despite his best efforts.

He hadn't been able to shake the disappointment that had crossed her face when her date had cancelled. Noah, she'd said his name was. Then the willingness to still go on the date when he'd rescheduled it instead. To see if there could be something more between them. Fitz hated that she was dating other people. He had no right to. She wasn't his. There was nothing stopping her from seeing whomever she wished.

And there was seemingly nothing he could do to wipe thoughts of her from his mind. The need to touch her, feel her lips press against his, their bodies sliding together as one. The desire for more that swallowed him whole.

The fact he wanted her was so far beyond his control he hadn't realised he'd lost his grasp on it until it was too late. He supposed he'd probably lost it a long time ago and it had taken being away from her for a few months to realise it.

When had he started falling for his best friend?

They'd always had a close relationship. She knew everything about him. Knew him better than he knew himself. Physical touch had never been strange for them. It had only been part and parcel of their friendship. He'd always found it nice. But when had that comfortableness stretched into something more?

He knew she didn't feel the same way. She was dating other men, which she wouldn't do if she had feelings for him. He knew that, because he hadn't been actively dating for a long while. It just took this damn long to realise why.

He waited, his breath held as he let his eyes drift towards the door. The shadow lingered a moment, shifted. Then disappeared. Shortly after, he heard her bedroom door close.

His throat burned. He wanted nothing more than to swing his door open and let her in, to talk about their days and let her share absolutely everything with him. He loved that about their relationship. About her.

But he couldn't.

He couldn't let her in knowing he was a thread away from begging her to stop seeing other people. To look no further than the man in front of her. If she didn't have feelings for him—which he was certain she didn't—he would only succeed in pushing her away. And frankly, her not being in his life at all would be more devastating than seeing her with someone else.

And if he was being honest with himself, she deserved more than he could offer. Deserved knowing that the man she spent her life with would walk through her door every damn day. Someone who didn't risk his life every time he put on his uniform.

Before Hattie had come home, Fitz had been looking up the predicted weather conditions for the next few days. That Flinders' fire was barely contained as is. All they would need is the perfect conditions for a nightmare to start. And though they had a chance over the next few days, the days following would be hell for the people fighting that fire.

Stanley McGrath and Nick had both stood before the whole shift earlier that day, telling them what to expect if things go south. They would only take volunteers, they'd said. The campaign could be difficult, long, and it might be a while before they could return home. They didn't want to force anyone to go, and wouldn't frown upon anyone who chose to stay.

Most of them had put their hands up to go, Fitz included. And he'd realised in that moment that none of them had even hesitated.

Fighting fires was what they were all called to do. It was what Fitz was called to do. And if there was a fire that could be disastrous if it wasn't dealt with quickly, then him going to help wasn't even a question. It never would be.

Yet it didn't stop the feelings that plagued him now, the thoughts that circled around in his head while he'd lain in the darkness, his bag already packed in the corner of his room to be able to go as soon as he got the call. If—and that's a big if—he put all his cards on the table and Hattie agreed to take a chance on him, that would be the life she'd be signing up for.

Of him fighting fires away from home, possibly not returning for weeks. Of running off to calls at the drop of a hat. Of long shifts and rotating rosters. Smokey uniforms and dirty boots. The lack of contact while he's away.

The not knowing.

Not knowing if he'd be home on time if he was still needed at a fire. Not knowing the severity of a call-out when she'd see the emergency notifications on her phone. If he'd be one of the firefighters attending that incident.

If he'd come home at all.

Or in what condition.

Fitz had been with his parents when they'd got the call about the incident that had happened a year earlier. The one that had left Dave badly burned and fighting for his life. Had left Nick battling PTSD for a long time afterwards. And Eric watching the woman he'd wanted to spend the rest of his life with being lowered six feet into the ground.

She hadn't come home that day.

Fitz was very much aware of the risk associated with his job. And he'd seen how losing Jade had destroyed Eric for so long. He was a lot better now, but Fitz could see that those memories still haunted him.

It wasn't the life Hattie should have.

She deserved endless happiness, security, knowing her man would be safe.

And he ...

He couldn't give her that.

No matter how he looked at it, he couldn't have her for himself.

So he'd refused to answer her knock, knowing he was not in the right space to stick to his guns. He needed time to regain the control he'd so steadily lost, to make sure he could talk to her without throwing all caution to the wind and taking her in his arms.

And he still felt like a dick for doing it.

# Chapter 19

Hattie's heart was heavy. She was supposed to have the day off, which would have been absolutely miserable if it had been how her day had ended up. Instead, she'd got a desperate call from Liz early that morning saying the hairdresser for the wedding she was working had come down really sick. The bride was frantic and about ready to postpone the wedding, until Liz had remembered that Hattie was available.

She'd agreed to work the wedding, relieved to have been given something to occupy herself with rather than trying to figure out what to do with the house to herself while Fitz was at work.

She'd knocked on his door after she'd come home from her outing with the girls. She'd been working herself into a frenzy the remainder of the evening, worrying about the possibility of Fitz going to the Flinders' fire. Worrying about what that meant for her. The way she was feeling. Because it sure as hell made no sense to her.

Whenever she was confused about, well, anything, she'd go to Fitz. Her best friend. The one person who had always known what to do.

So that's what she'd tried to do. And for a brief moment after she'd come home, she'd considered taking a chance. Of putting her feelers out there and seeing if there was even a whisper of substance to any of it.

But he'd been asleep.

And rather than knocking again and trying to take hold of whatever little bit of courage she'd found, she'd chickened out.

And that had only given her more time to think and realise what a terrible idea talking to him would be.

She'd rung her sister, Charlie, instead, and stayed clear of all topics to do with dating. It had been nice talking to her sister again. They don't get to talk as often as she would like, but truth was, they both had very busy lives. So they settled for their once-in-a-while phone calls. But she missed her sister.

And she missed Fitz.

God help her.

There were two extra cars parked out front of her place by the time she'd finished with the wedding and had come home. The bride had wanted her to stay until all the main photographs were taken—just in case—and Hattie wasn't able to leave until she'd touched up the bride's hair right before the reception. She was grateful for the distraction, but it still hadn't done much to assuage her conflicted feelings.

She was relieved to see Fitz's boots and jacket airing on the outdoor setting as she neared her door and eyed the second and third sets placed similarly.

She heard the premature cheer, followed by a collective groan of disappointment as she unlocked the door and let herself in. She smiled to herself as she saw Fitz and two other men—one with dark hair, one with blond—watching a game on the television. They each held a bottle of beer and passed a bag of chips between them. She supposed it was something she'd have to get used to now that she lived with a guy.

She caught Fitz's eye and waved as she flicked her shoes off and lined them up against the wall. His answering smile sent a warmth through her like there was a little flame permanently simmering inside her that flared to life when he was around. He was her centre, she realised. No matter what happened, how she felt, her world revolved around him.

And she loved that.

He said something to the guys and hopped to his feet, following her towards the kitchen. She went to the sink and poured herself a glass of water.

'Hey.'

She turned to face him, pressing back against the sink as she realised how close he was. He smelled faintly of sweat and smoke and soap and beer and barbecue chips and ... and Fitz. That heady concoction of woodsy spice and fresh seawater that her body had grown used to. Though he was still in his work clothes, his face was clean. Like he hadn't yet had time for a shower, but he'd washed the grime from his face. A smudge of dirt low on his neck only confirmed it. His stubble was growing back, and he was, quite frankly, hot.

Her breath caught in her throat, a surge of heat washing through her. She could rise up on her tiptoes and press her lips against his and it would seem like the most natural thing in the world. There were still many inches between them, but the effect it had was as strong as if they'd been touching. Those eyes—those gorgeous, stormy eyes—saw straight to her soul, and she'd let him see it.

'Hey,' she managed, her voice very much higher than usual.

He tossed his thumb over his shoulder towards the lounge room where his friends were still watching the game. 'Is it okay

I brought them here? I texted, but I didn't get a reply. I thought you would have been home when we got here.'

'Yeah, my, ah—' She lifted a hand to her hair, letting her fingertips slide through her ponytail. She could have sworn his eyes darkened as they followed the movement, but it could simply be the lighting. 'My battery went flat. I ended up working a wedding with Liz all day and didn't get a chance to charge it.'

He rested a hand on the bench beside her and dipped his head, that dark lock flopping over his eyes, and he smiled, his teeth showing as his lips curved higher on one side.

She swallowed hard.

She finally understood why all those girls were practically swooning over him in school. He was a teenage heartthrob then. But now? Well, he was the adult version of that.

'Yeah. Figures.' He glanced up at her through his eyelashes, and she could have sworn her heart stopped. 'Look, I know it's your night to cook, but there's extra mouths to feed and Gene and Justin have agreed to chip in for either Mexican or fish and chips. Your choice.'

She tilted her head back, examining his face like she might find the answer there, and indicated towards the television. 'Are we winning or losing?'

'It's tied.'

The boys let out a cheer, and Fitz's smile deepened, though he didn't look away, still holding her gaze with an intensity that made it difficult to suck in a full breath.

'Winning.'

'Mexican, then.'

'I'll order it up.'

But he didn't move, still standing close, still holding her gaze. She nibbled her lower lip, and his gaze dropped to study it. There was no mistaking it that time. Or the way his Adam's apple bobbed as he swallowed. And that damned lock of hair got the better of her. She lifted her hand to brush it away from his face, her lips parting as heat shot through her, her fingers lingering on his jawline before she let her hand fall.

'I heard about the Flinders' fire,' she whispered, not daring to speak any louder in case it broke the surprisingly intimate moment. He lifted his gaze to meet hers, his eyes troubled, and tilted his head back ever so slightly. It would have barely put another half inch between them, yet she'd felt the distance like it was so much further than that. 'Is it true? You might be going to it?'

'If conditions worsen, then yeah. I'll be going.'

He too had spoken softly, his tone serious and ... she couldn't quite place what else it was. Like he would be missing something if he did.

'How long?'

He shook his head. 'However long I'm needed.'

She wanted to ask him not to go. Not to risk it. But she couldn't. He'd trained specifically for moments like that. To help people. And asking him not to go ...

What would that achieve?

Aside from being purely selfish on her part, he would grow to resent her for holding him back. And she couldn't do that to him. To them. She'd supported his decision to become a fully trained firefighter. She'd known it was always that and nothing else for him. And damn it, it made him happy.

*It's part of the life.*

Rosie's words rung through her head. Hattie had been debating whether she had it in her to be part of that or not, but she realised now that she was in no matter how she looked at it.

'I have to go, Hattie. I can't just sit by and not help when I know one extra person can make a huge difference.'

She worried she'd said all her thoughts out loud, but she hadn't. She knew she hadn't. Words were too hard to form for that. He'd read it in her face. Like he'd always done. She'd never been able to mask anything from him.

'I know.' She wasn't even sure how she managed those words, as choked as they were.

His hand lifted to her face, his fingertips brushing her fringe behind her ear. He swallowed as his hand followed the line behind her ear to rest against the side of her neck, his thumb caressing her cheek. The touch was so tender, so intimate, and it just about undid her.

It was the first time he'd touched her like that, and God, she hoped it wasn't the last.

Her lips parted as she took in a sharp breath, very much wishing they were alone. Very much wanting to close that distance between them and see what would happen if they mingled a fantastic friendship with the passion of lovers. And very much wishing there wasn't so much to risk between them. Her shoulders dropped in resignation. Giving up or giving in, she didn't care. She just wanted Fitz.

And she wanted him to kiss her.

And for a moment, she thought he wanted it too.

He closed his eyes, his head moving so slightly, giving the impression he was counting in his head as he breathed. And pulled her close, pressing his lips against—

The top of her head.

Something he'd done many times before. As friends. Her eyes drifted to the new bouquet of flowers on the table. Yellow.

For friendship.

He rested his forehead against hers and took in a shaky breath. She was simply unable to take in a full breath at all. The flowers were a stark reminder of what their relationship was and would only ever be.

She just had to get it through her thick skull.

She dropped her head, breaking the contact, and stepped out of his bubble. The bubble she wanted to be in. Where everything made sense and there was nothing to worry about because it was Fitz, and he made everything better.

But not this.

'Hat.' He turned towards her, following her movements with his eyes. She refused to contemplate whether or not his expression was pained. Refused to allow eye contact full stop.

'I—'

'Hey, you want us to get that?' Fitz's blond friend said, pointing to the door.

It was only then that she heard the frantic knocking at the front door. She didn't dare look at Fitz. Couldn't bring herself to. But she felt his presence a few steps behind her as she made her way to the door and swung it open.

Bea stepped inside, one cheek redder than the other, her hair ruffled, her neck sporting the darkened imprints of fingers. She scanned the room, her eyes falling on the three men first, then Hattie.

And burst into tears.

'Oh, my heart,' the dark-haired one said.

# Chapter 20

Gene and Justin could go screw themselves as far as Fitz was concerned. Of course, he was stupid for taking their advice anyway, the self-professed love experts they thought they were. Neither of them had girlfriends, which Fitz had failed to point out when they'd offered their opinions on exactly what he should do.

He wished he hadn't told them anything. But the three of them shared a truck with McGrath, and while McGrath had been investigating a false call-out, the other two had grilled Fitz on his mood. Of course, they'd remembered about his being friend-zoned, and had automatically concluded that his mood was because of that.

They'd been surprisingly pretty accurate, which had only pissed off Fitz even more. They'd practically invited themselves over for the game, which he knew was so they could assess how he and Hattie interacted for themselves. He'd been hesitant to agree at first, but what did he have to lose? Despite the two guys annoying the hell out of Fitz at work, they'd grown on him, and he could see the three of them becoming good friends.

But they'd practically psyched him up to at least try something with Hattie. To see if he'd truly been friend-zoned. He'd bought her fresh flowers on his way home from work—bold, bright and beautiful. He'd seen those golden flowers and saw Hattie's smile. He'd looked at them and happiness and hope had filled him. And the bright yellows were like sunshine, which there surely wouldn't be any of if it weren't for Hattie.

She hadn't been home to give them to her, so he'd replaced the wilting ones on the table with them.

And perhaps it was the beer he'd had, but what Gene and Justin had encouraged him to do had suddenly started making sense. He'd been pondering it all day since they'd suggested it. Hadn't been able to focus on the game because his ears were tuned to hear her car and his eyes kept glancing towards the door for when she'd return.

He'd been sick to his stomach as he'd wondered if her date had called her up to see if she was free tonight after all.

Her date.

That was still a thorn in his side.

He took a swig of beer, his eyes drifting towards her room where her and Bea talked with the door firmly closed. The woman had only had time to burst into tears before Hattie had swept her off to her room to talk. Fortunately, the boys had the grace to turn the television down a little, clearly noting the seriousness of the situation.

'You're not friend-zoned.'

'What?' He blinked as he glanced towards Gene.

'Her reactions in the kitchen.' Gene shook his head. 'I don't know what you are, but you're not friend-zoned.'

Fitz frowned, bringing the beer to his lips again. He hadn't meant to get that close to Hattie in the kitchen. He certainly hadn't thought his friends were watching them instead of the game. In the moment, it had been private. Intimate. Like the two of them had entered some kind of sphere of energy with sparks flying between them.

He could have sworn she'd wanted him to kiss her, and damn it, he'd wanted to. But before he'd been able to, his stupid brain reminded him of why he couldn't even broach the topic with her. That he couldn't give her what she should have.

Despite Bea's unfortunate reason for dropping by, he'd been grateful for the interruption. And whatever Gene and Justin said, he could never make a move on his best friend. The guys might be willing to take that kind of risk, but he wasn't.

The game ended and Gene and Justin were tidying up their shit from the lounge room when there was a loud banging at the door, a fist pounding against the wood. He glanced at his friends, both of them straightening with a look just as curious as he felt. Yet something told him he already knew the answer.

The banging continued, and Fitz made his way towards the door, putting his beer bottle down so both hands were free. He didn't need to look to know the guys flanked him as he opened the door.

The man standing on the other side of the door was about as tall as Fitz. Though he had more flesh than muscle, he had no doubt the guy could inflict pain, especially on a woman significantly smaller than him.

'Where is she?' he spat out, his breath reeking of alcohol. Fitz stood firm, his frame blocking the doorway.

'I'd leave, if I were you.'

The man's eyes landed on Fitz like he'd only just seen him, his gaze scanning the two men standing behind him before narrowing in on Fitz once more.

'Who are you? You all fucking her too?'

Venom laced his words, and as the man launched towards him, Fitz shoved him backwards, sending him stumbling back a few metres. He took the opportunity to follow him outside, keeping him out of the house as much as he possibly could. The last thing he needed was for the guy to have another go at hurting the scared woman in his home.

'Go. Home.'

The man spat on the ground, his eyes turning malicious. 'The whore had it coming for her.'

Fitz blinked and almost missed the blur of dark hair flying towards the man, a string of expletives leaving Gene's mouth. A quick glance at Justin showed he hadn't been expecting it either, and both of them knew it was a bad move. Gene was the shortest out of the three of them, and Bea's ex had a good head-height on him. The smaller man got a decent shot in before copping a punch to the side of his face that sent him staggering backwards.

'Aw, fuck,' Fitz groaned, stepping between the two men, shoving the man back again with a fist in his shirt.

'Lyle!'

Each of the men's heads snapped towards the house as Bea shook free of Hattie's hold and stormed towards them. Fitz caught Hattie's terrified gaze for the briefest of moments, but didn't dare take his eyes off Lyle for long.

'Bea,' she called out, following her friend.

'Go home, Lyle,' Bea yelled at him, storming towards them like a firecracker about to go off.

Lyle waved a finger at her, seemingly having forgotten about Fitz's fist in his shirt. 'You're coming with me.'

'Like hell I am.' She stopped when she got level with Gene, her eyes burning with fury as she saw the blood trickling from the corner of Gene's mouth. She folded her arms across her chest, lifted her chin, and looked Lyle dead in the eye. 'We're done. I want nothing to do with you.'

Lyle growled, jerking towards her, his movement halted by Fitz's hold on him. 'You heard her,' he said, his voice steady and firm.

'I'm calling the cops,' Hattie said, tugging on Bea's arm to lead her back to the house. 'You need to get off my property, Lyle.'

Lyle's eyes darkened as they narrowed on Hattie, his body tensing. Fitz's grip tightened. '*You*.' Hattie lifted her phone to her ear, not releasing eye contact with the man. 'You're the bitch who put ideas in her head.'

'You did that on your own, buddy,' she said, then started speaking into the phone, listing the address and asking for the police.

Lyle yelled, launching towards Hattie with violence in his eyes. Fitz saw red, his protective instinct swamping him, consuming every fibre of his being. With as much strength as he could muster, he yanked the man back towards him, his hand fisting at his side.

And swung.

# Chapter 21

Hattie found herself standing outside Fitz's closed door once again, her fists clenching and unclenching at her side as she tried to work up the courage to knock. Her mind drifted to the smile he'd given her when she'd come home. The moment they'd shared in the kitchen. The way he hadn't hesitated to step in when Bea's ex had shown up. The way time had slowed right down when she'd seen the furious man lunge towards her, his attempt thwarted by the man on the other side of this door.

What a hell of a night it had been.

Gene and Justin had gone home after the police had left with Lyle, a bruise already forming on Gene's face. She'd missed exactly what had happened there and the guys were tight-lipped about it, but she probably didn't have to stretch her imagination too far going off the look he'd given Bea when she'd arrived. Like he'd seen a goddess. It would have been amusing if Bea's intentions for coming over had been different.

But that's not what held her mind captive now.

Rather, it was the look that had crossed Fitz's face when Lyle had lunged towards Hattie. The spark that shot through his eyes and charged his body as he'd leapt into action. One hit was all it had taken to daze Lyle enough to apprehend him. It was the ease and efficiency that Fitz had done it that had caught her by surprise. She'd never seen him move like that. Wasn't sure how she was supposed to feel about it.

But she knew how she did feel.

A tightness in her core that couldn't be swayed. A yearning to feel those hands on her, knowing just how gentle they could be. Seeing that possessiveness in his eyes as he looked at her like he had in that split second before taking down Lyle. The look that had screamed two words across the space between them.

*You're mine.*

His.

His to protect, and to hold, and to cherish, and to beat the crap out of any guy who dared threaten that. And God, in that moment, she'd wanted it to be true.

The fact they'd been so close to kissing in the kitchen earlier only fuelled it.

She lifted her hand to knock, her hand pausing before connecting with the door. She took in a shaky breath, realising the gravity of what she was about to do.

There was a lot suggesting even standing at his door was a bad idea.

It was late, for starters. They'd all been filled with adrenaline that was only now starting to wear off. He'd had a beer or two earlier, and she'd retreated to her room with Bea and a bottle of wine after Lyle's appearance. Their whole usual vibe had been off since he'd come back from training. And not necessarily in a bad way. But rather ... she was attracted to him. Feeling things for him she shouldn't be feeling at all.

There was also the fact she'd been around a lot of love stories lately with it being wedding season. Not to mention her multiple failed attempts at dating. And Fitz …

Well, Fitz was the perfect man.

And her best friend.

There really weren't many things that, on paper, pointed to this being a good idea. And with so much going on, including the fact he could be called out to the Flinders' fire at any moment, now wasn't the right time for anything.

But if she didn't explore this now …

If she didn't talk to him and feel out whether there was anything there for him as well, then she would never do it.

Blame it on the alcohol. Blame the adrenaline. Blame Bea saying that she wished she had what Hattie and Fitz had. Blame every damn thing she could think of.

But the fact of the matter was, she'd felt something.

She wasn't sure she'd reach so far as to call it a spark like she'd heard people talk about, but she'd felt *something*. Desire when he'd been so close in the kitchen. Yearning. A clear absence of his warmth when she'd stepped away from him like being doused with cold water.

And that look.

The look that shot straight to her core, consumed her whole being and made her want to throw everything to the wind and deal with the consequences later.

If she didn't do anything now, she would be wondering about this moment forever.

She let her hand fall against his door in a quiet knock before she could chicken out.

As soon as she heard the tap of her hand against the wooden door, the padding of his footsteps behind it, her heart leapt in her chest.

Oh, hell. What was she doing?

This was Fitz.

Not some random she could throw herself at and never see again.

Fitz.

The one guy who could very well destroy her if he wasn't in her life anymore.

There weren't normal consequences associated with this. The stakes were high. Very, very high. And this was an astronomically bad idea.

Her heart fluttered in her chest, the skin on her forehead prickling in the way it did when she was about to break out in a sweat, and her breath staggered. She couldn't—

The door swung open, and Fitz stood almost side on, his hand still on the door, those dark eyes assessing her with an intensity that made it even harder to breathe. He wasn't wearing a shirt, his shorts hanging low on his waist. And God, had he been hiding under those clothes.

She'd seen him without a shirt on. Before training. This was after training. His stomach rippled with abs, his muscles naturally bulging. A spattering of dark hairs covered his chest and formed a thin trail down his belly to the V in his muscles, dipping below his waistline.

She lifted her gaze, her eyes landing on the ink down his left side. The large dandelion head, a few seeds floating away from the rest and over the closest pec, and the stem that stretched down his ribcage, looping in just the right way to form one word.

*Breathe.*

'Breathe, Hattie. In—one, two, three.' A young Fitz had breathed in with her partway through a panic attack in their first week of school, holding the seedhead of a dandelion flower in front of her lips.

The world had ceased to exist around them, only Hattie and a boy in her class who'd decided to help her after he'd seen her being bullied. She'd known in that moment they'd have a special friendship. The young boy with the unruly brown hair would be her best friend. The image of the young boy turned into a teenager in their final year of school when she'd been stressing over exams. His eyes twinkling, his focus solely on her as he'd held a dandelion in front of her lips after instructing her to breathe in.

He'd leaned in closer, his lips curving higher on one side, a dimple in his cheek. 'Now make the bastards fly.'

Hattie blinked past the haze, her focus now on the fully-grown man in front of her, the tattoo that had sent her into her memories. Memories of Fitz. Their friendship. He'd always been there for her. Had always been the one helping her breathe when she'd forgotten how to.

A permanent reminder etched down his side.

The room was suddenly void of any oxygen.

'Hat?'

*Breathe.* He didn't need to say the words. The reminder stared at her in black ink. She sucked in a shaky breath, then another, tearing her gaze away from his body and to his eyes. Those stormy eyes that watched her with an unreadable expression. She swallowed.

None of it made sense.

And yet, all of it did.

Everything just made sense with Fitz.

And there was no way she could explain it.

He gave a slight nod, his eyes still assessing her. 'Good?'

She pulled herself together. Had to. She nodded, certain words wouldn't form if she tried.

His eyes flicked towards her bedroom where she'd closed the door behind her. Bea had eventually fallen into a restless sleep in Hattie's bed, yet sleep had been the furthest thing in Hattie's mind. She'd needed to defrag with someone who wasn't the person who'd just had her world fall down around her. She needed Fitz.

'How's Bea?' He'd spoken barely over a whisper, the deep baritone of his voice rippling through her.

'She's asleep.' The words came out more like a croak, but he didn't seem to notice.

He tilted his head, indicating his room, and stepped aside to let her through. She walked towards his bed, amazed her legs still worked, and twisted her hands together in front of her. He partially closed the door, leaving it slightly ajar so the click of closing it wouldn't wake up their guest while hopefully also stopping their voices from carrying.

She turned towards him, standing in the middle of the room, and he leaned against the wall beside his door, a thumb hooked in the waistband of his shorts. Her eyes hesitated on the bag packed in the corner of the room before she brought her gaze to meet his. Something told her it wasn't simply a bag he'd neglected to unpack. Instead, it looked like one ready to grab and go. His on-call bag, she assumed. For the Flinders' fire.

The thought lodged in her throat, and she tried her best to swallow it down. He studied her, but didn't say anything. Waiting. Waiting for her to speak first. She had been the one to knock on his door, after all. Her eyes flickered down to the dandelion seeds fluttering across his chest, over his heart.

'Fitz, I—'

She closed her mouth, not even sure what she'd intended on saying when she'd closed the distance between the bedroom doors. To think she'd been so close to risking all of this. She'd had such an outrageous courage earlier. She'd got in her head, thinking that she'd throw everything on the line just to test the waters. Yet that tattoo down his side only reiterated how very bad that idea had been.

Fitz was her everything.

Who would she be if she couldn't pick up the phone and call him whenever she needed his reassurance? His reminder to breathe? To tell him about her day or whatever issue is plaguing her and know that he would make it better. Or just to simply hear his voice. Just because.

That alone made everything better, brighter.

And that wouldn't be an option if she threw herself at him and he didn't reciprocate.

Yellow for friendship.

A sobering truth if ever she saw one.

She cleared her throat, swallowing again. 'Thank you for what you did tonight.' She hesitated, the lump stubborn in her throat. 'For Bea. I'm grateful you—and the guys—were here tonight. Guess us girls really know how to pick 'em, huh?' She forced a smile, a feeble attempt at humour.

He only held her gaze, his eyes darkening, his jaw tensing as he clenched it. Either her joke was too soon or just too true to be funny. She chewed on her lower lip, letting her arms fall to her side as she dropped her gaze to his right hand. The bruised knuckles.

'You're hurt.' She'd muttered the words, taking a step towards him before thinking better of it. She indicated towards his hand instead.

He lifted it to examine the bruising like it was the first time he'd noticed it. Perhaps it had been. He blinked at it, his throat bobbing as he swallowed. 'It's nothing.'

'It's not nothing.'

He'd done it for her. She closed the distance between them and reached for his hand. He let her examine it, albeit reluctantly. She pressed her thumb against his knuckles, not sure what she was checking for, but he didn't flinch, didn't wince in pain. Just bruising, she hoped. Though she wasn't sure he would've told her if it did hurt.

Her body grew hot at their closeness. He still didn't have a shirt on, and being this close had her engulfed in the scent of seawater and spice and Fitz. And her heart ached.

For some stupid reason, it ached.

She went to release his hand, but he turned his over, lacing his fingers between hers. The grey of his eyes were darker, troubled.

'You didn't have to do that,' she whispered, her gaze falling to their joined hands.

She'd said it because she didn't know what else to say. Fact is, she knew he would've done it regardless of who he was protecting. That's exactly the kind of guy Fitz was. Always helping those who need it. Always there at the right time. Her thoughts drifted back once more to when they were kids, when he'd stood between her and her bullies even then.

'Yeah, I did.' He still spoke low, his voice rumbling through her, and it tugged at her. Pulled to close the distance between them. 'He was gonna hurt you, Hat. Just like he'd hurt Bea.'

She nodded, the hands in her vision blurring, her mind an absolute mess. He would say that to her even if she'd been a stranger. But they were friends. Even if what she was feeling was not what friends should feel. Even if she wanted him to say those words to her and mean it in the way that she was his. And he protects what's his. A tear squeezed out despite her best efforts to suppress it, and he cupped her chin with his free hand, tilting her head back to look at him. He held her gaze with such an intensity it was impossible to break it.

'I can't let anyone hurt you.'

His voice broke on the last word as he wiped the tear away with his thumb. The touch left her cheek burning, an ember that simmered, slowly spreading, going deeper until she felt it within her. He closed his eyes for the briefest of moments, and his throat bobbed as he swallowed. When his eyes met hers again, they were torn. Stormy. Like he was fighting a losing battle and he knew it.

He dropped his hand from her chin and her body instantly missed the contact. She squeezed his hand to try to make up for it, but he didn't squeeze back.

'I can't vet your dates anymore.'

'What?' The word slipped out on a whisper before she could stop it, and his eyes darkened further, his troubled brow creasing.

Truth is, she didn't want him to be there watching her dates. She wanted him to be the one she was on the date with. And that hit her like a brick to her chest.

'I should never have agreed to it.' She blinked up at him. His eyes were on her lips, and his jaw was so tense. He slowly brought his gaze back to meet hers. 'I don't want to see you with other men. But I want you to be happy. I just ... I can't sit by and watch.'

Her breath caught, her heart skipping a beat. There were so many other reasons to explain this. So many other possibilities. But if she wasn't wrong ...

If she got that look in his eyes right, interpreted what he was saying correctly.

Was he voicing her thoughts?

Her heart pounded, the thudding of it loud in her ears as the prickle of heat washed over her. Her breaths were rugged, but so were his, she realised. It was all or nothing. And damn it, Hattie wanted it all.

'You make me happy.'

He shook his head, stepping to the side to put space between them. His hand dropped from hers, though he never broke eye contact. 'I can't make you happy.'

She almost laughed. And she would have, if it didn't come across as a rejection. As stupid as it sounded. But somehow, for some reason ... she couldn't let herself settle for a rejection. Because it made so much sense. And the more she thought about it, the more sense it made. She'd been looking in the wrong direction the whole time, when she should have been looking right in front of her.

She'd wanted someone just like Fitz. Someone who treated her like Fitz did. She'd thought it could never work. But how could it not when they had the relationship they already had?

'You already do,' she said, determined to make him see it too. He put another step between them, and her heart tried to push its way out of her chest. He was fighting it, but the look in his eyes told her he saw it too. 'I said I wanted someone like you, Fitz, but there is no one else like you. Just you.'

'Hat.'

'No, I can't fight it. I've tried to. And I've been getting mixed signals from you, but I'm pretty sure you feel it too.'

'Hat—'

'You're my best friend, and I don't want to screw that up, but we—'

She took in a shaky breath, her shoulders dropping. His eyes were wide and wild, his hand held up between them as though begging her to stop talking. But all or nothing. She couldn't stand to just be friends with him anymore. Her heart would break to see him with someone else. Just as he'd said he couldn't stand by and watch, neither could she.

'We don't do friend things, Fitz.' His jaw was clenched so tight she worried he might break a tooth, and his breath came out in a growl, his whole body tense. 'Friends don't do the things we do. They can last more than a day without talking to each other. I'm lost without you. They don't pretend to be on a date with you when you get stood up. They don't—'

'Stop talking, Hattie,' he ground out, his eyes drifting closed.

But she couldn't. Not now the floodgates had opened and she saw every non-friend thing they'd done. Even just since he'd come back from training. There was so much. And she knew there'd be more. Couldn't he see it too?

'They don't play your favourite song just so you can dance together, or snuggle on the couch while watching a movie. They don't kiss in the kitchen.'

'We haven't kissed in the kitchen.' Each word sounded hard to get out, a rumble to his tone.

'Friends don't want to,' she pointed out. 'Fitz, I wanted to.'

'*Hattie.*'

'And I know you wanted it too.'

His eyes darkened, his jaw clenching harder, and the way his gaze bore into her said she'd hit just the right spot. He had wanted it. It was clear as crystal when he looked at her like that. It gave her just a tiny bit of hope that she wasn't risking everything right now.

'We're not friends. We're more than that.'

'No.'

'No?' She did let out a laugh this time, though nothing about this conversation was funny. 'How do you see it, Fitz? Because

I'm pretty sure I—' *I love you.* The words died on her lips, her mouth still open as she took a moment to process it.

She'd said it to him so many times before.

*I love you.*

She'd always meant it as friends, but now?

It was all so clear to her now. She was in love with her best friend and she … she quite possibly always had been.

Recognition fluttered across his face, like he'd heard the unsaid words and it terrified him. Like it should terrify her. But as she waited for that terror to hit, it didn't.

'Don't go there, Hat.' A warning, but there was still that tightness in his jaw. The resignation creeping into his gaze.

Well, hell. If she was just realising it, then he should damn well realise it too.

She turned all her focus on him, letting the feelings wash over her. All or nothing, she reminded herself. And this would be the decider.

'Fitz, I lo—'

'*Stop.*'

Her words were cut off by his hand covering her mouth, the touch searing her skin, pulsing like a spark through to her core. A spark that she could hardly deny any longer. She felt his breath on her ear, heard the raspiness in his voice as she tilted her head back to look at him.

His eyes shimmered with battling emotions, his expression very much torn. Like the words she wanted to say just might break his heart.

It might break hers.

'Don't say it, Hattie.' He shook his head, holding her gaze, his eyes pleading. His face was so close to hers, and yet she wanted it closer. 'Please. If you don't say it, you can't regret it.'

Regret. She could never regret anything with Fitz. Certainly not telling him how she really felt. How she was sure he felt. But ...

If he did reciprocate her feelings, why would he try to stop her from saying it? She lifted a hand to rest on his arm, tugging on it to drop his hand from her mouth. He seemed reluctant, but he let it fall.

'Kiss me.'

His eyes widened with surprise, a flicker of anticipation and heat. His jaw tensed again, though he didn't pull away. Those grey eyes dropped to rest on her lips, and she sucked her lower one between her teeth. He growled. And it seared through her like the ember had been fanned alive.

'No.'

No? But his eyes still lingered on her lips, darkening with every passing second, his breaths quickening to match hers.

'You don't want to.'

He tilted his head to the side, his hand snaking its way around her waist. Did he realise he touched her like that? 'I never said that.'

Her tongue darted out to wet her lips, and that rumble in his throat started again. Or continued. Had it even stopped?

'Then kiss me, Fitz. Kiss me and tell me you don't feel anything.'

'I can't kiss you, Hattie.'

He pulled back only slightly, cupping her cheek in his free hand. He let the pad of his thumb brush against the corner of her lips. He looked as though denying her a kiss was denying him, too. Like he yearned to press his lips against hers and take their relationship to the next level. Yet something held him back.

'Why not?'

It came out breathy, but when he held her gaze like he did now, she didn't care how she sounded. She just wanted to wrap herself in him and let the world disappear around them.

'If I kiss you, Hattie, baby, I won't be able to stop.'

And there it was. The confirmation she needed that he felt the same way. That she wasn't just blowing things out of proportion. Her best friend had feelings for her.

And God, it made her heart soar.

She shook her head, lifting her hand to meet the one on her cheek, holding him there. 'I don't want you to stop.'

'Hattie.'

Her name was a plea, and she couldn't quite bring herself to determine what for. It was plain and simple, wasn't it? They'd both just admitted feelings for each other. Both admitted they wanted to kiss. So what was holding him back?

Nothing.

There should be nothing holding him back.

And if he wasn't going to kiss her, then she would kiss him.

So she did.

# Chapter 22

Hattie pressed onto her toes, closing the short distance between them, and pressed her lips against his.

Time stopped.

Fitz felt her slight gasp when her lips had made contact, like it had surprised her even though she'd initiated it. For the briefest moment, he couldn't bring himself to kiss her back.

He'd told her he couldn't bear to see her hurt. Yet if she pursued this—if he pursued her—she would only end up hurt. His stomach wrenched at the thought.

But with her lips on his, her body pressing against him, the control he'd had on himself faltered. She pulled back slightly, hesitantly, and the last of his control snapped.

The rumble came from deep within him. A hunger that had rested until this moment tore its way through him. He pulled her tighter against him with one hand around her waist and the other sliding to the back of her neck, her head tipping back into it as he closed the gap once more, kissing her with a fervour and hunger he'd never experienced before.

Hattie.

His best friend.

And it was so fucking right.

She wrapped her arms around the back of his neck and parted her lips for him. He tasted her, swiped his tongue between her lips. Heard her moan that only threw fuel on the already blazing fire inside him. He was wild for her. And with every press against him, every thrust to get closer, every stroke of her fingers as they glided across his bare shoulders, dove into his hair, he only grew more feral.

He let his lips trail across her jaw, relishing the gasp that escaped her perfect lips as he sucked on the sensitive spot just beneath her ear. His hand slid under her shirt, sliding against the smooth skin above the waistband of her shorts. The same spot his fingers had stroked the morning he'd woken up with her in his arms. But now ...

Now there was a heat that consumed him, stripped him of every logical thought, and he fucking loved it. Desired it. Begged to let the blaze eat him whole. Because damn it, there could be no one else for him. He was hers. Always would be.

Her hands slid down to his waist, tugging on the top of his shorts, and he trailed his lips back to meet hers once more in a dance that was practiced and perfect and—

And she could never be his.

He broke the kiss, jerking apart in one quick movement as he remembered why he hadn't let himself give into this in the first place.

'Fuck,' he mumbled, crouching down with his hands digging into his scalp. Stupid. *Stupid*. He'd given in to his desires. He should've remained firm, shouldn't have let her get too close. Shouldn't have opened the fucking door. '*Fuck*.'

'Fitz, don't you dare tell me to stop now,' she gasped. He only risked the briefest glance up at her before rubbing his hands over his face.

She was dishevelled, panting, her glasses askew on her nose. So damn beautiful. He couldn't look at her without wanting to throw everything in and show her just how perfect they could be together. But he could bring her nothing but pain.

And that was the hard truth he had to deal with.

'Hattie.'

'Don't you dare.' Her words croaked out, strangled by tears that she held back. Yet he couldn't bring himself to look at her.

If he did, he wouldn't be able to help himself. He would give her everything she wanted. He would give her the world.

But he couldn't give her this.

He lowered his hands in front of him, placing them together between his knees as he held his crouch. 'We can't do this.'

Silence was all that met him, yet he knew she hadn't moved. Felt the look she gave him. He'd tried to tell her before she'd kissed him. He'd seen the look in her eyes when her brain had made the connection only moments before. She loved him. Just as he loved her. But damn it, he couldn't hear her say the words. Couldn't let her. Not when there was no real future for them.

So he slammed that wall up between them, one brick at a time.

'You don't want this.'

The words broke his heart as he said them. He wanted nothing more than to have a life where he and Hattie spend it together. One that didn't end in pain and heartbreak. But they couldn't.

'Don't tell me what I want.' Fury laced her words, and she had every right to be mad at him. It was preferable, actually.

Much better than silence. 'I decide what I want. Not you. And I want this.'

His jaw clenched, and he rose to his feet, not daring to close the distance between them. They'd just end up back in each other's arms, and he could not let that happen again.

'No? Then let me tell you what you deserve. You deserve better than this.'

She scoffed, her arms folding over her chest. 'Oh, please. What is it with you boys and thinking that? Your brothers thought that too, and look at them.'

He was. That was the point. But he wasn't going to argue that with her.

'You deserve the best, Hattie. Happiness. Security. Love. A full life.' All things he could theoretically offer her. But that wasn't the extent of it. 'You deserve safety. Reassurance that your husband will come home every day. To not have to worry and scour the news every time there's a fire. Or that each time you see me might be the last.' He swallowed hard, his throat thick and his eyes burning. His heart ached so damn much. 'I can't promise you that. That's why this can't work.'

Tears trekked their way down her cheek, her lips quivering. He wanted to cross the room, to take her in his arms and kiss those tears away. But he couldn't. So he turned and reached for a shirt instead and pulled it on, feeling her eyes following his movements. He grabbed the duffel bag from the corner of his room. His wallet. Phone. Keys.

He turned to face her. She still hadn't moved, but he could visibly see the pain he caused her now. Damn it. He'd wanted to avoid all of it, yet he'd still hurt her anyway.

What a dick.

He drifted his gaze towards his bed, finding it so damn hard to look at her. 'I'll move out tomorrow,' he muttered. 'It'll be easier that way.'

He brought his gaze to meet hers, fresh tears flowing down her face, and gave her a slight smile. Surprising he even managed that, considering the pain in his chest at knowing what he was doing. What he'd done.

Would they ever go back to how they were? Could they still be friends after this? It would kill him not being a part of her life. But he wouldn't blame her if she never wanted to see him again. He'd been about to remind her to breathe. Something he'd always done when she looked like she was struggling. But he wasn't sure he could even still say that to her.

'I'm sorry, Hattie.'

His retreating figure blurred as tears burned Hattie's eyes. Her teeth dug into her bottom lip, trying her best to stop it quivering. From letting herself fall apart in front of him.

She'd glimpsed the tattoo on his triceps as he'd turned away from her. The one she'd only seen a hint of beneath his shirts. The silhouette of a firefighter surrounded by flames. Protected by the angel wings surrounding him. His job was dangerous. And it clearly weighed on him.

She deserved better than what he could offer her. That's what he'd said. Yet she struggled to see how she could get any of that with anyone else.

Her chest had been ripped open, growing tighter with every breath that failed to come. Knowing that the next breath would shatter her.

She heard the front door open. Close. Heard the rumble of his car as it backed out of the driveway. Stared at the empty doorway he'd left through for God knows how long. She staggered to the edge of the bed and lowered herself to it.

His bed.

Fitz.

Her tears dropped from her chin to the cover, a wet droplet soaking into it.

All or nothing.

She'd wanted it all. And she got nothing.

She heaved in a breath, her heart cracking on a sob.

And broke.

# Chapter 23

Hattie shouldn't be hurting like this. She shouldn't be wishing things were different. Fitz had tried to warn her. Hell, he'd even tried to stop her from saying everything she'd said in his bedroom. Had actually placed his hand over her mouth and told her to stop. That she would regret saying it.

Well, that was an understatement.

Did she regret it? She wasn't quite sure. If she hadn't approached it then, it would have simmered deep within her, eating her alive until she'd fallen for him more than she already had.

The heartbreak would have been worse then.

But what this meant for her and Fitz—the friendship she cherished so much—she had no idea. She wasn't sure she could look at him without remembering the feel of his lips on hers, his touch on her bare skin. Hearing the animal inside him trying to get out and knowing she did that to him.

It wasn't the rejection that hurt so much.

It was that she knew he felt the same way and still threw that wall up between them.

She glanced over to Bea's station where she worked silently on someone's nails, a decorative scarf looped around her neck to hide the bruises that still lingered. Hattie had hardly spoken to her own clients today, let alone her colleagues. What a sorry bunch they made.

She finished off with her client and took a moment for herself out the back. She wet a towel and dabbed her forehead, the back of her neck. It was a melting day outside, a hot, dusty wind making it feel a few degrees hotter than it was. It was the terrible conditions the firefighters had been dreading.

Hattie checked her phone, but there was no message.

Just like there hadn't been a message all week.

Fitz had, indeed, moved out and back in with his parents until he found another place. He'd done it all while she hadn't been home. While she'd been helping Bea get what she needed from her place while Lyle had still been apprehended. She'd got a restraining order put on him, but the police were vague about why they hadn't released him yet. Something about prior offences.

Hattie had told Bea she was welcome to stay with her for a bit, but the other woman had said she'd be moving in with her sister for the time being.

She hadn't told Bea about what happened between her and Fitz. Wasn't sure she could tell anyone at this point. The words were hard enough to think about, let alone say them aloud.

She couldn't think about him without that ache in her chest, the knife driving deeper. The knowledge that it was her own fault.

He'd warned her.

He'd made it clear they were just friends.

Yellow for friendship.

She'd thrown those flowers in the bin the moment she'd come home and found his room empty. She'd stood over the bin staring at them with blurry eyes for longer than she cared to admit, wanting to hate him and knowing she never could.

Fitz had been such a big part of Hattie's life before she'd risked it all on a whim. And now …

Now there was a huge emptiness inside.

She hadn't just lost the person she loved, but her best friend. The man who'd always been there for her no matter what. The most important person in her life.

He was gone.

And no amount of tears and heartbreak could change that.

Her heart skipped a beat as a message came through, then fell to her stomach when she read the name that popped up.

Noah.

Not Fitz. And it may never be Fitz again.

A fresh sob shook her, and she blinked up at the ceiling, desperate to not cry while she was at work. She'd refused to wear mascara, knowing it was more likely to run between the heat and her tears, but she didn't fancy her eyes being red for the rest of the day.

Sucking in a shaky breath to steady herself, she glanced down at the message.

Noah had listed a place and time as a suggestion for their date on the weekend.

Their date.

A lump lodged in her throat, her eyes burning. She hadn't forgotten about the date, per se, but it certainly hadn't been at the top of her list.

How could she go on a date with someone else, feeling how she feels about Fitz? Even if they weren't together—if he'd made it extremely clear there wouldn't be an *us*. How could she sit there in front of someone else and give him her sole focus when her heart—as broken as it was—belonged to another?

She bit into her lower lip to stop it wobbling.

If she'd met Noah earlier, would she be hurting like this now? If he hadn't rescheduled their last date, would she have gone out on a limb with Fitz?

She couldn't answer her own questions. But something told her that breaking it off with Noah would have been a hell of a lot messier if she'd been involved with him earlier.

Because her heart had always been Fitz's.

Whether he wanted it or not, it had always been his.

And it would have only been a matter of time before she'd realise it.

It sucked, because Noah was already a thousand times better than all her other failed dates. He was a nice guy, genuine, and he'd made her smile.

But not like Fitz had.

Had.

Past tense.

Her heart split again.

She should be trying to move forward. Perhaps she should go on that date with Noah, fall head-first into a relationship just to move on. To get over Fitz.

But she couldn't.

She didn't want to rush into something else when she hadn't finished grieving what she'd lost.

Hattie swallowed hard, tapping out a message to Noah before she let herself get too far into her own head. Because the answer was obvious for her. She wasn't ready to date. Not now. Not after what had happened with Fitz. And she wasn't sure when she would be ready—if she would. And it wouldn't be fair of her to string Noah along on a maybe.

She reread the message, making sure it didn't come across too terribly.

*I'm sorry, I can't make it. Something came up.*

She hit send before she could think twice about using his own excuse on him, and opened the dating app to delete her account, ignoring the unread messages. She dabbed at her face with the wet towel again, checking the mirror to make sure she hadn't made a mess of herself.

Noah's reply was quick, and she hesitated a moment before opening it.

*Is this a rescheduling message, or cancelling?*

Her thumb hovered over the keypad as she bit harder into her lip. If she rescheduled, she'd just be finding herself in the same position next week. And the week after that. And again. An endless cycle of rescheduling and feeling bad about it because she was ninety percent sure she wouldn't be over Fitz anytime soon.

If ever.

*Cancelling. I'm sorry.*

She watched as the dots appeared on the messages. Disappeared. Appeared again. Like he was writing something out and thought better of it. Eventually the dots stopped appearing, and no message came through. She swallowed hard. Clearly, she wouldn't be hearing from him again. And yet, as disappointed as she was with the timing and the fact she'd probably have what ifs plaguing her down the track, she didn't feel anywhere near the emptiness she had with Fitz's absence.

She gripped her phone, turning the screen off as the loneliness swept in.

If she didn't have Fitz in her life, she couldn't expect to still be close with any of the Harrows. Rosie. The woman who'd been like a mother to her. Her throat ached as she held back more tears. Even if he didn't care if she stayed in contact with his family, she did. She couldn't face any of them without her heart breaking over and over again.

God, she hadn't thought that through when she'd practically thrown herself into his arms.

She sniffed as Eliza—another hairdresser—poked her head into the back room. 'You okay?'

Eliza didn't know the specifics of what had gone down with Bea and her ex. She didn't know about her and Fitz, either. No one did. Yet she'd picked up on the vibe when she'd walked into the salon that morning and had set the playlist suitably.

Hattie nodded, though she was far from okay.

Eliza didn't look convinced, but she gave her a weak smile. 'Your next appointment is here.'

'Can you see her to the chair, please?' Her voice wobbled as she spoke, but if Eliza noticed, she didn't point it out.

'Sure.'

She muttered a thanks, though she wasn't sure if Eliza had heard. Hattie took a few shaky breaths and went out to her client, doing her best to act like everything was okay.

She was almost through with the client's appointment when the bell dinged over the door. She looked towards it out of habit rather than anticipation, her heart dropping when it wasn't her best friend.

Could she even call him that now?

It dropped even further when she realised who it was.

Noah gave her an awkward wave and an unsure smile. He'd ...

He'd come to the salon to talk to her.

When she'd thought he'd simply given up on her and hadn't bothered replying her message, he'd been on his way to the salon. Via a café, going by the tray holding two takeaway cups in his hand.

'I'll be right back,' she muttered to the client before heading towards Noah. 'Hey.'

'Hey,' he said slowly, his smile hesitant. 'Can we talk?'

Hattie swallowed. She didn't want to. Not really. But he deserved that much, at least. She nodded. 'Give me ten minutes to finish up and I'll meet you out front.'

He nodded, and she heard the bell ding again as she headed back to her client.

It was closer to twenty minutes before she'd finished up and was able to make her way out to meet him. Noah sat on the bench outside of the salon studying his phone, his brow creased as he tapped something out. A quick glimpse as she sat indicated he'd just written an email.

'Sorry, work stuff,' he muttered, finishing it up and tucking his phone into his pocket. He handed her one of the takeaway cups as she sat next to him. 'Sorry if it's cold.'

'Thanks. I'm used to drinking cold coffee.' Her coffees were always cold by the time she got to them, sipping them through-out the day while she worked. 'Noah—'

'Was it something I said?'

She blinked, his eyes focused on her. 'What do you mean?'

'I just—I thought we hit it off. If it's because of something I said, I'm sorry. If it's because I had to reschedule, I really did have something come up. Imogen's husband, Paul, broke his leg on the last day of their honeymoon. I had to fly out to help her bring him back and get him set up at home.' He took in a shaky breath, gave her an awkward smile. 'Call me hopeful, I guess.'

Realisation dawned on her. He thought she'd cancelled the date because of him. God, they were more alike than she'd first thought.

'No, it's nothing you said.' She took a shaky breath, cradling the coffee in her hands. 'I—'

She considered giving him excuses, but she'd rather the truth if she was in his position. She tried not to acknowledge the irony in that his own excuse had been legitimate after all.

'You're a nice guy, Noah,' she started.

He dropped his gaze, eyes focused on his own cup in front of him. 'Ah. Right.'

'You are. Just—' She chewed the inside of her cheek, trying to find the best way to word it. She sighed, staring in front of her, letting her vision blur. 'My heart belongs to someone else.'

'Oh.' She sensed his gaze on her. Saw the question coming before he asked it. 'You didn't—' He let out an awkward chuckle. 'I mean, I can live with it. But you didn't know that when I asked you out?'

She could see where he was coming from, and she smiled awkwardly herself. He was absolutely right, of course. Someone should know whether or not their heart was actually available when they agree to go out with someone.

'Clearly I was in denial,' she said, trying to find the humour in it. It was there, but it was smothered by the ache in her chest. 'No. I only realised it a few days ago.'

'Okay then.' He cleared his throat, standing. 'Well, thank you for making the time to talk. I understand what you're saying, and I wish you the very best.'

He smiled at her, extending his hand for a handshake. She took it. And she realised that he meant it. He wasn't just using it as a throwaway line. But he clearly wasn't going to be holding his breath for her to change her mind.

'Same goes for you,' she said. He smiled again, nodded, and turned to leave. But one question still irked her, and she wasn't sure who else she could ask about it. 'Hey, Noah?'

'Mmm?' He turned back to look at her, pausing mid-step.

She chewed on her lip, then sighed. 'What do yellow flowers mean to you?'

He considered the question for a moment. 'Um. They're pretty. Bright.' He shrugged. 'I don't know. Is it supposed to have a meaning?'

She nodded. 'Yeah. You know, like red for love. White for peace.'

His shoulders lifted to just below his ears before he dropped them again. 'Guys don't really think about that stuff, Hattie. Flowers are flowers.'

'Right. Thanks.'

He smiled, waved, and then he was gone, leaving her and her thoughts running wild.

Could it be?

Was it possible she'd had it wrong all along? Had Fitz only been buying her flowers for the sake of buying her flowers? Had it meant something else for him?

If the bouquets that had kept appearing on her table had alternated in colour, she might believe Noah. Might have believed that perhaps Fitz was the same and didn't think about that kind of thing.

But the bouquets had all been yellow. Like he'd been making a point.

And what point would he be making aside from the meaning of the colours itself?

Her phone buzzed with an incoming message and she opened it without thinking anything of it, her mind distracted.

Only to have her heart plummet to the ground as she read Ainslie's message.

Their boys had just left for the Flinders' fire.

# Chapter 24

Fitz grunted as he axed a particularly stubborn shrub. He'd been cutting a line in the vegetation for hours along with Gene and Justin and a good handful of other firefighters while the bulldozers worked further along the line to get through the thicker stuff.

The Flinders' fire had taken advantage of the bad weather conditions, and the crew hadn't managed to get it under control before it did. It was moving fast, and hard, and Fitz could feel the temperature of the fire approaching. Feel the heat in the dirt beneath them.

It had been two weeks since they'd left home. Had climbed in the trucks with their duffel bags and headed straight towards the biggest wildfire they'd had in the area in a long while.

Two weeks and three days since he'd moved out of Hattie's place. Since they'd kissed.

He could still feel her fingers in his hair, gripping close to his scalp as she'd deepened the kiss. Had let him in. Told him how she felt.

It had hit him to the core. Sent him in a panic when he'd realised what direction she was going.

He'd thought it had all been one-sided. Thought he was the only one toeing the line. And it would have been easier to keep his feelings in check if that were the case. But then ...

Then she'd come right out and asked him to kiss her.

And when he'd tried his damnedest to refuse, she'd kissed him anyway.

And damn.

That.

Kiss.

He could still feel the fire blazing deep within him when he remembered it—and it was never far from his mind. Could feel the hunger it drove, the primal need that threatened to take over.

And he'd pushed it away. Suppressed it deep down. Denied them both something that could be incredible—would be incredible—because it came with an expiration date. Because there would be an expiration date. Whether he didn't come home from work one day, or if she got tired of the life and the stress and worry that came with it.

Ending things before it truly started was the best thing for both of them. At least, that's what he told himself. So he threw himself into his work, focusing on the task at hand. And if thoughts of her—of their kiss—crept in, he just worked harder. If anything, the physical exertion helped get his mind off things.

His tasks had changed each day, but he was mostly cutting through vegetation. Occasionally he caught a glimpse of his brothers. They'd been assigned to a different part of the fire. He knew they'd be working the hoses, the grunt work generally being reserved for the ones who were less experienced. Fitz didn't care. He'd cut through the vegetation even if he'd had years of experience like his brothers did. It was a job that was just as important in fighting fires.

He dug harder, feeling the strain of his muscles as he put everything he had into his work, his mind once more drifting back to that night.

When he'd first arrived here, he'd thought the work would be just what he needed to get Hattie off his mind. To forget about what had happened between them. The feel of her mouth against his, her body pressing against him. The tug of her fingers against the waistband of his pants.

But it had done nothing to ease the ache. And when he'd drop into his makeshift bed at night exhausted and barely able to keep his eyes open, he'd fall into a restless sleep, plagued with dreams of her. Them. More of what they'd done. What could have happened. And damn it, it wrecked him.

Without Hattie, he was empty inside. He still saw the pain in her face before he'd left her standing in his room. Knew he'd caused that. And that only made him feel worse.

He wished things could be different.

Wished he'd been called to do something less dangerous. To give her the life she deserved. But it had never been an option. Not for them. But now he wasn't sure they even had their friendship. She could hate him, and she had every right to. Even if it killed him inside.

It hadn't taken Gene and Justin long to find out what had happened. They'd taken one look at his sorry love-sick expression, found out he'd moved back home, and had put two and two together. He'd spilled it all to them then, half expecting them to tease him relentlessly about it. But they didn't. And it had been good to get it off his chest. To talk about it. Especially if he was going to be risking his life each day he put on his clothes.

There'd already been too many close calls since he'd arrived. He was fairly certain every single firefighter here had had a close call of their own. Himself included. And the longer they were here, the more exhausted and tired everyone got. Mistakes were being made. And the fire was still raging.

The next few days were expected to drop in temperature again. God knows they needed it. They needed all the help they could get if they had a chance of getting it under control. It had been looking positive a few days ago before the temperature changed. The wind had picked up. Just like it did now.

He felt the sudden shift in the air around him. A shift that couldn't easily be explained. Yet he'd grown to be able to identify it. As had the rest of the crew he worked with now.

'Time to go!'

No one hesitated at the command, knowing every second wasted could be the difference between getting out of there alive or not.

Various commands were called out around him, but his eyes drifted up the hill, the red of the flames cresting into view. Embers fell around them, starting multiple spot fires that didn't seem bothered by the line in the vegetation they'd spent hours working on.

He picked up the pace, putting out as many spot fires as he could while he moved. Just like everyone else did. Sparks fell on his shoulders, and he looked up, the top of the tree he stood near a red blazing ball. His heart pounded against his chest, adrenaline coursing through his body as he anticipated the danger they were all in. And still, Hattie was the one he thought about. It was her face that urged him to get out of there. Begged him to come home safely.

He heard the calls of his retreating crew, saw the wall of fire barrelling towards them.

Heard the crack of the falling tree.

# Chapter 25

Hattie's heart lodged in her throat as she heard the breaking news intro. Everyone turned almost as one towards the television behind the bar. She'd spent the last two weeks moping. Aching for what could have been. Desperately missing her best friend.

She'd been lost. She still was. And nothing had appealed to her. Not work. Not going out to the shops. Not hitting the gym every morning before work. Food was bland. Her house felt empty, all traces of Fitz ever living there erased. She'd broken down one day when she'd bent down to pick something up and came eye-level with the rock he'd thrown through the window when he'd come home from training, right next to the picture frame sitting on her bedside table. Her and Fitz were smiling, sitting together on a picnic table at a waterfall nearby. His arm was around her, as it always had been, her head resting against his shoulder.

The image had blurred in front of her, her knees growing weak. She'd lowered herself to the ground, still staring up at that picture frame, wishing things were different. Wishing things could go back to how they were. Knowing they couldn't. She'd struggled to suck in air, gasping for breath, forced herself to remember to breathe. In. One, two, three. Out. Struggled more at the ever-present reminder of her best friend. Of how he'd once been there to help her breathe and now she had to figure it out herself.

There was an ache in her chest. Her stomach constantly feeling like she wanted to throw up. Her heart felt like it was breaking every time he filled her mind. Every time something reminded her of him. And God, a lot reminded her of him.

He'd been her safe place. Her home. And now ...

Now he was gone.

And she had no idea whether or not he was safe. What was happening up at the fire. Grasping for straws as she took in only what she could find from the news platforms. Which, admittedly, hadn't eased her anxiety.

She'd deliberated sending him a text. Ringing him. Aching to hear his voice. His laugh rippling through the phoneline. And each time she'd picked up her phone, she remembered their kiss. The unchecked passion in it. And that he'd pushed her away.

She didn't even know if she could call him her best friend anymore. But without him, she didn't have one. She had friends, sure, but none like him.

And despite the heartbreak that plagued her every breath, she still checked her phone for news on the Flinders' fire almost every hour. Still kept whatever television she was near on the channel where breaking news would pop up as it came in. She was desperate for information. Desperate to know he was safe.

To know she would see his face again. Hear his voice.

'Hey, turn it up, please,' Ainslie called out, catching the bartender's attention. Her and Hattie had met for lunch at the pub, the other woman feeling the emptiness at home as well, particularly while Cliff was at school.

Hattie struggled to breathe as she saw the images of the uncontrolled fire flicker across the screen, the reporter's voice louder now that the volume had been turned up.

'The Flinders' fire has taken an unexpected turn ...'

She watched the screen carefully as the camera flickered past some firefighters. Was Fitz in there? She didn't dare blink in case it was the only way she'd know he was safe. Her heart pounded in her chest, anxiety threatening to take over as none of the faces shown were Fitz's. Neither were they Nick or Dave or Eric. Ainslie tensed beside her.

'... a crew was trapped ...'

'Oh, God.' Ainslie clutched a hand to her chest.

'It's a sad day, indeed. We've just received the stats. Three firefighters have been taken to hospital with serious injuries and one fatality ...'

Hattie's heart lurched, her ears roaring. She stared at the television, the images blurring in front of her. The reporter kept talking for another moment, but Hattie couldn't make out what she was saying. Only that they didn't know the identities of those injured or ...

She couldn't even think it.

God, Fitz.

She sucked in a breath, and it was like she was inhaling acid. The next breath was worse. Oh, God, let him be okay. What if she never got to see him again?

What if she never got to tell him that she loves him? That she wants him and only him, the whole package, risks and uncertainty and all.

If she never got to see that smile again.

Without thinking twice about it, she picked up her phone and dialled his number. Nothing. Not even a call signal. She tried again. Still nothing.

'Come on!'

She dialled again.

Nothing.

A sob shook her, her fingers fumbling with the touch-screen of her phone. She needed to know. Needed to know he was safe.

Needed to know that there was something to that tattoo on his triceps.

That he was—

'Breathe, Hattie. They've got no reception there,' Ainslie said, putting a shaky hand on her shoulder, worry etched in her own face.

No reception. Right. Of course they wouldn't be easily contactable.

She forced her breaths to deepen, forced them to slow down. Ainslie stood, gathering up her purse, their meals forgotten. 'Come on, let's go to Jeff and Rosie's. I'm pretty sure Jeff still has an old radio. They might know something.'

She tugged on Hattie's arm, and Hattie let her guide her out of the pub. They hopped in Ainslie's car, and Hattie was able to somehow tap out a message to Eliza asking her to reschedule her afternoon. There was no way in hell she'd be able to focus on her clients when she was in this state. She was surprised she'd even managed the message. Her thumb hovered over her text message thread with Fitz, her eyes blurring once more as she opened it and reread their last messages. They were from that night. His asking if it was okay if Gene and Justin came over. Her telling him she'd be late home a few days earlier. His saying dinner would be waiting for her.

Her hold tightened on the phone. Would she ever be able to have those kinds of messages with him again? Could they ever share simple moments with each other again?

Her chest tightened as she sent him a new message. The first one in weeks. Weeks that had seemed like a lifetime. Regardless of what was or wasn't going on with them, she still cared about him.

*Please tell me you're safe.*

She hardly noticed when Ainslie swerved into the driveway of Jeff and Rosie's place and struggled to keep up as Ainslie flung herself out of the car after it had barely stopped moving.

She swallowed as they neared the front door. The door that had always felt like home more than her own did. She supposed it was Fitz who had felt like home, not the house.

Ainslie didn't bother to knock as she flung the door open. It was already unlocked, like Rosie was already expecting them. Hattie closed the door behind her, and the two of them rounded the corner to the kitchen. Rosie and Liz were already sitting at the table, their hands cradling cups of tea, and Jeff was talking on a radio. A teapot sat in the middle of the table.

Hattie wasn't sure he was supposed to still have a radio, but God, she was glad he did.

'Tell us you know something,' Ainslie said, seating herself next to Liz.

'Jeff's trying to get hold of someone now.'

Rosie's gaze fell on Hattie as she spoke and she gave her a gentle smile. Hattie wondered if she knew about her and Fitz. She suspected she knew something was going on, considering Fitz had moved back in with them. But rather than asking questions, she simply pulled the chair out beside her and patted it, indicating for Hattie to sit there.

So she did. Taking a seat at the table with her fami-ly-who-wasn't-her-family. The family she'd always wished she could be a part of. She just hadn't realised what that had meant until now.

'Do you want a cuppa, love?'

Rosie's eyes were kind, and she'd placed a hand over Hattie's. She squeezed the older woman's hand back and nodded, the gesture meaning more to her than Rosie probably realised.

'I'll get some cups,' Liz said, pulling herself to her feet.

'I can get them,' Ainslie said, placing a hand on Liz's arm.

Liz scoffed. 'I'm pregnant, not incapable. Besides, this baby starts kicking hard if I sit for too long.'

Liz returned with two more cups and poured tea into both. Hattie cradled hers in front of her.

It had been weeks since she'd made a pot of tea for her-self. Usually she shared it with Fitz or made it whenever Rosie popped by. The woman beside her had been the one who had started Hattie's love for teapots and tea in general.

The four women sat in a sombre silence, sipping their tea, their eyes on the man at the edge of the room talking into his radio. Their breaths caught in unison as he lowered the radio and turned towards them.

'They're safe.'

Relief washed over her, and a glance around the table said it was the same for everyone. They were safe.

Fitz was safe.

'The life, huh?' Ainslie said, chuckling. Her shoulders were visibly more relaxed. She lifted her cup towards Rosie. 'You did warn us.'

'Well,' Rosie said, bringing her own cup to her lips. She glanced around at the three other women, her eyes lingering on Hattie for a moment longer. 'It helps having each other for support. You girls will never be alone in this. You have each other.'

'Here, here,' Liz said, reaching across the table to grasp Rosie's hand and beside her to take Ainslie's.

Ainslie reached across to Hattie, and Hattie and Rosie finished the circle. Hattie didn't miss the extra squeeze Rosie gave her. Like she knew more than she'd let on. She respected the woman more for not bringing it up in front of the others. And if the others suspected, they also didn't say anything. But in that subtle squeeze, the look Rosie had given her ...

She'd included Hattie when she'd talked about the girls not being alone. She wanted Hattie to know that she meant her as well. Hattie's expression alone—the fact she'd come just as worried as the others—would have given away more than she'd intended. But in that moment, she hadn't cared who knew. She just needed to know Fitz was safe.

Then she could figure out the rest.

'He refused to tell me what happened,' Rosie muttered when the other women had scurried to the kitchen to find the sweet slice Rosie had baked earlier. Rosie reached out to tuck a stray tendril of hair behind Hattie's ear and patted her cheek. 'I can see you both care about each other. Whatever happened, you'll work it out.'

Hattie nodded, unable to form words, and gave her a wobbly smile. God, she hoped they could work it out. Because the prospect of not having him in her life—not having this—would destroy her.

Her heart already ached from the distance they'd had these past weeks. Knowing that it could be forever ...

She would never recover from that.

Fitz's arm ached as he ploughed through the ground cover, the scabs already pulling tight on his skin. It had been yet another close call when that tree had fallen. A branch had knocked him over, slicing his forearm. He hadn't needed stitches, thank God. He'd done a few days of lighter work before returning to his usual work.

A scratch.

He could have been trapped. The branch had knocked him over. If he'd been a few inches over, the whole tree would've fallen on him.

His crew had been able to help him up and they'd got out of there before they'd been trapped. Another crew hadn't been so lucky. Which only drove home how dangerous his work was.

It could have been him.

It very nearly was.

And yet ...

It didn't deter him from getting back out there. From pushing through pain and exhaustion to deal with the fire before it took more lives. Civilian lives. They were getting closer to having the Flinders' fire under control. When it was controlled enough to be managed by the local crews, he could go home.

He could see Hattie.

His chest heaved, though from the thought of her or from physical exertion, he wasn't quite sure.

Would she even want to see him again?

He hated the idea of not having her in his life. And yet, he wasn't sure he could manage having her in it without being the one he shared his life with.

He loved her.

Loves.

There was nothing else to it.

And maybe ... maybe that would be enough to step back and see her happy with whatever she chose. But he knew that this fire only proved each of the points he'd made to her. Why she deserved more.

A drop landed on the back of his neck. Sweat. He'd forgotten what it was like to not be sweating. For his skin to be properly clean. He couldn't get the smell of smoke out of his hair, and he knew there was no point trying to while he was there.

Another drop landed on the slight bit of skin visible between his gloves and his jacket. He kept ploughing, ignoring the sweat that crept down his neck. It wasn't until he saw another drop land on the dirt in front of him, and then another, that he looked up. Another drop fell on his face, and he straightened.

The crew moved almost as one, each slowing their work, each looking up as the rain fell harder with each drop.

A smile pulled on his lips as the drops turned into a steady rain. He tugged off his helmet just for a moment. Just to feel his hair dampen. The water streaming down his face. Stuck out his tongue to taste it.

And let out the biggest whoop he could muster.

He wasn't the only one.

They all knew this wouldn't be the end of it. Knew the rain alone wouldn't be enough to douse the flames they'd been fighting for weeks. Knew they still had a lot of work to do. But it would be pretty damn helpful. And it would considerably increase their chances of getting it controlled quickly.

Gene slapped his back and threw his head back in a howl, many of the crew joining in. Fitz howled too, if only to let out the pure relief that flooded through him. The surge of motivation and hope that filled him. And God, it felt good. Exhilarating.

And despite everything, the only person he wanted to share that feeling with was Hattie.

# Chapter 26

Hattie didn't bother moving from the kitchen before she downed the first shot of bourbon. It burned her throat as it went down, warmed her chest and then her stomach. To say she was in a bad mood would be putting it lightly.

Another week had passed since she'd been terrified about Fitz's safety. She still hadn't heard from him. Didn't expect to.

And yet, she hadn't realised how much more she could miss him until now. Until after the day she'd had.

She was still catching up on the appointments she'd rescheduled from that afternoon a week earlier. And while some of those clients were understanding, some weren't happy about being rescheduled at the last minute. Those clients had been particularly vocal about their disappointment and had been picking fault with their haircuts, making Hattie run late for her next appointments. Today seemed to be full of them.

It was the domino effect, and with each passing hour, it seemed that whatever could go wrong, had. She poured another shot and knocked it back. It was the shittiest of days, and she had no one to talk to about it.

She didn't want to go to Liz or Ainslie with it. They both had enough worries of their own with the guys being away. She didn't know Eliza well enough to offload all her problems on her. And Bea was particularly stressed today too, considering she'd just found out Lyle was no longer being held in custody. Hattie had reminded her about the restraining order, but Bea had simply told her a restraining order could only go so far. She'd considered calling Charlie and talking to her, but she'd never vented to her sister about things like this. Rosie would be a listening ear in a heartbeat, but she didn't want a solution. Didn't want someone to console her. She needed a good hard vent and Fitz—

Fitz had always been the one who'd been there for that.

And now she didn't even have him.

Tears pricked her eyes. She'd still been scouring the news all week. Still felt that lurch of panic in her chest every time she heard the breaking news intro. She'd been relieved to know they'd got the fire under control a few days earlier, but she still hadn't heard from him. And after how they'd left things ...

Her lower lip wobbled as she poured herself another shot and decided on bringing the whole bottle to the couch with her. She could put on a sappy movie and sob into her glass, deal with the hangover tomorrow.

The life.

It had haunted her all week. She knew the words were thrown around in the local firefighting community. She knew what they meant, knew not everyone was cut out for it. If she was being honest with herself, she'd never even thought about it before Fitz had come back from training. She'd always known her best friend was going to be a firefighter. Always known he'd be putting his life at risk each day.

But she'd never thought she could say she was part of the life as his friend. But she realised now, she absolutely could. She cared about him. Loved him. And even as friends, she'd have worried about him. He was that much a part of her life that it would have been impossible for her not to. The fact he was more to her than simply a friend only added to that.

She realised now that she was always going to be a part of the life. Always going to be affected by what happened to him. And, she realised as she plonked the bottle on the coffee table and took a sip from her glass, she always would be, even if he was no longer in her life.

She missed him.

So damn much.

She missed her best friend. The easiness they had. The way he made everything better just by being him. How he healed her with just his proximity. She missed calling him up after a hard day and watching a movie together. They would talk about it—or not, depending on what was needed. Sometimes they just sat in silence. And even that had been healing. Had made everything seem less daunting.

Now she was drowning.

She swiped at her eyes as a knock sounded at the door and straightened her glasses. She took another sip as she moved to open it.

She blinked twice. Was she imagining things? Had she drunk more than she realised? She must have.

How else could she explain what she was looking at?

The smell of soap and spice and seawater mingled with the scent of Chinese takeout was heady as she caught the hesitant smile on his face. She let her gaze fall over him. He was in one piece. He had no visible injuries that she could see. He was ... here.

In one hand, a plastic bag with the Chinese food in it looped over his fingers, his phone cradled in his palm. In his other—

Her heart plummeted as she eyed the bouquet he held in front of him.

*Yellow.*

Fitz wasn't sure what he'd expected when he'd shown up at Hattie's door. He'd wanted nothing more than to see her. It had always been normal for him to show up at her place whenever. He'd always gravitated towards her. He'd never been able to explain why, but now he knew it was because he loved her.

He'd been torn when they'd told him he was going home. His first instinct had been to go to Hattie's. And then he'd remembered why he couldn't. He'd spent the hours driving home fighting it. Had banged his fist against the wall in the shower as he'd washed grime and smoke off himself, feeling like he was in the wrong place. Hated himself for letting things get out of hand. For losing her.

But as he'd dried himself off and let his phone turn on after charging for a while, his chest had tightened at the message that trickled in.

*Please tell me you're safe.*

He'd had no reception at the fire. Hadn't bothered to charge his phone because of it. He'd grown tired of watching the battery drain quickly while it searched for service. He wasn't sure when she'd sent the message, but it didn't matter. She'd sent one.

His hand had gripped his phone, droplets of water falling from his hair to his shoulders. And he still hadn't been able to tear his gaze away from the message.

He hadn't even told her he'd been called out to the fire. She would have once been the first person he'd told. He'd deliberated with the message for so long he'd run out of reception before he'd even found the words to say it. Hadn't been sure she'd wanted to know. Not after how they'd left things.

But despite all that, she'd messaged him.

She'd still cared enough about him that she'd wanted to know he was safe.

His thumb had hovered over his phone, ready to tap out a reply, to tell her he was home and he was safe.

That he missed her.

That he wanted to see her. To fix things. To at least go back to how they were—if it was even possible.

That he loved her.

But the words didn't come. He'd tossed his phone on the bed instead and got changed, a new plan forming. The words didn't come because none of that should be said over a text message. Ma had raised him better than that.

So he'd dressed and called ahead to order food, catching the florist just before they'd closed.

And now he stood on her doorstep, trying his best to decipher whether or not his visit was welcome.

Surprise fluttered across her face as she opened the door, like she couldn't quite believe he was there. Perhaps she'd finally forgotten who he was in the weeks they'd been apart. If she did, maybe he stood a chance. But she'd once told him she never forgot anything to do with him, despite her terrible memory. Her eyes darkened as they fell to the bouquet in his hand. The one he'd stretched towards her without fully realising it. That look was unreadable, yet when she lifted her gaze to meet his again, he could see the pain laced in it.

She didn't take the bouquet, merely lifting her glass to her lips. She took a sip. But said nothing.

He cleared his throat, desperate for something to say. Anything that might ease the tension between them. To heal the pain. To fix what had broken. He lifted his phone, turning the screen on so she could see her last message to him. See the timestamp on it that showed he'd only just received it.

'I'm safe.'

There was more silence as her shimmering eyes drifted to the phone. Back to him. Then she dropped her gaze to her drink, lifting it again.

'I'll get another glass.'

She moved towards the kitchen after picking up a bottle of bourbon off the coffee table, leaving the door open. As good of an invitation as he could expect, he supposed.

He followed her in, closing the door and kicking off his shoes. He nudged them to the side where some shoes sat lined up against the wall, her normal work shoes left askew. He placed the food and flowers on the bench, keeping it between them, but his eyes were on her.

Her hair was still tied back. Unusual, considering she usually let it out as soon as she got home. She'd changed into her pyjamas and he caught a whiff of her vanilla soap. She'd obviously showered since she'd knocked off work, but something clearly bothered her if her hair was still up and she was drinking with no food in sight. Her eyes drifted to the flowers as she uncapped the bottle and started pouring into a second glass. There was something unreadable there. And he couldn't help but feel that she didn't like them.

Perhaps he'd overstepped. Perhaps it was all too much for a repair attempt. He needed to think. Damn it, he needed to fix this.

'I, um, only received your message after I charged my phone. I didn't have reception.'

'I heard.' Her tone was flat as she slid the glass across to him.

He held it in his hand, watching his best friend. His heart cracked at the tightness in her expression. The usual joy and happiness gone. Had he done that? Had he been the one to wipe that smile off her face?

'Hattie, I'm sorry.' She held his gaze a moment, her eyes glistening, and her throat bobbed as she swallowed. She was fighting tears and he'd caused that. His heart lodged into his throat, making it difficult to breathe. To talk. 'Tell me we can fix this.'

She sniffed, lowered her gaze, then indicated towards the glass in his hand. 'You've got some catching up to do.'

He lifted the drink, eyed the double shot and a bit in the glass. Knew what she meant by catching up.

It had always been their way. An inside joke of sorts. If one started drinking without the other, the other had to catch up. She wanted him on the same level of tipsiness as her. Especially if they were going to be having this kind of conversation.

He downed the liquid in one go, wincing at the burn that trailed through him. He only just held back from coughing. 'How much have you had?'

She lifted an eyebrow in a challenge, tipping more of the bourbon into his glass. 'As much as you.' Her words were still flat. Cold.

She capped the bottle, picked it and her glass up, and headed towards the lounge room. He followed with his.

'Hard day at work?' He was reaching for reasons for her mood, but he couldn't bear to think that he was the sole reason her light was struggling to glow.

'Among other things.'

She placed her glass and the bottle on the coffee table, began a search for the television remote. He swallowed hard, his heart cracking in his chest. This wasn't his Hattie. This was a broken, weary lookalike of his best friend who could barely stand to look at him, let alone talk to him.

'Can we talk about this? About what happened?' He placed his own drink on the coffee table, but didn't help her search. He needed her to look at him. To see if there was a chance of fixing things.

Her gaze was still averted as she searched behind the pillows on the couch. 'I don't know how to.'

'Yell at me. Throw something at me. Call me the biggest dick you've ever met.' He ran a hand through his hair, still damp from his shower. He could feel the pressure building in his chest, needed some kind of reaction from her. Something that might hint that he hadn't lost it all. 'Anything but this, Hattie.'

He refrained from begging her not to say she hated him. He couldn't stand it if she did. Would never forgive himself. But she had every right to say it. If that was what she felt.

'You want something, Fitz? Fine.'

She turned towards him, her eyes flickering with challenge and fury. Good. If she was angry at him, she would talk to him. It was still better than silence and curt answers.

'You. Weren't. There.' She put a hand over her mouth, pinched her nose, squeezed her eyes shut for the briefest of moments before letting her hand fall. 'I needed you, and you weren't there. You—' She brought her hand to her forehead, let it run over the top of her head to her ponytail. 'You've always been there. It's the one thing I've ever been able to rely on. And maybe that's not fair of me to say, and I get it, you were away and you had no reception, but what about before that? What about now?'

She threw her hand in the air in frustration, staring down at the couch like she'd wondered if it had swallowed the remote. His throat worked, but he kept his lips shut tight, letting her get it all out.

'You left without telling me you'd been called up. We hadn't talked for days before that. And after how we left it—' She sniffed, bringing her gaze to meet his. The hurt in her eyes pierced him. 'I've spent weeks worrying about you. Weeks. And I know it's part of the job, but I was terrified of losing you like that. It's worse—so much worse—worrying about someone who's not even talking to you. You didn't want me in the life, Fitz? Well, I'm already there, whether you like it or not. And after today—' She swiped at her eyes, her voice cracking.

His jaw clenched as he thought of the tree falling beside him. How close he had been to not returning home. He'd wanted to save her all the worry, but it seemed she'd done nothing but.

'I had the worst day today and all I wanted to do was call you so I could hear your voice and I couldn't even do that.'

'I'm here now, Hattie,' he managed.

'But you're not, are you?' She pierced him with a look that made his blood cold. 'I know we can't go back to how things were, I just wish it didn't hurt so much.'

His throat worked to push through the lump there. She was right. They couldn't go back to how things were. Now he knew what it was like to have her lips against his. He knew what she tasted like. Felt her body pressing against his, begging for more. Her sigh against his lips.

She shook her head, her eyes going wild. 'Of course, it's all my fault.'

He blinked.

What?

'You *did* try to warn me.' She let out a shallow laugh, though there was nothing funny about it. Just pure irony. 'I should've listened to you. Should've seen the signs for what they were.'

Signs?

He shook his head, his brow creasing. 'What are you talking about?'

'The *signs*,' she repeated, her voice raising. She was clearly getting more heated, which could be a good thing. If he knew what the hell she was on about.

'There were no signs, Hattie.'

'You literally made me stop talking.'

She was yelling now, her eyes wild as she held his gaze. Her expression kept switching between anger and hurt and disbelief. Like she couldn't decide which emotion she felt.

'So you wouldn't regret what you said.' His own voice had risen, tension crackling between them like a spark might set them alight.

'Because you don't have feelings for me, right? Because you couldn't stand to see me crossing that line without you.'

'No,' he ground out. She couldn't be further from the truth.

Tears fell down her cheeks, her face scrunching as she tried to hold it all together. He could see her body shaking, ached to wrap her up in his arms and make it all better.

'Because you'd seen it coming and dropped all the hints you could that you're not interested, right down to the stupid flowers.'

He threw his arms out beside him, the conversation lost on him now. 'What's wrong with the flowers?'

'They're yellow!' she yelled, more tears coming. She let her arms fall to her side, defeated. And he realised that look on her face was no longer a mix of emotions, but heartbreak. 'Yellow for friendship.'

He swallowed hard, his body vibrating with the urgency to ease that heartache. Screw all the ideals he'd had. Screw wanting to keep her from worrying about it. She'd admitted it before. She was already in the life. Whether he wanted it or not, she was there, and she would be worrying. And she'd be hurt if anything happened to him. At least—

He rubbed the back of his neck, dropping his gaze as he realised something he hadn't before.

She would have his family's support if anything happened to him. She would not be facing life alone. Would never be alone if she was part of his family.

'It's not for friendship.'

'What?'

He brought his gaze back to meet hers, seeing the whole situation in a new light. It had only been his fears stopping anything from happening between them. He'd pushed her away because of his own presumptuous fears. Fears that weren't as bad as he'd thought.

She'd said they couldn't go back to how they were, which meant it could only be one of two things.

Either this was the end, or they picked up where they left off.

He studied the surprise in her eyes. Those beautiful honey eyes. The flush in her cheeks that had appeared while she'd been yelling. Hell, even having her yell at him.

'I don't need flowers for friendship, Hattie.'

'Then why'd you get them?'

Were they seriously arguing over the colour of the damn flowers? He dug his hand through his hair in frustration.

'Because I thought you'd like them.'

'But they're *yellow*.'

'Like the fucking sun, Hattie! Like the—' He'd thrown his hand up between them as though emphasising his point. He let it fall to his side now. 'You light up my life just by being in it. Your rays chase away the shadows in my life. Wherever I am, I gravitate towards you. You're the centre my world revolves around, Hattie, because you're the most important person in my life. My life doesn't exist without you in it. It's just dark and cold and a terrible, terrible place.'

He hadn't noticed that he'd closed the distance between them until his hands fell on her upper arms, gripping them gently. Begging her to look at him. To understand.

'Yellow like the sun. And, Hattie—'

He let one hand lift, pressing his palm against her cheek, swiping the tears away with his thumb. He swallowed, knowing there was no turning back now. Her honey eyes met his, darkening a shade. Her lips parted as he cupped her face between both hands now, brushing tears away with both thumbs. He felt it deep within him first. A flicker of a flame that he'd been desperately trying to put out for her benefit. And then it grew, building inside him until it consumed him, incinerated him from the inside out. He inched closer, his eyes holding hers as their lips grew closer.

'Hattie, I love the sun.'

# Chapter 27

Hattie didn't even have time to close her eyes before his lips were on hers, pressing against them so tenderly, softly. Hesitant. Waiting for her response.

*Yellow like the sun.*

Not for friendship. But because they'd meant something so much more to him than that. Than any typical flower meanings. They'd been personal, and thoughtful, and so very ... Fitz. And she'd thought he'd been dropping hints, telling her in no uncertain terms that he only saw her as a friend.

What did that make her?

She'd blamed the fact he'd come back from training different. Her emotions had been haywire since. And the value she'd placed on their friendship. Having one-sided feelings would very much be crossing a line.

But when those feelings were reciprocated ...

She melted into his kiss, the surprise ebbing away. She parted her lips, letting him in, devouring the taste of him that she couldn't quite describe. Sweet. Full. And the hint of bourbon.

Hattie tensed. She'd been tipsy last time they'd kissed too. Would he still want her without an ounce of alcohol in their systems? God, she hoped so. For her, the kiss was sobering. And frankly, she'd barely had enough to even say she was tipsy. But the thought still lingered.

His chest rumbled beneath her palms as his lips moved against hers, and her knees went weak. Right now, she wouldn't care how drunk she was. Not if it meant he kept kissing her like this. Like he wanted her as much as she wanted him. Yearned for her like the very thought of him consumed her. He shifted one hand to the back of her neck, tilting her head back to deepen the kiss further and snaked his other hand around her waist, tugging her closer.

God, she loved it. Loved him. She wanted more. Wanted to let that fire burning between them explode into something unforgettable. Unmistakeable.

Because when it came to Fitz, she was all in.

Hattie slid her hands up and over his shoulders, diving her hands into his thick locks. She spent every moment of her workdays with her hands in other people's hair, but none of them were like his. None of them sent flames skittering up her arms, down to her belly. That spark—zing—coursed through her. That thing she'd told herself she didn't believe in.

Fitz tore his lips away from hers, and she moaned in protest, only to gasp as he brought his mouth to the sensitive part of her neck. Her legs threatened to give out from under her, and yet, there was something so perfect, so delicate in the way he held her. Kissed her.

He reached for her ponytail, tugging her head back just enough to gain better access to her neck, to trail kisses across her collarbone.

'Fitz.'

Her breath caught in her throat as his hand slipped under her shirt, pressing on the small of her back. Fire coursed through her, and she felt like she just might combust if she didn't have more of him.

'Mmm?'

His hum vibrated through her neck as he kissed the column of her throat, inching closer to her lips.

'I need—' She gasped again as he nipped, then kissed her in the same place. God, they hadn't done more than kissing and she was about to come undone.

'You taste so fucking good.'

His voice rumbled through her, the baritone doing things to her she never knew sound could.

*Oh, God.*

'I need more,' she managed, pulling back just enough to catch his eyes. Those dark, hungry eyes that made her stomach flip. Made her burn for him.

His jaw tensed, his eyes darkening just a shade as they dropped to her parted lips. 'How much more?'

It came out more of a growl, really. Like he was trying his best to control himself. To stop himself from letting that hunger, that wildness come out of him. But damn it, she wanted it. Wanted to be wild with him.

'All of it.'

She tugged on the waistband of his shorts, pulling herself against him. She felt his need—his want—press into her belly. She lifted a hand to his cheek, directing his gaze to meet hers so he could see the conviction in her eyes.

'I want everything, Fitz.'

The rumble grew louder, working its way up his chest and into her mouth as he crushed his lips against hers, kissing her with no abandon. She let his hand slide up her side, to her breast.

A wicked grin found her lips as he realised she wasn't wearing a bra. His groan urged her on, and she nipped his lower lip and dug her hands under his shirt, her nails scraping along his back.

In one smooth movement, he lifted her by her thighs, bringing her higher, wrapping her legs around his waist until there was nothing between them but layers of fabric.

'Here or the bed?' he ground out between kisses.

'What?'

'Choose where, Hattie, baby, before I take you like this.'

Holy shit.

She was so grateful she was no longer standing because there was no way in hell her legs would still be holding her weight with that.

'Bed. Now.'

'Fuck yeah.'

His lips didn't leave hers while he carried her to her room. Had barely opened his eyes to see where they were going. He'd been at her place so often he could probably navigate his way around her house with a blindfold on. But right now? With him holding her like this? His hands sliding to cup her bottom while he carried her? That rumble deep within his chest like he couldn't get enough.

She couldn't imagine being here with anyone else.

It was Fitz.

Always Fitz.

She'd half expected him to throw her on the bed like he'd playfully done when they were just friends, but as they came to the edge of her bed, he slowly lowered her to her feet, his hands sliding higher under her shirt until he'd lifted it over her head and dropped it on the floor beside them.

His eyes dropped to her breasts, and she bit into her lower lip, feeling the warmth flood to her chest, her face. Everywhere.

He swore as he exhaled, lifting his hand to cup one breast, his thumb brushing over the peak.

'So fucking beautiful, Hattie, baby.'

Heat coursed through her, filling her with a need so great she just might get there from his look alone. She tugged at his shirt.

'Shirt for a shirt, Muscles. Or have you forgotten how this works?'

His eyebrow shot up, his lips curving into that grin that promised he'd do all kinds of wicked things to her. Her core tensed in anticipation. 'Muscles?' His shirt was off in one quick tug, and he flexed his arm between them. 'These ones?'

She rolled her eyes, but let her hands fall on his biceps. Squeezed them. 'You're so full of it.'

He stepped closer, nudging her back towards the bed. The back of her knees hit the edge and threatened to give out. He caught her around the waist with one arm.

'Oh, yeah?'

'Yeah,' she said breathlessly, her hands sliding up his chest. Her fingertips dragged over the flying seeds of his dandelion tattoo. The ones over his heart. 'When did you get this?'

He leaned closer, nudging her cheek with his nose before kissing the corner of her lips. 'First week of training.'

Her heart fluttered as his hands drifted lower, his thumbs hooking in the top of her pants.

'Why?'

It came out on a breath, barely audible, and her heart stopped beating for just a moment, waiting for his response. Wanting to know why he'd had something so personal inked so close to his heart.

He pulled his head back just enough to study her face and tugged her closer. 'Because I wanted to feel you with me all the time. And I figured I couldn't have you any closer than that.'

Until now.

Had Fitz known he had feelings for her even then? Months before? She'd only realised her own recently, but looking back on it, she could see she'd had them for a very long time. No one else had ever compared to him. No one else had ever been good enough because they weren't him. No one else had even come close.

'I missed you.'

His words rippled through her, reached her centre and swirled there before spreading through her body.

'I missed you, too,' she whispered.

His fingers brushed against her cheek, his thumb caressing along her jaw. 'Are you sure about this, Hattie, baby? I'll stop if you want me to.' His eyes darkened another shade as they dropped to her lips, and he tugged her against him again with the hand still hooked on her pants. 'But I want this. I don't want to stop.'

'I don't want you to stop.'

'Still on the pill?'

She nodded, her face flushing at the fact he remembered she was taking it. He reached for his wallet in his back pocket, flipping it open with one hand. Her heart dropped.

'I've got protection, too.'

She put a hand over the wallet, stopping his one-handed search for the foil packet. 'I want to feel you, Fitz.' His body tensed, his eyes filling with a new hunger. She flushed again, her body growing hotter by the second. 'I—I'm clean, if that's what you're worried about.'

'I never doubted it,' he said, letting his wallet fall to the ground. 'I am too, for the record.'

She gave him a shy smile, slipping her hand to the button on his shorts. 'Then what are you waiting for?'

'You, Hattie, baby. I'm waiting for you.'

He slammed his lips against hers again, guiding her onto the bed, resting himself above her, one leg between her thighs. They kissed like the world didn't exist around them. And it didn't. Not for Hattie. She hoped not for him. She moaned as he kissed down her neck, her collarbone, down to her breast, and sucked a nipple into his mouth. She arched against him as he licked and sucked, tweaked her other one with his thumb and forefinger.

God, it felt so good.

So good she had no words. It was …

It was perfection.

His hand slipped from her breast as he continued kissing, nipping, sucking her other one, his fingers trailing down her belly, slipping underneath her pants, her underwear. Her legs trembled as he slid a finger against her entrance. He groaned as he found how wet she was for him. She felt what it did to him as his own need pulsed against her leg, begging to be let out of his own restraints.

'God, Hattie.'

She gasped again, her back arching as he slipped the finger in, then another. Flames seared through her, setting alight every nerve ending, every muscle fibre. He crooked his fingers as he moved them, his thumb working the swollen nub. Pure fire, raw and hot, consumed her, aching to be set free, pushing her closer and closer to her release. He brought his mouth back to hers as he worked her, brought her closer to the edge, swallowed her scream as she tumbled over the edge, her body shattering around him as she came completely undone.

Gently, slowly, he eased her back to reality, back to safety, and made to pull away. She slung an arm around his neck to bring him back, arching herself off the bed to kiss him, not wanting to feel his absence again. Ever.

His chuckle was delicious, beautiful, and promised her the world. 'You want everything, baby?'

She nodded, unable to form words. He'd sent her careening into another world just with his fingers. Of course she wanted more.

'Then I'm gonna need to move.'

She released him reluctantly, her breaths coming hard and fast as her body still worked its way back from her orgasm. Fitz had been mesmerised by her, hardly able to hold himself together as he brought her to the pleasure her body craved. He made quick work of both of their pants, and settled in between her legs, his own tip moist and begging to be buried deep.

Holy fuck.

He was about to make love with his best friend. And damn if that didn't feel right.

She held his gaze, her skin flushed, her eyes wild for him. She was so stunningly beautiful. Perfection personified. And the smile she gave him. The knowing in her eyes that what they were about to do would feel a thousand times better than what they'd just done.

What he would give to see that look every damn morning. Every night.

To see her lying beneath him like this. Straddling him. Against the wall. On every damn surface they could get to. But this—that look in her eyes? That would always be his favourite.

She bit into her lower lip as she tilted her hips up, bringing his tip to her entrance. God, she was wet. And it was all for him.

'What are you waiting for?'

Her fingertips traced the tattoo on his side, his chest, and his arms grew weak as he held his weight above her. He dropped to his elbow, bringing one hand to cradle her face, his other between them.

'Just savouring the moment, Hattie, baby.'

He guided himself into her, and she arched against him. God, it was incredible. He could feel her stretching to fit him, her body still pulsing, taking him in like they were always meant to be.

Perhaps they were, he realised.

She tightened around him, and it almost sent him soaring over the edge. He grit his teeth to hold it all together, moving slowly against her. Picking up the pace to meet the one she set beneath him. He kissed her, her body quivering as they moved, pulsing around him. She was close, and *fuck*, so was he. Her nails scraped down his back, the bark of pain pushing him closer.

But he was too close.

And he refused to get there without her.

He scooped his arm beneath her and rolled onto his back, bringing her up above him until she straddled him. Her cheeks—her breasts—were flushed, and he lavished the look of pleasure that flowed through her. The way she tipped her head back as she moved.

He gripped her hips, guiding her along his length. 'Yes, baby, take what you need,' he ground out. He slid one hand up her chest, reaching behind her to release her hair from its restraints. Her golden locks fell over her shoulders, and it took his breath away.

Beautiful.

So beautiful.

He slipped his hand between them as she moved, working the swollen nub with his thumb. Circling, flicking, pressing until she moaned, showing him what she liked.

Loved.

God, he fucking loved this. Loved her.

'Oh, God,' she cried out, her body tensing, fluttering around him.

He hissed through his teeth, holding it together for just a few more seconds as she rocked on him, her arms shaking as she pushed against his chest, driving harder onto him.

*Fuck*.

'Fitz!' She pulsed, her movements staggering as she tipped over the edge once more, her whole body shaking with her orgasm.

'Right there with you, Hattie, baby.'

He thrust inside her once more, arching off the bed as he pressed their bodies together, meeting her there, tumbling through time and space and oblivion with her. He scooped a hand behind her neck, bringing her lips to his in a kiss to seal their lovemaking. His body burned with his release, the euphoria sweeping through his body as he emptied himself inside her.

Home.

She felt like home.

And damn if he didn't want to spend forever there.

# Chapter 28

Life was decidedly better with their new arrangement. After their first night together—well, the first night they'd slept together—Hattie had felt lighter. Free. Even with moody clients and the usual issues at her workplace, she just couldn't bring herself to let it get to her.

She made her way around the salon, checking the scented candles that had been lit earlier that day. It was a gentle touch they'd brought in months earlier, one that certainly helped with the mixed chemical smell of hairdressing.

She was particularly elated today after Fitz had spent the night. They hadn't got much sleep, but she was far from restless. Sated, more likely. Every cell in her body still vibrated from the pleasure he'd brought her to once more before they'd started their day. The only downside was that he was on the evening shift tonight, so she'd be eating alone for the next few evenings.

She chewed on the inside of her cheek as she made her way towards the back room of the salon. After almost a week of making love with Fitz, her body housed a new ache. One in her deepest of muscles. A reminder of the way he'd felt inside her. Of what his kisses did to her.

They'd agreed to take things one day at a time. Not slow. Not fast. Just however it happened. But they were, as it seemed, officially in a relationship. They hadn't left her place the day after that first night. Had reluctantly agreed to tell his family the day after that over Sunday roast. They were bound to figure it out sooner or later. It was just one secret they couldn't have.

His brothers had teased that it was about time they'd got together. His mother had only given Hattie a knowing smile and said she was glad they'd worked it out, then had made Fitz promise not to elope with her like his older brothers had done with their wives. He'd laughed and said he'd be making no promises as his gaze had connected with Hattie's. Her cheeks had grown hot. They hadn't even talked about marriage. And yet ...

The idea only seemed logical.

Even if she hadn't told him she loves him. If he hadn't said it either.

Spending forever with Fitz ...

It just made sense.

She checked the time as she passed by Bea's station. It had just been the two of them at the salon today with Eliza only working four days a week. Her last appointment had cancelled that morning, and for once she hadn't had any walk-ins. But the idea of going home early to an empty house just didn't appeal to her.

She wondered if she could pick something up and sneak into the station for a late dinner but decided against it. Fitz probably wouldn't be getting a break until later. Still. She would be lonely without him.

She sighed as she started taking inventory of all the stock out the back. She would need to put in an order for more products soon and she didn't want to miss anything. Perhaps she could catch up on all the laundry and cleaning she'd neglected while her and Fitz had been exploring each other. This new thing between them. Her cheeks flushed at the reminder of all the exploring they'd done. The scratch of his stubble as he'd buried his head between her legs the night before, tasting her, bringing her to pure ecstasy with his tongue ...

She shook her head, shaking the thoughts away in case someone walked in and found her hot and bothered in the supply room.

Fitz hadn't moved back in, but he had spent almost every night with her since that first one. Still hadn't changed the fact he had a few changes of clothes at her place and toiletries in her bathroom. She supposed that was the keeping things slow part. Everything else had had them powering down the relationship highway.

He'd taken her on a real date.

It had been exactly how she'd imagined a date should be. Easy. Comfortable. Chemistry flying between them. Sneaking glances at each other across the table. His foot had rested against hers for the entirety of their dinner, and she'd loved the reassurance it had given her. And after eating, they'd danced. Close. Slow. And kissed. The way she'd wanted to kiss him when he'd helped her out with her failed date.

Those dates seemed a lifetime ago now. Everything just fit with him, felt so right. It's hard to imagine they'd ever only just been friends now that they were something more. Still, nothing about a future with Fitz scared her.

She knew there would be times she'd worry about his safety. Where she might not hear from him. But at least now she knew he would be right back with her as soon as he could. That he'd contact her whenever and wherever possible. And she had Rosie. And Liz and Ainslie. The way they'd banded together while the men had been at the Flinders' fire …

Hattie would be a part of that now.

She stared out the window they'd often open to let out the fumes as they mixed dyes, letting her gaze fall on the tree in the corner of the backyard swaying in the breeze.

It really was something, feeling like you belonged to something special. Knowing that it was for real.

'Hey, taking inventory?' Bea said, poking her head into the back room.

'Need anything?' If Bea noticed her voice sounded wistful, she didn't let on.

'Yeah, some polishes. I'll get a list to you shortly.' Bea tapped her fingers against the doorframe. 'Hey, I just need to pop out for a few minutes. I want to catch this shop before it closes. They had a dress in the window I desperately need.'

Hattie chuckled. It was good to see Bea getting back to how she was before she'd got with Lyle. Things hadn't completely resolved on that aspect. The restraining order still held, though that didn't stop Bea from seeing him around town every now and then. She'd told Hattie about the uneasiness she'd felt whenever she'd seen him across the street. In the supermarket. The way he still looked at her.

Hattie had tried reassuring her, told her to tell the police if it looked like he was doing it purposefully. She'd grumbled something about wishing those other charges hadn't fallen through.

'He could've gone to jail for those other offences, you know,' she'd said. 'They let him out on a technicality.'

Surely Bea thinking about buying a nice dress meant she wasn't worrying about her ex so much now. And that would be a good thing. Bea needed to move on. Needed to find someone who'd treat her right. Like Fitz treated Hattie.

'Sure, go ahead,' she said, waving a hand at her absently. 'There are no more appointments today, so it should be fine. Just turn the music up on your way out, okay? It'll make this all a little less boring.'

'Sure thing,' Bea said, grabbing her bag from behind the supply door. 'I'll be back soon.'

'I'll be here,' Hattie muttered, though her friend had already left the room.

She let her hips sway from side to side as the music turned louder. Closed her eyes as she imagined Fitz swaying with her, his lips on hers.

She didn't hear the ding of the bell above the door.

Hattie would love this, Fitz decided. He could almost imagine the way her eyes would widen when he told her about his day. Who he'd saved this shift.

But for him, right now, as he lowered himself into the semi-blocked storm drain on the side of a backroad, well, he wished just thinking about how Hattie smelled could fill his nostrils with that scent instead of the putrid smell of the still water he lowered himself into.

They'd been coming back from a false alarm when the job had been called through to their truck. They were the closest to the street, so it had made sense for them to go instead of dispatching another truck.

Ducklings.

Someone had called them up about ducklings.

He'd still been expecting calls for rescuing cats from high places like the children's shows would all have you believe. But ducklings? He hadn't heard about that one.

Someone had spotted the parent ducks panicking near the drain. They'd got close enough to hear the peeping from inside the drain, but the slab was too heavy to lift themselves. Fitz had drawn the short straw for being the one to climb into the drain when his crew had finally shifted the slab. He hadn't minded, until he went almost knee-deep in putrid water. He worked on his circular breathing, trying to block out the stench as much as he could as he scooped up each of the five ducklings and lifted them to the road. With the fifth duckling, he noticed the parent ducks had neared the drain, one of them nuzzling his hand as he placed the duckling in front of it.

Like it was thanking him.

Yeah.

Hattie would love that.

He saw Justin snap a photo of the family of ducklings, of him in the drain, but didn't dare dig his own phone out of his pocket with his hands covered in dirty, slimy water.

'Send those to me, won't you?' he said, heaving himself out of the drain. He watched the family of ducks waddle down the road, peeping and quacking as they hopped onto the footpath and across to the nearby park. There was a small lake there. Probably their home. Maybe he could take Hattie there one day and see if they could see them.

Hattie.

His heart had never been so full than when he was with her. She completed him in more ways than one.

Ma had tried to make him promise they wouldn't elope. It wasn't the first time he'd thought about marrying his best friend.

They'd already known each other so long. Knew everything about each other. And the sex? The sex was fucking incredible. He wasn't sure how long he should wait before proposing. He knew he would. It was inevitable. But they hadn't talked about it. Hadn't discussed how long they should date before getting engaged.

He saw no point in waiting, if he was being completely honest. What more did they need to explore before taking the next step? He already knew he wanted to spend the rest of his life with her. And if her screams as he brought her to absolute bliss were anything to go by, he was pretty sure she wanted it as well.

'Done.'

His phone vibrated in his pocket as Justin tucked his own phone away and helped shift the slab back into place. Hopefully those ducklings don't fall down again. They might not be so lucky next time. He made a mental note to report the drain blockage to council when they got back to the station. It was something they'd want to get fixed up before they got inundated with heavy rain.

Victoria's voice crackled through the radio as they neared the truck. Her tone alone told them there was a fire. He heaved himself up into the back seat, the others climbing in. His heart lurching into his throat as she listed off the address. The name of the shop.

Hattie's salon.

He checked the time. She wouldn't have left yet. His chest tightened at the thought she could be in danger.

He heard nothing but roaring in his ears. Couldn't form the words that fought to get out. Only saw Gene indicate towards him, saying something to McGrath. McGrath took one glance at him, flicked the sirens and lights on, and turned the truck towards the centre of town.

# Chapter 29

The entire front room of the salon was full of smoke, red flames licking out the front window. A mixture of adrenaline and fear coursed through Fitz as he jumped out of the truck. His brothers' truck had beaten them there, thank God, and were already pouring water onto the flames.

What the hell had happened?

He scanned the crowd gathering around, couldn't see her. Couldn't see Hattie. His heart threatened to tear out of his chest as his eyes landed on her car parked just down the street in her usual spot.

She hadn't left yet, so where the hell was she?

Behind him, he heard the rest of his crew working on crowd control, putting some distance between the fire and spectators. He beelined for Nick, the most accessible of those already working the fire. Dave was closer to the fire, manning the hose along with Jeremy. Everett was over by the truck, getting out supplies they might need.

'Where is she?' Nick looked up in confusion as Fitz neared him, his jacket already done up, his helmet in his hand. 'Hattie,' he said, firmer this time. Though he shouldn't need to tell his fucking brother who he meant. 'Where is she?'

'Haven't seen her,' Nick said. 'Whoever called it in said the shop looked empty.'

Empty. He could only hope. He looked towards the building as he heard the kerfuffle behind him. He spun towards it. His heart rising to his throat as Bea ducked through the crowd and ran towards him.

'Fitz!' she called. 'Hattie—'

'Where is she?' he growled, slamming the helmet on his head, because he already knew the answer.

'She was in the back room when I left. I didn't—'

'Gene!' he called, directing him towards her. He was already running towards the salon.

'Where are you going?' Nick called out after him. He ignored him, no time for explanations. No time for wasting his breath.

'Make a path,' he yelled to Dave and Jeremy, both of them directing the hose to make the salon more accessible for him.

He threw his arm out in front of him as he ran through the door, being hit with heat and roaring flames.

Hattie keeled over, coughing unbearably as her feet hit the ground beneath the window. She hadn't heard anything obscure over the music. Hadn't left the back room since Bea had left. She'd only noticed something was wrong when she started smelling smoke. And by then, the front of the salon had been ablaze, not safe for her to get through.

She would've been completely trapped if she hadn't been able to squeeze through the window in the supply room. The only thing she could think of being that she had to get out of there.

At that stage, she'd had no idea if help was on the way. She sure as hell wasn't going to wait around to find out. She'd managed to grab her bag before climbing out the window, thankful it had been within arm's reach.

She struggled to catch a full breath as oxygen burned her lungs, and urged herself to move. The next alley accessing the main street was a few doors up, and she pushed herself towards it, her movements not seeming quick enough. Never quick enough. It seemed like forever before she'd managed to make her way back to the main street, pushing her way through the crowd to see the fire trucks parked out front. It was a flurry of commotion. She saw Nick yelling something to the firefighters on the hose, commands being issued seemingly from all direction. She scanned each of the faces. The bodies of the firefighters as they moved. Desperate to find the one she knew was here. The rest of his crew was here. But he—

Fitz was nowhere to be seen.

She caught Bea's eye in the commotion as she ran closer to it, breaking past the crowd and the relative crowd control.

'Oh, God, Hattie,' she said, releasing herself from Gene's arms and running towards her.

'I'm okay,' she said, though her lungs burned and she felt dirty. 'Have you seen Fitz?'

Bea's face was terrified. 'He went in there looking for you.'

The blood drained from Hattie's face as she registered her friend's words. He'd gone in after her. He wouldn't fit through that window. Not with all his gear on.

It happened in slow motion. Gene rushed towards Nick. Nick looked back at her. Said something into the radio. Directed where the second hose that was now unwound should go.

It didn't take a genius to see whatever pathway out he might have had would very quickly be blocked off.

There was an explosion.

And someone let out an ear-piercing, heartbreaking scream.

Hattie had a feeling it was her.

Fitz wedged himself out the now broken window and fell to the ground seconds before the explosion. Heard the ear-splitting scream despite the ringing in his ears. He pushed himself to his feet and broke into a run behind the shops until he reached the alleyway.

He'd searched every part of the salon he could until he'd ended up in the back room, desperate to find Hattie. To make sure she was safe. He'd been working into a panic until he'd seen the flyscreen on the narrow window was no longer there. He'd stuck his head out the window to see it on the ground outside. There was a disturbance in the gravel underneath the window that looked as though someone had climbed out.

She'd escaped.

Thank God.

'Good girl, Hattie,' he'd said, pride filling him.

A quick look back into the front of the salon had told him escape the way he'd come would be too risky even with his protective gear. He'd have to go out the window.

Except he wouldn't be able to fit through the same space she had. He'd rummaged around until he'd found something to break the window with, smashing a space big enough to squeeze through.

Now he rounded the corner, shoving past the crowd that had gathered around, racing towards the scream that still hung in the air.

It was like he was drawn to her. Knew where she was without looking too hard. His Hattie. His legs burned as he pumped them, racing towards the two women in a tangled heap on the ground. He saw the golden head of hair rocking in Bea's arms. Knew it was her.

'Hattie!'

He threw his helmet off and hit the ground as he neared her, sliding to a stop and pulling her into his arms in the one movement.

'Fitz,' she sobbed, bringing her hands to his face, tears streaming down her face as she touched his face, his arms, everywhere she could reach. 'You're okay.'

He crushed his mouth against hers, pure need and hunger driving him. Relief swamped him to feel her kissing him back. She was safe. God, she was safe. He broke the kiss, pulling her into him, closing his eyes as he told himself the same thing over and over again. She was safe. She wasn't harmed. No one was harmed.

She was safe.

'You ran in there for me,' she sniffled, her body still shaking.

'Of course I did.' He stroked the hair back from her face, tilted her chin up to face him better. 'I love you, Hattie. I would run through hell for you.'

Her lips parted, her cheeks flushing pink as she straightened ever so slightly. Her red-rimmed eyes softened, shimmered. 'I love you, too.'

He kissed her again, slower this time. He registered his coworkers around him, registered the jobs being done. The fire would be extinguished before too much longer, but he didn't care about that right now. All he cared about was that Hattie was safe. She was in his arms. He didn't dare let her go. She was safe.

And she loved him.
His heart soared at the admission.

# Chapter 30

'What will I do?' Hattie murmured, staring at the smoking building as she sat nestled in his lap.

'We'll figure it out. Together.' Fitz surveyed the building. He'd seen the damage inside. It would be more by the time the fire was completely dealt with and it could be cleaned up. 'Insurance will cover a lot. And if the salon owners close down because of the fire, we'll figure that out too. Offering mobile hairdressing services could be an option.'

She leaned into him, letting her head fall back against his shoulder. Her body had stopped shaking, weariness making her shoulders slump. He held her close. He didn't dare attempt to move. Couldn't bring himself to. The rest of the crew had handled the fire quite capably, and none of his coworkers had tried getting him to help. McGrath had glanced over at him at some point. He'd given Fitz a nod. Confirmation that he was exactly where he needed to be.

He caught Justin's eye from across the street. He was talking to a couple of police officers and a shop owner waving his phone around. He sighed, said something to the officers, and made his way over to Fitz and Hattie.

'What have you got?' Fitz said, registering the look in his eyes.

'Arson,' he said flatly. 'Looks like an accelerant was used for the fire to act like that. The shop owner across the road who'd called it in accessed his security cameras from his phone. He'd seen a man leaving the salon right before he noticed the fire.'

Fitz's blood chilled as he wondered who could be after Hattie. 'Have they identified the man?'

'I did it for them,' Justin said. 'Took one look at the security feed and recognised him instantly. Lyle. Bea's ex. They called it through immediately. They'll find him. Knowing what he's like, he's probably down at the pub having a beer.'

Fitz held Hattie a little closer just in case.

'Thanks, mate.'

'Bea was supposed to be in the salon,' Hattie said quietly when they were alone again.

'Mmm?'

'I wasn't supposed to be there. Bea was. But I worked late, and Bea ducked out to catch another shop before they closed.'

Fitz tightened his hold on her, stroking a hand up and down her arm. If Lyle was the arsonist, that made sense. He still had a thing against Bea, and the restraining order she had on him probably pushed him towards doing something stupid.

He took in a shaky breath. Hattie wasn't the target.

Hattie was safe.

And the police would find Lyle before long. He wouldn't be getting away on a technicality with that one. Not with security footage as proof.

'Why do you smell like sewerage?' she said, watching the movements around the salon. The last of the fire had been put out, and the sun was dipping beyond the horizon, basking them both in an orange glow.

His smile widened, his heart skipping a beat as he pulled out his phone and opened the messages. 'Baby, you won't believe the day I've had.' He tapped on the image, enlarging it.

She let out a squeak as she took in the ducklings, taking his phone from him as she flicked through the images. But he couldn't take his eyes off her. His sunshine that chased away the darkness. The light he followed blindly.

His Hattie.

His best friend.

Nothing made sense without her. And with her, everything did.

'Marry me, Hattie, baby,' he said into her ear.

She pulled back, a crease in her brow as she lowered the phone to her lap. 'What?'

He traced her jaw with his fingertips, wiped a smudge of dirt from her cheek. 'Marry me.'

She blinked at him, her mouth working but no words coming out.

'Marry me,' he repeated, no hesitation within him. He wanted forever with this woman. And he wasn't about to waste any more time with her.

'We—we just started dating,' she stammered, her cheeks flushing. Her lips were swollen from their kissing. It suited her. Looking kissed. Ruffled. God, he loved her.

'We've known each other forever.' He tilted her chin up with his hand, brought his lips closer to hers, never breaking eye contact. 'Marry. Me.'

'Yes,' she whispered, leaning into him.

'Yes?'

She nodded, fresh tears welling in her eyes. 'Yes.'

He kissed her then, his heart soaring. Flying. Burning for her like a wildfire within him. She completed him. Consumed him. And made him the happiest man alive.

Her smile was wide as they broke apart, her fingers twining with his. 'I don't want a big wedding,' she said, her cheeks flushing.

'Ma may actually kill us if we elope.' Ma had been furious when Nick and Liz had eloped, then Dave and Ainslie had as well.

'So we'll have a small wedding.' She lifted their joined hands and tucked them under her chin.

'Whatever you want, Hattie, baby. I just want to call you my wife.'

'I'd like that,' she said, squeezing his hand. 'I want a simple dress, nothing too fancy.'

'What colour bouquet will you have?'

She gave him a mischievous smirk, her honey eyes looking more golden as they reflected the sunset. 'Yellow, of course. Like the sun.'

The smile pulled at his lips, his heart expanding in his chest. God, he would love this woman until the day he died. Then he'd keep loving her afterwards. There was no end for them. She'd be his wife. And that was the sweetest name he could call her.

His lips tilted higher on one side as he rested his head against hers, realising he would have to move his stuff back into her house before long. But he didn't mind. He would do anything for her. Moving a few bags of belongings didn't make a dent in what he would do for her.

He held her close, where she belonged, and his heart was at peace.

'Yeah. Like the sun.'

# About the Author

Australian author R.J. Groves has been passionate about writing since she could put pen to paper and can usually be found jotting plots and stories down on anything she can get her hands on. Describing herself as a mum, wife, author, and coffee lover, her other passions include music, cooking, books, adventures, and searching for plot bunnies in even the most mundane activities.

To find out more about R.J.'s current and upcoming releases, sign up to her newsletter on her website and receive a free novella as her gift to you.

www.rjgrovesauthor.com

Are you on social media? Follow R.J. for more updates.
Facebook: rjgauthor
Instagram: r.j.groves_author

# Also by R.J. Groves

*Outback Firefighters Series*
A LOVE SO FIERCE
A LOVE REKINDLED
A LOVE LIKE WILDFIRE

*Ash Gully Series*
ASH GULLY
MOUNTAIN LODGE
WATTLE BROOK

*The Bridal Shop Series*
SAVE THE DATE
BE MY VALENTINE
SAY YOU'LL BE MINE

*Jilted Brides Series*
FINDING A BRIDE
WRITTEN IN THE SAND

*Cities of the World Series*

IN PARIS
THE IRISH MAIDEN

*Set Ups Series*
THE SET-UP

*Mail Order Brides Series*
THE CALM IN THE STORM
THE WARMTH IN THE WINTER
THE SONG IN THE SILENCE

*Standalones*
WRITING YOU
TWO BABIES TOO MANY
SECOND CHANCE
THE BOYFRIEND APPLICATION
SWEETER THINGS
HOME BOUND
STAY WITH ME
HER FIRST NOEL
WHEN DREAMS COME TRUE
TO FALL FOR YOU